the hurt of letting go

Copyright © 2023 Lexi Bissen
All rights reserved. No part of this publication may be reproduced, distrusted, or transmitted in any form or by any means including photocopying, recording, or other electronic or mechanical methods, without the prior written permission of the publisher, except in the case of brief quotations embodied in the critical reviews and certain other noncommercial permitted by copyright law.

This novel is fiction. That means all its content inducing characters, names, places, and brands are products of the author's imagination or used in a fictional manner. Any similarities to actual people, living or dead, places, or events are purely accidental.

Editing: Lawrence Editing, Rumi Khan, and My Brother's Editor
Cover Design: Wildheart Graphics
Formatting: Swoonworthy Designs
Cover Image: Lindee Robinson Photography

PROLOGUE

CONRAD

SIX MONTHS AGO

Glancing down at my phone, I groan at the caller ID displaying the number one person I want to avoid most in the world. My father. Each time I talk to him, my blood pressure rises and it takes everything in me not to throw the phone against the wall. He either wants to talk about what a disappointment I am or what he's doing to prepare for me to take over the Dugray business—one of the largest and most well-known luxury hotel chains across the world that my great-great-grandfather started.

My family comes from old money and ever since I was born, there have been expectations of me as the oldest son. After college, I am meant to join my father in Boston, where his main office is located. I'm lucky enough that he allows me to play soccer in college because he sees it as a wasteless talent.

I grew up near Boston in Blackburn, Massachusetts, and would love nothing more than to never go back to that town. It is filled with the most stuck-up people I have ever met, who only care about their money and what they can buy with it or who they can manipulate.

Groaning, I answer the phone on the fourth ring. "Hello."

"Took you long enough to answer. When I call, I expect you to pick up right away," he chews out. There is never a greeting when I answer his calls. He's also not once asked about my life since moving to Braxton.

"Sorry," I grind out through clenched teeth. Arguing or giving my father excuses is a waste of time. Howard Dugray does not do well when people come at him with either of those. I choose to avoid confrontation as much as possible with this man.

He ignores my not-so-sincere apology. "Listen, your mother has picked out a variety of well-bred women for you to meet. I expect by spring, you will have at least gone out on a date with each of them and be able to make your decision by summer. We want to announce the engagement by this time next year."

Being the oldest son of a well-known, wealthy man means there are expectations of me. Not only to take over the family business but to marry a "proper" woman who also comes from a family like ours. The only problem? I want nothing to do with that life, not with his business nor the women my mother has picked out for me.

My jaw twitches. I want to say no. Tell him to shove his business and arranged marriage up his ass. All my life, I have been told what is to come and what is expected of me, but that does not make it any easier. It's why I have never gotten close enough to a woman and always found a new one when I felt myself or them catching feelings. I don't do relationships and need to keep women at arm's length.

My biggest issue…I like Emree. Too much. I never should have given in to her at the first party before the semester, but she was too beautiful with her sweet face and curves for days.

Sometimes it's difficult to even look at her for too long. Those ocean-blue eyes and that bright, white smile paired with her sweet, Southern belle personality. Except she doesn't have the accent and is a spitfire. I think that's what keeps drawing me in. Emree doesn't know about my family or where I come from, and she treats me like any normal guy at our college.

"Do we really have to go through with this arranged marriage thing?" I groan, refusing to even think about breaking it off with Emree. We haven't confirmed we're exclusive, but I know she wants that. She's aware I'm not known for having a girlfriend and that I keep it casual, but it's starting to bother her, even though I haven't slept with anyone else since we met.

"Don't question me, boy. You have known this would come, so do not think about changing the plan. You were born for this and will continue the family business. You will need someone from a proper background by your side and an heir to take over after you."

The way he talks about this, you would think we're the royal family or something. It's how old-money families handle things, though. They join other wealthy ones to continue their empires and preserve their strength.

"Fine," I tell him, making sure not to show that my breathing has increased. I'm tired of being controlled and having all these rules.

The sound of rustling papers comes through the line.

"I'll have my assistant send you a file with pictures, names, and a description of each woman. These are the ones your mother has approved, so if there are any you do not think will work, let her know." He pauses, and the paper noise stops on his end. "Personally, I think you should consider the Hawthorne girl. Her father owns hundreds of casinos across the country, and a merger like that with our hotels would be beneficial. She is easy on the eyes too, with a tight body, and her mother has held up over the years."

The way my father talks about women is disgusting. While growing up, he made sure to point out to my mother if she was not put together or if her hair needed to be done. Image is important to him, and I am sure the Botox injections he and my mother have had over the years are because of that.

"I'll take a look. Listen, I really have to go. We have people here." A party at our house started about an hour ago, and I have been stuck up here talking to my least favorite person.

"Be responsible. You have an image to uphold." He hangs up. No goodbye. No "I love you." To say the house I grew up in was cold would be an understatement. It was the goddamn tundra in the Dugray house.

After tossing my phone on the bed, I get up from my desk chair I've been sitting on. The conversation with my father has put me in a horrible mood, and I want nothing more than to get plastered drunk and forget about what I need to do soon. Breaking off what I have with Emree is going to suck because she is everything I want in a woman. She is hot as hell, funny, quirky, and I enjoy being around her. Finding a smart woman with a sense of humor that I'm attracted to is like winning the lottery.

After changing out of my sweats and into a pair of loose jeans and a button-down shirt, I head downstairs through the people milling around and go straight to the kitchen, ignoring anyone who tries to stop me for a chat.

Spotting a bottle of vodka on the island, I grab it and start chugging. The burn in my throat as it goes down is just what I need. Chloe, our most famous ball chaser, saunters up to me and slides her hands along my chest.

"Where's your team captain? Haven't seen him all night," she purrs.

Chloe is a beautiful woman, and she knows it. Her shoulder-length hair is an unnatural blonde color. Her body is what society deems to be the "perfect image," with her thin frame and hefty breasts that I am sure she was not naturally endowed with. Her brown eyes are large, with several coats of mascara lengthening her lashes, and her lips are nice and plump. She is most guys' wet dream, and I know how wild she is in bed from past experiences.

I take another swig of the vodka, already feeling warm all over from the alcohol. "With his girl tonight."

She rolls her eyes, her hands drifting lower on my stomach. "That virgin. No clue what he sees in her. Guys like you and Cam need a real woman. One who can keep you…satisfied." She licks her lips as she says the last word, her intentions clear.

As I maintain eye contact with Chloe, I take more chugs from the bottle and know exactly what I need to do. From how much of the bottle I have consumed, I will be numb enough to go through with this. I have tried, and I can't break it off with Emree. I need her to hate me. She has to be the one to leave me because, clearly, I'm too much of a pussy to do it.

Grabbing Chloe's hand and the bottle, I drag her to the living room. While most people in here are dancing, some are occupying the couches to talk or make out. A freshman from our soccer team, whose name I've forgotten, has a new ball chaser in his lap, and when I approach them, his eyes widen.

"Up," I tell him.

He neglects the girl on the seat beside him and stumbles away, readjusting his pants.

Without saying a word, I take his seat and pull Chloe onto my lap so that she is straddling me. She smiles, seemingly happy with me being plan *B* since Camden is off the market. I chug more of the vodka before placing it on the table beside the couch and pull Chloe's mouth to mine with my hand on the back of her neck.

She comes to me greedily, and it brings me back to the last time I slept with her. I said it was going to be the last time I would touch her because I am not a fan of being used, but right now, I need that. After the phone call with my dad and the realization that my life is almost over, I need to get out of my head, even if it is only for a moment.

Chloe runs her hands through my hair and starts grinding her hips against mine, and if I wasn't already so buzzed, she might be able to get a reaction out of me. Though her overexaggerated noises are having the opposite effect on me.

Hands glide across my chest and another pair of lips latch on to my neck. When I open my eyes, I see the abandoned new ball chaser wanting to join in. Grabbing the bottle from beside me, I chug some more, welcoming the burn as both women touch and lick at my exposed skin.

Chloe's hands are inside my button-down shirt, trailing my pecs and up my shoulders. New Girl nips and sucks at my neck and ear. Chloe smiles, running her hand through New Girl's hair before pulling me back to her with a tug at the hair on the back of my head.

Over the music, I hear a loud gasp, and when I peek one of my eyes open, I take in the face of the girl who has consumed my every thought for over a month. Her mouth is wide open, and she brings her hand up to cover it. Tears well up in her beautiful blue eyes, and something inside me breaks. I should have never done this. I should have manned up and told her the truth, that I needed to break it off for family obligations. Anything but whatever the fuck I'm doing right now.

Chloe looks behind us and smirks at Emree. "You know, it's rude to stare."

That seems to snap Emree out of it because before anyone can say another word, she turns and runs out the door, my heart leaving with her.

I don't move, even though I know I should. My legs feel like jelly, my head cloudy from all the liquor I consumed.

Chloe turns to me and smiles. "Now, where were we?" she purrs as she tries to pull my face back to hers.

Without saying anything, I get up, dumping her on the floor.

"What the hell, Conrad?"

Shaking my head, I grab the bottle of vodka. "Just get the fuck out."

Breezing through the crowd that has abandoned their dancing to watch the drama, I make my way upstairs. After shutting and locking my door, I head toward my bed and collapse on top of my comforter. With the bottle of vodka still in hand, I take a few sips while I lie there, regretting everything that went down in the last hour.

I can't hurt this girl. Emree is important to me, and I keep fucking up. She doesn't deserve this, and yet I keep begging her to forgive me after I try to push her away. Isn't that what I want? For her to leave me and hate me so she won't take me back.

My life has been planned out since before I was born, and there is no way I can change the path my parents have for me. If I had a choice, I would give myself to Emree completely. She is the girl I could see myself with. And I've just devastated her.

Maybe this is for the best. Her hating me will make me playing *The Bachelor* with the list of women my mother sends me easier. I need to stop hoping for a future with Emree and accept my destiny.

THE NEXT MORNING, after sobering up with a large glass of orange juice and a handful of pain medicine, I sit at the kitchen counter and reflect on my actions of last night. Emree didn't deserve that, and even though I was trying to get her to hate me so that ending our relationship was easier, hurting her by fucking around with someone else was not how I should've handled it.

"Oh, you look rough," Levi announces as he walks into the room.

My roommates and I are usually good about not overindulging in alcohol during the soccer season, but last night was a mishap for me.

"Thanks. I love hearing how great I look."

Levi grabs the egg carton from the fridge and a loaf of bread off the counter. "Any particular reason why you were drinking so much last night?"

Sighing, I hang my head and stare at the countertop. "I fucked up with Emree."

He laughs. "Dude, when aren't you fucking up with her? I swear you've never acted like this with a girl. It's like you're doing everything to get her to not want to be with you, but you actually want her."

The truth is, he's right. I've never been in a relationship before, but Emree has been different. She came to one of our parties before the beginning of the semester, and the moment my eyes landed on her, it was as if none of the other girls there mattered. Her skin was sun-kissed, and she was wearing a pair of jean shorts that hugged her thick thighs perfectly. Her looks may have had me gravitating toward her, but Emree's personality is what makes her stand out. She is loving and loyal to a fault. She cares deeply for the people around her, and you can see it right away with her best friend, my roommate's girlfriend, Blaire.

Running my hands through my hair, I groan. Last night should have never happened, and I don't want what we have to end. She is going to hate me for hooking up with Chloe, but my heart is with Emree. Hurting her like I did crushes me inside.

Getting up from my seat, I grab my keys and stuff my feet

into my shoes as fast as possible. "I can't fuck this up like that. She can't get hurt because of me. I need to fix this."

Levi is standing by the stove cooking some eggs as he watches me fly around the room, gathering my things. "Just make sure you're honest with her and she knows how much you mean to her. Oh, and maybe actually ask her to be in a relationship with you rather than this bullshit dating. Girls don't want that. They want commitment."

I freeze at the front door. A relationship? How could I even be in a relationship with someone when our time together has an end date already? Do I want to be with Emree?

The thought of ending what we have, or could have, completely has my heart clenching. She's everything someone would want in a woman, and for some fucked-up reason, she chose me. She could have anyone in school, and she wants to be with the one guy who can't have what he wants.

While our time may have an expiration date, I know breaking it off with her isn't an option for me right now. It may be selfish, but I need more time.

More days. More nights spent together. More laughs. Just… more.

CHAPTER ONE

EMREE

"My legs don't bend that way. You're stretching me too much," I say through the pain.

"Just relax. You'll enjoy it."

I roll my eyes. "Nobody would enjoy this. For real, get my feet out of the straps. I'm not ready for something this advanced."

"Em, seriously, relax and let me do what I need to do."

"Jules, you've been doing Pilates for years. This is my first time. You need to get my legs out of these straps before I pull something." Currently, both my feet are locked into some torture contraption, and she has my back on a sliding board. I must have gone too far down because there is a burning pain on the inside of my legs.

She rolls her eyes. "You are such a baby. Blaire is handling this like a champ."

I look over at my best friend, and she is on her side, pulling the straps up and down as she lifts her legs to the side. She has a smile on her face, and I want to punch her for that.

Jules releases me from what I can only describe as my own personal hell.

"Good for her. Now, I'm going to go grab some more of that cucumber water and drool over the men in the kickboxing class. Maybe those sweaty, shirtless bodies will help me forget the burning feeling in my thighs."

As I'm leaving the room, Jules calls out to me, "You'll never get to enjoy it if you quit on the first day."

Not stopping, I wave her off without turning around. "Hot, sweaty bodies, Jules. Hot, sweaty bodies."

Blaire laughs as I round the corner and head toward the front to the reception area. Hope Gym is unlike anything I have ever seen. Past the front, it looks like an everyday gym with its machines and weights, but beyond that, there are several rooms that host different types of classes. On the right side of the building, there are Pilates, yoga, and Zumba classes. Toward the back are kickboxing, cycling, HIIT, and CrossFit. While I have never been someone who partakes in the gym, the fact that this place offers more than the usual boring stuff intrigued me. That is until Jules locked me into a torture machine and then proceeded to call it exercise.

Once I have a nice, chilled glass of cucumber water in my hand, I smile at the sweet teenage receptionist and make my way to the back. Several men are letting out unnecessary grunts as they lift weights in the open area, and there is a row of people using the treadmills and other cardio machines. The place is packed for a Saturday afternoon. I would think more people would want to be out, enjoying the sunshine and touching some grass.

It is March in Florida and while some states are still stuck shoveling their driveways in the morning, we get to enjoy the most perfect seventy-degree weather. The water is still too cold to swim in, but being outside at this time of year is perfect. Spring break is approaching, and I can't think of anything better than seven days in the sun, working on my tan.

While not every room has a window from the hallway, I

have been blessed that the kickboxing one does. Fifteen beautiful men are facing away from me as they punch and kick some kind of large bag. The music is loud and I can hear it through the closed door. There is an instructor on the other side of the room, and when he spots me, a smirk graces his chiseled face. I have been caught, and I'm not even ashamed. Who says a woman can't ogle some sexy men? They're just putting themselves on display with their low-hanging shorts and shirtlessness. A girl's eyes have a mind of their own sometimes.

For the next few minutes, I sip on my delicious water and enjoy the view. All too soon, the instructor ends the class and the group of men walks to the side of the room. Many of them grab shirts from their bags and cover their beautiful bodies. I may have pouted.

The instructor looks over at me again, and now I feel like a creeper still hanging around when the class is over. I drain the rest of my water and toss the cup into a nearby trash can. The men in the class begin to exit the room. A few look my way and some smile. While I thought my bright-pink leggings and tank top with a cat lifting dumbbells on it were cute for a day in the gym, now I'm wondering if I look absurd.

Just as I'm about to walk back to my friends, the instructor comes out and stops when he sees me standing there. He looks at me from head to toe and smiles, showing off a picture-perfect smile. He is an attractive guy. A few years older than me, maybe late twenties, with jet-black hair hanging in his face and a full beard. His beautiful, dark-bronze skin glistens with sweat.

I must have been staring for too long because he heads over toward me, wiping the sweat from his face with the white towel resting on his shoulder. He's tall, much taller than my five foot four, and his legs are long as he strides over.

"You enjoy the class?" he asks, still showing the most perfect set of teeth. His lips are full and now that he is closer, I can see a dimple in his right cheek hidden behind his beard.

Ducking my head, I try to cover my blush at being caught. "A room full of half-naked men? Who wouldn't enjoy that show?"

He laughs, and it's a deep, manly sound. "I'm pretty sure that's why they put the kickboxing class in one of the few rooms with a window. Helps me gain a lot of new clients." He smiles. He's looking at me like a guy who is attracted to a girl, and I can't help but feel good inside.

Growing up, I was never known as an attractive girl. My choice of clothing was considered weird. My body has never been perfect. I'm short and was always the chubby kid. While I have filled out more, I am still self-conscious about my stomach and the jiggle in my underarms. I was hoping joining the gym with the girls would help me tone up like I have been saying I'll do for years.

Hot Kickboxing Instructor leans forward, and with his height, I have to strain my neck. "You looking to join? I teach a women's self-defense class on Monday nights. You should come check it out. It's fun, but you also learn a lot of techniques that can be useful."

Biting my lip, I duck my head. "Maybe. I've never done a class before. Is it okay for beginners?"

"It's perfect for beginners. Stop by. It's at seven, but if you come earlier, we can grab a drink at the juice bar or something."

Instant guilt washes over me as I realize I may have been flirting with this guy. "Oh, um, I kind of have a boyfriend."

He raises an eyebrow. "Kind of?"

Shrugging, I answer, "It's been a complicated relationship, but I would like to come to the class. I think it'd be good to learn some self-defense."

He nods, taking a step back. "Yeah, for sure stop in. It fills up quickly, so I would still be sure to come early. If you have any friends, bring them too. Learning self-defense is always useful." He gives me a kind smile and sticks his hand out. "I'm Andres, by the way."

I accept his offer, and my small hand gets swallowed up in his. "Emree. And thank you. I'll see you Monday."

He walks away and I watch him, smiling that I was asked out by a handsome, older man. Never has that happened. Until college, I had never had a guy ask me on a date or even kissed someone. While I have been on a few dates here and there and have had some hookups since attending Braxton University, I have been longing for a relationship. I'm twenty-one years old and never had a boyfriend. While the guys I went on dates with said I was nice and sweet, they didn't want to be in a relationship with me but would rather text me in the middle of the night for a booty call.

When I saw Conrad Dugray my freshman year in our math class for the first time, I thought I was dreaming. No man had ever been that perfect looking. He is tall, a couple inches over six feet, and has the most intoxicating eyes. They're a dark brown, almost black, and compared to his tanned skin and blond hair, they feel out of place, yet fit him. When he walked into our class talking to a friend of his, he passed right by me. I was far too used to people, men especially, not seeing me, but Conrad did. He glanced down at me sitting at my desk and smiled, showing off a set of straight, sparkling teeth. As he made his way by, he winked one of those dark eyes at me and then took his seat with his friend.

That was the moment my crush on Conrad Dugray developed. As the years went by, I came to learn that the boy I fell hard for was a player, on and off the field. Conrad is the starting left defender for the Braxton University soccer team, and at this school, soccer is everything. We lack a winning football team and with it being Florida, college hockey isn't too popular. We have a decent baseball team, but their season is in the spring. Fall at Braxton is all about soccer.

When I finally got up the courage to approach Conrad last fall, I never knew it would lead to where we are now. What started as a hookup at his party led to us now dating. We had a few hiccups along the way, including me walking in on him kissing a girl we all detest. Conrad was persistent that he did not want to be in a relationship, but I told him I deserved more than what he was giving me. It wasn't until Conrad's roommate and my best friend's boyfriend, Camden, told me to stand my ground with him and tell him he needed to let me go or finally take a chance at a relationship. He chose me, and for the last six months, we've had a great time together.

"Girl, what are you doing all the way over here? We've been looking for you," Jules asks as she and Blaire come down the hallway.

I smile at them. "Was enjoying the nice view of a men's kickboxing class."

"Well, well, well, you have my interest." Jules is smiling and has a gleam in her eyes. "I'm going through a crazy dry spell. Did you see any potential in there?"

"Plenty," I tell her. "Actually, the instructor asked me out. He said they have a women's self-defense class he teaches Monday nights. We should all go."

Blaire's eyes are wide. "Wait, he asked you out? You didn't say yes, did you?"

I roll my eyes at my best friend. "Of course not. I wouldn't do that to Conrad. But the self-defense class does sound interesting and maybe we can learn a thing or two."

"I'm in," Jules answers. "Since you're both off the market, maybe Hot Instructor will ask me out."

Jules is beautiful, so I am sure she will have no problem

catching his attention. Her medium-length hair is thick and jet black and always silky straight. She is tall and has impossibly long legs. Her body is fit and her skin is a glowing medium-brown shade. Jules spent her high school years playing volleyball and you can tell by her athletic build. Back during Halloween, she was dressed as Princess Leia in a gold bikini, and Blaire and I were envious of her toned stomach. That's when she told us about Pilates and how we should come to a class with her. I don't care how in shape it can make me. I won't ever be doing that again. My soft stomach and I will live our lives happily together forever.

Blaire bites her lip. "Um, I'll need to check with Camden. He was talking about going to see his mom before spring break since we'll be gone, but I'm not sure what day."

"Tell him you're booked Monday for girls' night. He'll understand."

She rolls her eyes. "Yes, because that has worked so well in the past. Remember when we tried to have a girls-only night on the Saturday after my birthday? He showed up at the country club with Maddox and Levi as if it was a total coincidence." That was a good night. Jules and I wanted to take Blaire out for her twenty-first birthday since she was the last in our group to be able to drink legally, but we wanted to do so without the swarm of guys that always surrounded us. Camden couldn't let Blaire out of his sight for more than ten minutes, though, and he swooped in, taking her from us.

"Your man needs to get over his obsession with you and let us have our friend sometimes."

"Don't even give him any ideas, Em. I love how much he cares about me."

"Whatever. You both done with your torture workout? I wanted to go to the mall and try to find a new bikini for our trip."

Jules smirks. "Trying to find something sexy for Conrad?"

I can't help but smile. "Maybe." While I do need a new bathing suit for our spring break beach trip, I will definitely have the beautiful man I'll be spending my nights with in mind when picking one out.

CHAPTER TWO

CONRAD

As I stare at the truckload of suitcases and supplies, I can't help but wonder how we are going to fit the eight of us and all our stuff into two cars. Levi said there was no reason for us to waste gas and money and drive three vehicles out to where we're staying in Wrightsville Beach, North Carolina. When he sees how Mateo's SUV trunk is filled to the top and Maddox's truck has no space left after Emree and Blaire bring their bags over, he's going to rethink his two-car rule.

For spring break this year, our group is heading to Maddox's parents' new beach house since they only use it over part of the summer. He said it was large, with six rooms and plenty of space for all of us. We've all been looking forward to seven days of no class assignments, no work, and no stress. I, especially, need this week away.

My dad's calls have been coming in more frequently. Since my mom sent me the list of potential women last fall, I have pushed off meeting any of them. He is growing impatient and I know after this trip, I am going to have to fulfill my family obligations. Thinking about it puts a sour taste in my mouth. I made the mistake of getting close to Emree instead of pushing her away like I was supposed to, and now I went and fucking fell for her.

In the six months Emree and I have been dating, not once have I brought up my family or the arranged marriage my parents have planned for me. She has asked about where I'm from and I kept it simple, telling her I grew up in Boston and my parents are in real estate, and that we aren't close and I haven't talked to them much since starting school. She understood I didn't like talking about my parents and eventually stopped asking.

Although I know I need to break it off soon, I keep telling myself I'll do it the next week, and then the time comes and I can't go through with it. She is too perfect. From her beautiful looks to her weird sense of fashion and the fact that she is always keeping me entertained. Emree is unlike anyone I have ever met and the more time I spend with her, the more I fall. I can tell she feels the same way and it pains me to know I'm going to have to hurt her like this.

"You want to tell Levi 'I told you so' or want me to?" Maddox asks as he comes up to stand beside me.

"Go for it. Remind him that we still have Camden's sister's stuff to try and fit, but unless she sits on her bag, I don't see that happening."

"H-his...sister," he stutters. Maddox's eyes are wide, face pale.

"You okay, man?"

He straightens his face and nods. "Uh, yeah. Just didn't know we were having more guests." Maddox stuffs his hands in the pockets of his khaki shorts and walks off without another word.

Emree's blue Honda Civic comes down the road and she pulls off, parking on the side of the street. Smiling, I start walking over to her as she gets out.

My girl is looking more beautiful than ever in her bright-pink leggings and blue tank top with pink stripes going down it. Emree is always wearing some crazy kind of outfit and while I think it would look insanely ridiculous on most people, for some reason, they work on her. From her bright-colored leggings with weird designs on them to her shirts with some funny saying on the front. You would think someone who looks like Emree would wear the most basic outfits, maybe even some cowboy boots, but she is all about her colors. She is a contrast to her best friend, Blaire, who is dressed in her usual jeans and black T-shirt.

"Hey, baby," she greets me with a wide smile as I walk over, throwing her arms over my shoulders. I wrap mine around her waist. She is soft all over and I love the feel of her in my hands.

I bend down and glide my lips along hers, getting a taste of the cherry lip balm she is always wearing. Em's arms tighten around my neck as she goes on her tiptoes to deepen the kiss. Our almost a whole foot height difference makes it interesting when kissing her, but I wouldn't have it any other way. Her soft, sweet lips against mine are one of the best feelings.

Pulling back, I stare down at her and smile. "You ready for a fun trip away?"

She steps back and claps her hands, jumping up and down. "Beyond excited. I can't wait to lie out on the beach and enjoy seeing you in nothing but a pair of swim trunks." She winks and I laugh.

Hand in hand, we head toward the house where Blaire has joined Maddox, Levi, Mateo, and Jules. Camden should almost be back from picking up his sister, Trazia. Maddox tells Levi we're going to have to take another car because his truck is overflowing, but Levi argues, thinking we have plenty of space.

"Do you want people's things flying out on the highway? Because I can guarantee you, these ladies are going to be pissed if they lose their skincare products. Don't you remember the night Blaire forgot hers and Cammy had to drive to her apartment at one in the morning?"

Levi rolls his eyes. "You all packed way too much shit. Downsize. Do we really need that giant umbrella? It takes up half of your truck bed."

"Don't you dare think about removing our sun protection," Blaire chimes in. "I am a pale individual, Levi Mariano, and I will not get sunburned during this trip." She's right there. Even though she grew up in Texas and has lived in Braxton for a few years, Blaire looks as if she has never seen the sun before.

"Then sit on your bags because taking three cars is dumb. Or put a seat down in Mateo's car and three people can sit in the front of Maddox's truck," Levi suggests.

Maddox looks over at Mateo's large SUV and then back at the group. "That could work, but don't you dare think about cuddling up to me, lumberjack. Knowing you, you'd fall asleep on my shoulder and drool or something." Disgust crosses Maddox's face. "Put one of the hotties beside me." He looks at Emree, Blaire, and Jules and winks.

I pull Em closer to me. "Not happening, man."

"Aw, don't be like that, Conny. I wouldn't cop a feel or anything, but having her beside me is better than your stinky asses."

Camden's Jeep pulls up, distracting us from our conversation. He and his sister open their doors and get out at the same time. While Camden goes to his trunk to get her bags, Trazia rounds the front.

"Holy shit," Maddox whispers beside me. His jaw is completely slack, eyes wide as he stares at his best friend's sister. He's taking her in from head to toe.

Trazia's thick, long hair is a pale pink. She has it hanging down straight over her shoulders. She's average height, but her long, toned legs make her look much taller. She's wearing a white, fitted tank top and black cutoff shorts paired with some beat-up Converse sneakers. If I didn't know they're three years apart, I would think she and Camden were twins. They both have these clear green eyes and matching full lips and straight noses. Besides the hair and the fact that she's a woman, they look almost exactly alike.

"You okay there, Mad?" I ask him.

He shakes his head as if coming out of a trance. "Uh, yeah. Let's get the fuck out of here." He storms off to his truck, getting into the front seat.

"Oh, this is going to be interesting," Levi says with a laugh.

"Okay, so it wasn't just me who saw his reaction, right?" Emree asks.

Blaire looks between all of us. "What are y'all talking about?" she asks, a little bit of her Texas accent coming out.

I laugh. "Oh, nothing, just that Maddox is crushing on your future sister-in-law."

Blaire's eyes bug out as Emree and I laugh. "Wh-what? But she's barely eighteen."

Emree wraps her arm around Blaire's shoulders and drags her toward Mateo's SUV, whispering something to her. I follow them and climb into the front seat. After loading his sister's bag into the trunk, Camden takes the driver's seat. Maddox, Levi, Mateo, Jules, and Trazia load into Maddox's truck. Mateo ends up bringing a surfboard, so they have a tight squeeze in the cab of the truck over there. Luckily, Trazia is pretty small, and Levi suggests she sit in the middle in the front...right beside Maddox.

Emree leans forward, positioning herself above the center console beside me. "Let's get this show on the road, boys. I need to be lying out on the beach in my new bathing suit ASAP."

Images of Emree in whatever bikini she bought recently flash through my mind, and I grin, thinking about her wearing nothing but that all week.

Leaning forward, I place a kiss on her cheek. "Drive fast, Camden. My girl is ready to be wet and sandy."

Emree laughs, throwing herself back into the middle seat. "Oh, that was bad. Keep the cheesy comments to a minimum this week, will you?"

Looking forward, I can't stop the smile on my face. Being around Emree does that to me. I'm happy when we're together, and she makes me forget about the fucked-up family I come from and their demands of me. "No guarantees, baby…no guarantees."

CHAPTER THREE

EMREE

Over nine hours in a car is absolute torture. My neck is cramped and my knees are in desperate need of some stretching. Camden wanted to stay on a tight driving schedule since we didn't leave until nine this morning, and that meant only two bathroom breaks and drive-through food. When Blaire asked for an unscheduled restroom stop, you would have thought she asked him for an organ. He then started a lecture about not drinking so much, and now the two haven't spoken in almost an hour. It has been extremely awkward, but luckily, we entered Wrightsville Beach not too long ago and the house should be close.

"GPS says the place should be up here on the right," Conrad tells Camden.

Looking out the window, I take in the houses as we pass by them, my jaw slackening slightly. Never have I seen such extravagant homes before. Most are three stories high, with wide staircases leading up to the front door. One had six garage doors and I can't help but wonder how someone would need so many cars.

Camden turns the car into a long driveway and a house

much like the ones I have been looking at comes into view. It is also three stories, but only three garages line the front on the right. The staircase leads up to a yellow double door with a chandelier hanging from the top. The house is bright white and has shutters that match the door. It seems like a perfect beach house. A very *large* beach house, but from what I have heard about Maddox's family, they come from money, though I never asked what they do.

After Camden parks, I nudge Blaire with my elbow to get her to move. "If I don't get out of this car right now, I am going to go crazy. Scoot your butt, woman."

She huffs but kicks open the door and gets out. Once my feet touch the ground, I stretch my back and arms above my head. Nothing feels better than being able to move around after being stuck in a car for a long period of time.

Arms snake around my waist, and I open my eyes. Conrad is smiling down at me. "Let's go to bed," he says with a knowing look on his face.

I laugh. "It's just after seven."

"Don't care." He nuzzles his face into the nook of my neck and plants open-mouth kisses along the column.

"Conrad," I whine, but there is little fight in me. The moment his hands or mouth are on me, I turn to mush.

"Yo, break apart and come help unload this shit!" Camden calls out.

He and Blaire are at the back of the SUV, and Maddox's truck is pulling into the driveway. Maddox jerks the truck to a stop and before anyone else is out, he swings his door open and is jumping away as fast as he can. From the front seat, I can see Trazia staring at the seat he was occupying with a confused look on her face.

Over the next twenty minutes, we unload the insane amount of stuff from both cars. Everyone in the other car stopped at the grocery store on the way here and picked up enough food and supplies for the rest of the week. Us girls are in the kitchen unloading and organizing the groceries as the boys bring in the last of the bags. Maddox bought more food than we need, but with five athletes in the house, I am sure they will blow through these.

Maddox plops down on one of the five barstools at the island. The kitchen is a work of art and straight out of a magazine. With white marble countertops, deep-green cabinets that go up to the ceiling, brand-new stainless steel appliances, and a large floor plan with a butler's pantry, there is enough space in this room to comfortably fit all of us.

"Which one of you beauties wants the honor of cooking me food?" Maddox asks with his ever-so-charming grin on his face.

I can't help but roll my eyes. "You are more than capable of cooking for yourself."

Blaire laughs. "You may want to take that back. Mad will either end up burning the place down or getting food poisoning from whatever he tries to make. He has officially been banned from cooking during the week for family dinners."

His jaw drops in offense. "How dare you. Blaire baby, never have I caused a fire or been close."

She points her finger at him. "What about that time you put two pieces of toast in the toaster with cheese and then got melted cheese stuck all over inside?"

"You put cheese in a toaster?" Trazia, who has been quiet since we got into the house, asks.

He looks over at her, his eyes raking up and down her body. "Was trying to make a grilled cheese sandwich, peach."

Her eyebrows pull together at the nickname he calls her.

Conrad walks into the room. "Are you all talking about Mad's lack of cooking skills?" He makes his way over to me and wraps his arms around my waist.

When he started casually touching me like this, I wasn't sure how I felt about it. Never has a guy had his arms around me in public or held my hand. Conrad does it so effortlessly and it's something that warms my heart.

"How about this? I will make dinner tonight. We will all agree that Maddox won't touch a thing in the kitchen all week unless he is grabbing a drink. I saw enough ingredients to make tacos, so unless anyone objects, that's what we're having," Blaire announces.

We all nod, agreeing. Since it is getting late, I am sure everyone is hungry. Trazia insists on helping Blaire prepare the tacos, and Maddox remains in his seat, claiming he is taking notes on what to do. In reality, I think he enjoys watching Trazia. His eyes follow her as she brings items out of the pantry and sets them on the island. Not once has she glanced at him, nor does she seem to notice him watching her.

"Want to bring our bags upstairs and pick a room? Camden already claimed the owner's suite, but we can beat the rest of them and pick the second best," Conrad whispers in my ear.

I turn my head to the right and kiss his smooth cheek. "Let's go. We're not being left with two twin beds or something like that. Leave that to those suckers."

He buries his face in my neck and I giggle, pulling away because his breath is tickling me.

We grab our bags, Conrad making sure to carry the two largest ones and head upstairs. The first two rooms at the top of the landing are large, but there are two full-size beds inside of them. We decide to leave those for Mateo and Jules or Maddox and Levi. The third room is smaller, with a queen bed against the wall and decorated in a light-blue design. There is already a bag on the bed, and I assume Camden brought up Trazia's stuff for her to stay in here.

The last room on the right is beautiful. There is a window on the left side of the room with a perfect view of the ocean. A queen-size bed is against the center of the wall across from the door and the bedding is fluffy and inviting. This room, much like the owner's suite downstairs, has its own private bathroom. Besides the accent wall with large green tropical leaves that the bed is set against, the rest of them are off-white. There is a vanity just outside the bathroom and a dark-green velvet reading chair in the corner by the window with the ocean view.

This room is everything I could have dreamed of.

"Damn, this is nice," Conrad comments as he walks in, setting our bags on the bench at the foot of the bed. "Maddox said his mom spent most of the summer having professional interior decorators completely redo this place. Got to say, they did a damn fine job." He kicks off his shoes and jumps onto the bed, settling on his back with his hands linked behind his head.

"Crazy how this is their second home. I can't imagine what their house in Boston is like."

A strange look comes across Conrad's face, and he looks away. "Probably twice the size, and I'm sure they have people working there, doing the cleaning and cooking."

I smile as I unpack one of my suitcases. "Must be nice. While I can't imagine living in a home this large and extravagant, I could get behind someone cleaning and cooking for me. I despise cleaning a bathroom. Blaire and I take turns each week, and I dread when it's my time."

Pulling out my bathroom bag, I bring it into the private restroom and set up my shower products, skincare, toothpaste, and toothbrush by the sink. Looking around, I can't help but notice this bathroom is twice the size of the one Blaire and I share in our two-bedroom apartment. There is a double sink with two circle gold mirrors above them. A walk-in shower takes up the entire side of the room. Something I've never seen before is a bathtub inside the shower area, but that's what this one has. Behind the glass enclosure, there's a white claw-foot tub on one side and the showerhead on the other. It looks inviting and I am excited to soak in a nice hot bath later.

When I come out of the bathroom, Conrad is shirtless, pulling clothes out of his duffel bag. I lean against the doorframe, taking in his half-naked state. Being a defender for the Braxton soccer team means that Conrad must be in top physical condition. He works hard for the body he has and it shows. His skin is naturally tan from hours in the sun at practice, and while he doesn't have the giant muscles and ripped abs some guys have, he is lean and muscular. His torso is wide and he has little body fat on him. All the years of running have left him with thick thighs that are straining against the sweatpants he changed into.

He looks up at me with a wicked smile. "Found something interesting while unpacking your suitcase."

Raising an eyebrow, I question him. "What would that be?"

Lifting his hand, my new bright-pink bikini top hangs from his fingers. "Oh…just a thin piece of fabric I can't wait to see covering that beautiful body."

Ducking my head, I hide my blush. "I still haven't made up my mind if I'll be wearing it this week."

He strides over, desire darkening his eyes. Wrapping both arms around my waist, he pulls me to him so my body is flush against his. "You'll be wearing the suit, baby. It's going to look sexy as fuck on you." His voice is low and sends shivers up my body. Conrad notices and smirks. "Actually, on second thought, maybe not. Seeing you in practically nothing out on the beach will only make me want to carry you back into this room."

I throw my head back, laughing. "Don't you dare think about it. I'm using these few days we have to work on my tan and relax. You and your dick are going to have to control yourselves."

"Oh yeah?" he questions as he pulls me even closer.

Sliding his hands down the back of my thighs, Conrad lifts

me up effortlessly and I wrap my legs around his waist. He crushes his lips to mine in a hungry kiss, and I wrap my arms around his neck, running one hand through the short hair on the back of his head. His tongue explores mine as he walks us over to the bed and lays me on my back, coming down on top of me and settling between my legs. Since he isn't holding me up anymore, his hands are greedy as they run up the outside of my legging-covered thighs and to my waist. My shirt has ridden up and his hands circle my waist.

Pulling back, I take a deep breath. I'm practically panting as Conrad's lips move from my lips to my cheek and down to suck on my neck. His hips move against me, and my body heats at the friction, even through my pants.

Something vibrates against the inside of my thigh and I try to ignore it and focus on Conrad's hands and mouth on me and the delicious feeling between my thighs.

Conrad drops his head onto the bed beside me. "Fuck," he whispers, clearly annoyed.

Standing up but still remaining between my open legs, he pulls his phone out of his pocket. I can tell he isn't happy about whoever is calling him by the anger coming over his face. He looks at me, torn between wanting to continue where we left off and speaking to whoever is on the other end of the line.

"I need to take this. Why don't you go downstairs and I'll meet you in a few minutes for dinner?"

Without another word, he walks away toward the window. In hushed tones, he answers the call, and I can hear an angry voice on the other end.

Not wanting to bother him or eavesdrop, I leave the room and make my way down the stairs to join our friends as they make their tacos from everything Blaire and Trazia put together.

It's more than half an hour before Conrad comes downstairs. He is cold and distant as he gets his own food, and when he sits beside me—the only open seat—I can tell something is different. He doesn't look or touch me as he sits there eating his tacos. Too immersed in conversation, I don't think anyone else notices the change in him. After he scarfs down his third taco, he excuses himself and goes to bed.

No look in my direction. No kiss good night. No offer for me to come up with him.

I have grown accustomed to Conrad having these weird distant moments during our six months of dating, but they are becoming too frequent, and I don't know how much more I can take. Sometimes he makes me wonder if he even wants to be with me, but then there are the sweet moments. And those are the ones I live for. The times he tucks my hair behind my ear when he wants to see my entire face or when he comes to my work to drop off my favorite foods because he knows I always forget to pack a meal. Anytime I'm feeling down about our relationship, I try to remember the sweet times, and I know he cares for me deeply.

Something is wrong, though, and I'm worried about the state of us because of it.

CHAPTER FOUR

CONRAD

Day fucking one of our trip, and I get a call from my father. It's put me in a horrible mood, and I know it is unfair to Emree, but pretending there isn't something wrong is becoming harder.

Two nights ago, my dad called to inform me that because of my delayed responses to my mom regarding the women I would like to meet, he had made the decision for me. One woman has decided on the arranged marriage already without meeting me, and, luckily for him, it was his top pick.

The casino man's twenty-year-old daughter. Liliana Hawthorne.

Liliana is a year younger than me and we went to prep school together. I vaguely remember her, but she seems to know me enough to agree to become my wife. The thought of that alone makes me feel queasy. The whole idea of what our parents have planned for us is wrong, but anytime I bring that up to my dad, he leaves no room for argument and goes into a lecture on family obligations and what my role is as his oldest son. How he did the exact same thing for his family when he married my mom, who came from a well-known family that made millions with their air and cruise line, as well as luxury resorts all over the world.

I'm too lost in thought about my impending future that the ball Maddox kicked back to me goes flying past me on the right and rolls through the sand.

He throws his hands out. "Dude, what the hell? You should have been able to stop that."

Shaking my head, I clear all thoughts of my family and focus on the now. "Yeah, sorry. Spaced out there for a moment."

Running through the sand, I reach the ball and kick it back to Maddox with the inside of my foot. It flies through the air directly toward him and he stops it with his shin, dribbling it with the top of his foot before kicking it over to Levi.

Leaving them to continue their game, I head over to where everyone else is hanging out in chairs and on towels. Blaire and Trazia are reading, something the two of them have been doing every day since we got here, while Camden, Mateo, and Jules are lying on towels, absorbing the sun. Emree is reading a fashion magazine in one of the low-sitting chairs, which she bought at the gas station up the street yesterday.

Heading toward her, I drop down into the seat beside hers.

She looks up and smiles. "Hey, you. You were looking good out there."

I lean forward and softly kiss her lips before pulling back. Licking my lips, I savor her cherry flavor. There are going to be many things I'll miss about Emree, but that is going to be at the top of the list. Never have I met a girl who not only always tastes good but smells good too. "Good for us to mess around like that since we have no practice this week."

She nods, agreeing, and goes back to reading the article in front of her.

With her focus on whatever she's reading, I take in the girl who has me breaking my own rules. We only have a few more days at the beach house, and I hate that I've already wasted two keeping myself at a distance. I know this is the last week before I have to come out with the truth and not only break her heart but mine as well. Instead of being distant, I need to relish these moments with the girl I am crazy about. Losing her is going to hit me hard.

Leaning to the side, I kiss Emree's bare shoulder, making my way to her neck. She giggles but tilts her head to allow me better access. Her skin is slightly damp from the heat, and she smells like the bronzing oil she's been using.

"What are you doing?" she asks me, not looking away from her magazine.

"Oh, nothing," I tell her, my breath against her neck causing her to shiver. "You look sexy in your new suit, baby."

Emree decided to wear the skimpy bathing suit after I told her several times this morning it was hot and looked perfect on her. The top's cups are triangle-shaped and trimmed with white ruffles. It's secured against her body with thin strings around her neck and back. The shape showcases her amazing, full breasts. The bottoms are high-waisted and pink, matching the top, with the same white ruffles along the edges.

She's been a distraction for me since she came out here. She and the shitstorm that is my life.

Emree closes her magazine and turns her head toward me. I capture her slightly parted lips with my own and swipe my tongue along the seam of hers, seeking entrance. She eagerly opens, leaning closer to me so I'm able to amplify the kiss. Lifting my hand, I wrap it around the back of her neck, holding her against me as I get lost in the feeling of her full lips against mine.

Panting, I pull back and rest my forehead against hers. "Thinking we should head upstairs for a bit."

Emree smiles and nods.

"Thank the heavens because if we had to sit here and listen

to you two moaning and breathing heavily any longer, you'd clear the beach," Jules says with her eyes closed the entire time.

Mateo chuckles beside her. "Honestly, it was turning me on some."

Everyone joins in and laughs while Emree ducks her face, hiding the crimson that is dusting her cheeks. Without saying a word to our friends, I stand and reach my hand down to help Em up. She accepts, and together we walk inside through the back French doors.

As we make our way through the house, I'm basically dragging her behind me. She laughs at my eagerness, but she wouldn't think it was funny if she knew why I needed her so badly. I want to make the most of these five days we have left.

Walking into our room, I kick the door closed with my foot and push Emree against it, my hands going to her face and cupping her jaw. My lips crash to hers and she snakes her arms around my waist, pulling me close. My erection pushes against her stomach, and I grind, enjoying the feeling of her against me.

Emree claws at my naked back, trying to get me closer. Sliding my hands down, I find the bikini ties at her back and neck and let them loose. The thin material falls to the ground, revealing her bare breasts to me. Reaching forward, I cup them both in my hands, testing their heavy weight. She moans and drops her head back against the door. Her mouth is slightly open as she relishes the feeling of my hands on her.

With my mouth and hands, I worship Emree's beautiful body. She is soft and warm all over, and I don't think I could ever get enough of her. Her body is responsive to mine as I lift her by the back of her thighs and bring her over to the bed, where I lay her down. With her blonde hair spread out against the comforter and being naked from the top up, I can't think of a better view. I could stand here and stare at her for hours and never get bored. Emree is every man's dream and the most beautiful woman I have ever known, inside and out.

She smiles up at me and my heart breaks, seeing how happy she is, even with me being a dick to her in the past and the hot-and-cold attitude I have given her. She looks at me like...like she loves me. Part of me is worried she fell in love, and if she ever said those three words to me, I fear it would be impossible to do what I need to do.

I focus on the stunning woman below me. The one who makes me smile the moment I see her and who has put up with more bullshit from me than anyone should. Slowly, I pull her bathing suit bottoms down, and in no time, she is completely naked in front of me. I bend down and kiss her, trailing my lips down her neck and to her chest, moving one of her hands and taking her into my mouth. She is panting as I shower her with attention.

Blocking the negative thoughts about my family, my now future wife, and losing the first girl I caught real feelings for, I center my thoughts on this moment right here. Being with Emree, just her and me, makes me happier than I have ever felt. As I give her body much-needed attention, I make sure to memorize every dip, every mark, and every sound that comes out of her mouth. After making her more than satisfied with my mouth, I kiss her on the lips hard as I remove my trunks.

Nothing has ever felt more like home than being with Emree. Whether I'm with her intimately or just hanging out beside her, she gives me this feeling of pure comfort. Being with her in every way feels right, and I fear what it will do to me when I lose that.

CHAPTER FIVE

EMREE

"That smoky eye is seriously hot, Jules. You have the perfect look right now. The sexy black dress, straight, dark hair, and your skin is glowing from being in the sun this week." Jules is looking like a runway model tonight.

The four of us girls have been getting ready in my room for the last hour and a half, but the time and effort are worth it. We all look banging, and with Jules's and Trazia's help, our hair and makeup are pure perfection.

Trazia admitted she has been doing several of her classmates' hair for the past two years. Even though she hasn't taken professional classes or gotten her cosmetology license, you wouldn't think she's an amateur. She not only styled my hair with full, perfect curls, but she also colored it with fresh highlights yesterday and gave me some curtain bangs that she said would frame my face well. I have to agree with her because my new style fits me.

She did a half-up, half-down style for Blaire, and it showcases my best friend's long neck, which I'm sure will make Camden happy since he constantly likes to attach his lips there.

Paired with a white, knee-length dress held up by thin straps, Blaire looks like a dark-haired angel.

Trazia is wearing a pair of high-waisted black jeans that are like a second skin to her body. She's paired them with a low-cut, dark-green crop top and some seriously sexy strappy heels. By looking at her, you would never know that Trazia is still in high school and turned eighteen years old only a month ago. It helps because the club we're going to is twenty-one and older, so she should have no trouble getting in now.

I grab my pale-pink velvet dress and head to the bathroom to change. Jules made sure to match my eyeshadow to the dress and contoured the fuck out of my face. Looking in the mirror, I barely recognize myself. My cheekbones are more defined, nose slimmed, and jawline sharper.

Disrobing, I shimmy into my dress and strap on the silver wedges I brought. Twisting around while looking in the mirror, I check to make sure everything is in its place. Last thing I want is for the bottom of the dress to be stuck in my underwear.

Exiting the bathroom, I hold my hands up. "Are we ready to get our club on or what?"

They all cheer and Jules holds up the bottle of vodka we have been pregaming with. Conrad and Levi volunteered to be the designated drivers this evening. Maddox has been complaining for the past two days about how he needs to get out of this house. While many of us are happy lounging on the beach all day and spending time on the patio at night, we understand Maddox's caged feeling.

"Let's get this party started," Jules announces just before she takes a pull from the bottle.

The four of us head down the stairs and as we enter the room, the conversation halts. Camden and Maddox are the first to see us, and Camden has a hungry look in his eyes as he takes in his girlfriend from head to toe. Blaire bounces over to him and sits sideways on Camden's lap.

Maddox looks down and stands from his seat. "Let's get going."

The rest of the guys stand and start heading to the front door. Conrad approaches and rests his hands on my hips. "This dress is far too sexy," he rasps out by the side of my face.

Sliding my hands up his chest, I settle them on his strong shoulders. "That's the plan. By the end of the night, you're going to want to be tearing it off me."

"End of the night? I'm ready to do that now." He laughs.

"Well, you're going to have to control yourself. I want to have some fun with our friends and that means drinks and dancing. Then I'm all yours." Reaching up, I kiss him on the cheek and follow everyone out of the house and hop into Mateo's car.

Conrad and I need this night. A few hours to relax and have some fun. Something has been sitting heavy on him, and if he won't tell me, then I want to try to get whatever it is off his mind, even for a little while.

THE CLUB IS a bit of a drive away in Wilmington since Wrightsville Beach is more of a small town than a city. Traffic is light and we make it there in no time.

Since it's Thursday night, the parking lot is not as busy as I'm sure it would be on a weekend. It's a little over half-full. Conrad finds a spot and the moment our doors open, the music from the club fills the otherwise quiet night. It sounds like some techno beat, and I cringe because this may not be the scene for our group.

Camden, Blaire, Conrad, and I meet up with the rest of our friends. Levi is staring at the club as if it has some kind of disease.

Trazia is clapping her hands and skipping toward the building. "This place looks better than the clubs in Gainesville."

Camden's head snaps in his sister's direction. "Excuse me? What clubs have you been to? Better be the Mickey Mouse Clubhouse."

She turns her head back while still walking. "Oh, big brother, this isn't my first rodeo." With an extra sway to her hips, Trazia leads the group and heads toward the beefy bouncer at the front door. He blatantly checks her out, resulting in a groan from Camden. His baby sister is now a woman—a beautiful one, at that—and he is not going to be handling that too well.

Bypassing the ID check, Mr. Bouncer Man lets us all in. The techno tune gets noisier when the door opens, and I know the guys are going to regret coming here. They're more rock or country fans versus what this club is about.

Inside, it's dark, but there are several neon lights in various areas, making it bright enough to see. Several bodies are on the dance floor, some people standing at the high-top tables, and the bar has a few people there ordering drinks. Everyone is highlighted, thanks to the black light above the dance floor.

"We're going to put in some drink orders. Anything special you want?" Conrad all but shouts in my ear.

"Cranberry vodka. We'll grab a couple tables."

He nods and heads toward the bar. Levi and Mateo are right behind him.

Camden and us girls make our way into the club and snag two tables beside each other. Camden stands behind Blaire and whispers in her ear. She turns and smiles at him. With Blaire's past, I know places like this are hard for her to enjoy. She was raped in high school, and crowds have made her uncomfortable since then. It wasn't too long ago that she would never even entertain the thought of coming here with us. Before Camden, it was me who reassured her that it would all be okay and I was there for her, no matter what. Now she has a man who loves her enough to drop anyone who touches her to the ground. It warms my heart to know she has found her person.

The song changes, and instead of the same techno tune that has been playing, "Watermelon Sugar" by Harry Styles spills from the speakers. Trazia cheers and grabs my hand.

"Come on. We *have* to go dance. It's sacrilegious not to let loose during a Styles song," she shouts as she pulls me into the crowd. Our friends watch as I'm being dragged away, smiles on their faces that I know are matching the laughs coming out of them, but I can't hear over the music.

Once we're on the dance floor, Trazia lets go of my hand and throws hers in the air. With her eyes closed, she tilts her head back and loses herself to a man singing about oral sex and the female orgasm.

Trazia's energy is infectious and before I know it, I'm moving my hips to the song and getting lost in the music. She grabs my hands and spins me around, molding her body behind mine. Never have I danced this intimately with another woman, but Trazia knows how to move her hips and helps me move mine in a more seductive way.

A new set of hands grips my waist and pulls me into a hard chest. "Not a fan of you dancing like that with anyone but me," Conrad growls in my ear.

The song has changed, and luckily, they have drifted away from more techno. "Then don't let me go."

Conrad's grip on my waist tightens and his nostrils flare, but he doesn't respond. He holds me tight and everything around us fades away as I get lost in the feeling of being in Conrad's arms. He makes me feel safe and loved. Even though we haven't said those three words to each other, I know in my heart that I love Conrad. Never have I said those words to someone romantically, and I've been scared to do so because I know if he doesn't feel the same way, it will crush me.

Our friends join us on the dance floor, and Blaire hands me my drink. I sip on my delicious vodka and cranberry as we all move our bodies to the beat of the music. The guys create a secure barrier around us girls, even though no one is near our group.

The night goes on and we dance to song after song while consuming several drinks. Conrad and Levi guzzle down water, making sure to honor their promise to be the group's DDs. Camden has been strict with Trazia, but between Jules and me, she is able to sneak in a couple drinks. She's surrounded by friends, and we're here to make sure no one gets into any trouble.

The copious amounts of alcohol have gone to my head, and it starts to get fuzzier. Resting my arm on Conrad's shoulder, I lean up to whisper in his ear, "I'm going to head back to the table."

He nods and grabs my hand, guiding me through our friends and to the tables we have been occupying off and on. Currently, Camden, Blaire, Levi, and Trazia are off the dance floor and enjoying drinks at the tables.

Trazia smiles when she sees us heading in their direction and bounces toward me, wrapping her arms around my neck. "My dance partner. Cammy is being a dud and not letting me dance with any of the guys."

Her brother groans. "Not a fan of you rubbing your ass against my friends, Traz."

With her arms still around my neck and her basically hanging off of me, Trazia turns her head toward him. "I'll rub my ass on whoever I want."

Blaire and I laugh, but Camden rubs his hands down his face. "I think it's time we head out. Apparently, someone has been sneaking my *underage* baby sister alcohol." He looks directly at me, and I fight hard to hide my smile.

Conrad volunteers to go round up the rest of the group. No one seems heartbroken to leave as we toss back the last of our drinks before Maddox goes over to the bar and closes our tab. Once everyone is ready, we walk back—some of us stumbling—to the cars. Camden is dragging a drunk Trazia, who keeps mumbling about how she is completely sober, while Mateo is trying to keep Jules from running toward the McDonald's next door.

Our mess of a group makes it safely into our cars and back to the house. Trazia passed out between Blaire and me and has been snoring the entire drive back to the house. When we park, Camden struggles to get her out but finally manages to haul her over his shoulder.

"Well, this has been a fun night. Jules, don't try to escape again. There is no fast food near here and Conrad ordered you enough nuggets for the rest of the trip," Camden states as he heads up the stairs with his sister still slung over his shoulder and Blaire right behind him.

We all retire back to our rooms, and the buzz I have had from the alcohol is starting to wear off. Conrad closes our bedroom door and sets a bottle of water and orange pills on the nightstand beside my bed.

With a groan, I flop down on the bed and stare up at Conrad. "I think I drank too much."

He laughs and starts removing the throw pillows from behind me. "Those vodka cranberries are dangerous."

Conrad begins moving around the room and grabs a pair of his sleep pants as well as an oversized T-shirt for me. "You're looking sexy," I tell him as he removes his clothes before pulling on the sleepwear.

Chuckling, he makes his way over to me. "And you're

drunk. Here, change into this and I'll grab your wipes so you don't have to sleep in your makeup."

My heart swells with how sweet this man can be. Reaching for the bottom of my dress, I lift it over my head before tossing it on the floor. Conrad comes back from the bathroom with my makeup wipes in his hand and takes in my naked body on the bed.

"What the fuck is on your tits?" he asks, trying to hide his laugh.

Confused, I look down and quickly grab the comforter to cover myself. "Oh no. I forgot these were on. I was trying to be sexy for you."

Unable to cover his laugh anymore, Conrad walks over with a wide smile on his face. "Baby, you're always sexy, but seriously, what are those?" He pulls the comforter back and stares at my chest.

"They're pasties. I couldn't wear a bra with this dress and didn't want my nipples to be saluting everyone."

My arms are crossed over my chest and Conrad pulls them apart. His fingers toy with one of the pasties and start to pull the edge away from my skin until my nipple is freed. "This is the least sexy thing. But I'm glad your nipples weren't on display for everyone."

With another groan, I rip the other pastie off. "How about now? Sexy enough to bang?"

"You will always be sexy enough to bang, Em. But right now, you're going to wash your face, change into that shirt, take the meds I put on your nightstand, and then we're going to bed."

Lifting myself up, I crawl to the side of the bed and wrap my arms around Conrad's neck. "But the ugly pasties are gone and I want to have sexy time."

Too fast for me to object, Conrad slides the T-shirt over my head, covering my naked body. "You've had a lot of alcohol tonight. Time for sleep. We can have sexy time later when you're sober." He leans forward and kisses my nose. "Now go take the pills I brought up so you don't have a headache in the morning and get under those covers. I'm going to shower and I'll join you after."

Listening to his instructions, I take the pills and chug half the bottle of water. All too soon, my eyelids get heavy, and as I snuggle under the comforter, I drift off to a deep sleep while listening to the sounds of water falling from the bathroom.

CHAPTER SIX

EMREE

The last six days have been more perfect than I could ever imagine. While it started out with Conrad in one of his weird moods where he seemed guarded, something changed on Tuesday when we were on the beach, and since then, he hasn't left my side. In the mornings, I either wake up with his arms wrapped around me in a tight hold or his mouth on some part of my body. Almost every day started and ended perfectly with the most beautiful lovemaking we have ever had. It was as if he couldn't get enough of me and while I'm not sure what changed, I'm not complaining either.

For so long, I have tried to get Conrad to take our relationship seriously. While we haven't said those important three words to each other, I know I have been in love with him for a while now. My biggest fear is that when I tell him, it will send him running in the opposite direction. Conrad is not prepared for that kind of serious relationship, and I don't want to push him before he's ready.

It's our last night at the beach house and we all decided to have a bonfire. Camden mans the grill and makes several steaks for everyone. Jules and Trazia took care of the sides and made some mashed potatoes and corn. Blaire, Maddox, and I went to the store to get supplies to make s'mores. It's a perfect night with no clouds in the dark sky, making the moon and stars shine bright.

The beach house has a large porch that is the length of the entire home. It has a large outdoor kitchen with a grill, sink, refrigerator, smoker, wood-fired pizza oven, and several cabinets filled with supplies. There is matching patio furniture and a ten-person outdoor table and chairs. Much like the rest of the house, everything is extravagant and expensive, yet beautiful. It's something many people dream about.

It's a chilly night, and Blaire and I have been enjoying the fire to help warm us up. In contrast to how I dress during the day, tonight I have my thickest leggings and a tie-dye T-shirt on with a throw blanket wrapped around my shoulders. Blaire is wearing a pair of jeans and a long-sleeved Henley T-shirt. Her feet are covered in fuzzy socks, and she is wearing her brown Birkenstock sandals since they're all she packed.

Looking over toward the grill, I see Conrad. He's changed into a pair of gym shorts and a blue hoodie with our school's name in gold on the front. He's chatting with Camden as they keep an eye on the meat cooking. He must feel me staring at him because he looks over his shoulder and smiles at me. Before turning back to Camden, he winks at me and resumes their conversation.

"That boy is sure smitten," Blaire tells me with a smirk on her face.

Leaning back against the wooden lawn chair, I close my eyes, thinking about Conrad. "Blaire, I can't explain to you how much I've fallen for him. I'm just scared he doesn't feel the same way about me."

Turning my head, I look over at my best friend. She waves her hand at me. "That is crazy. The way he looks at you is a man falling in love or already there. You two have been dating for far too long for him not to have fallen for you."

A weak smile grows on my face. "It's been six months and sometimes I feel like I'm still fighting to get him to acknowledge that we're even a couple."

When Conrad and I first started seeing each other, he only wanted a friends-with-benefits relationship, even though he would treat me like a girlfriend and say things that made me think he wanted more. While I desired a real relationship with him, I held off on asking for more to wait for him to come around. It wasn't until I walked into a party at his house and found him making out with two girls that I stood up for myself. When he came to my door the next morning apologizing and saying what a mistake it was, I told him he was either with me, or he had to let me go. He struggled to make the decision because he had never been in a monogamous relationship before but ultimately agreed to be with me and only me.

Blaire's eyebrows pull together as she thinks. "Maybe he's still struggling with being in his first relationship. Conrad was Mr. Playing the Field for years. You can tell he cares about you, but I'm sure maneuvering a relationship has been a struggle for him when it's a new experience."

"It didn't seem to take Camden long, and doesn't he have just as much relationship experience?" I ask, my voice barely above a whisper.

Her eyes drop to her hands in her lap. "No, I guess it didn't." She takes a deep breath. "I know I've said this before, Em, but you deserve someone who knows what they want. You're incredible and one of the most amazing people I know, and to keep fighting for a man to grow up and see the prize he has right in front of him is unfair to you. He needs to open his eyes to the woman who loves him right here."

My heart hurts at her truthful words. Blaire has always been honest with me about my relationship with Conrad. While she likes him and sees how sweet he can be, he also frustrates the hell out of her with his wishy-washy attitude toward us being together.

"Maybe I'll try talking to him tonight. I don't know how much more of this back-and-forth I can handle. Sometimes I don't know which Conrad I'll get on any given day, the standoffish or loving one."

Camden calls out to announce the steaks are ready. Mateo and Levi take over, setting the table, and Camden sets the pan of steaks in the middle beside the mashed potatoes and corn. We all grab our own drinks and settle around the table. Conrad comes to sit beside me, kissing my temple before settling in his seat. He grabs my plate and puts a steak on it before getting his own. I smile at his thoughtfulness.

We pass around serving dishes filled with food and load up our plates. Having steak reminds Mateo of the time Maddox was on duty for their weekly "family dinners" and how he burned it, causing them to order out that night. Since then, he has been banned from cooking on his own and needs supervision.

Conrad's left hand rests against my thigh as he eats his food. His thumb strokes the inside, causing me to burn up all over. Anytime his hands are on me, my body lights up. It is one of the reasons it's hard to resist him when he would come back after hooking up with someone else when we were in the friends-with-benefits stage. Conrad knows he has this power over me that makes it hard to say no to him.

"Do y'all ever wish life could be like this all the time? No stress from classes, work, or soccer. Just peaceful days," Blaire says with a faraway look on her face.

"Yeah, except for the fact that only rich people live like this and we need to make money," I reply with a laugh. I glance over at Maddox to make sure he isn't offended, but he's laughing alongside us. Conrad tenses beside me but covers it up with a fake laugh.

"That's true," Blaire agrees. "Although if I didn't have to carry a tray full of heavy cocktails again a day in my life, that would make me happy."

I laugh because this is something we have both talked about. Being a waitress is straining, but I'm used to working hard. Since I was fifteen, I've had a job. It started at a fast-food chain near my house since I couldn't drive and would have to walk to work. At seventeen, I was able to move away from the food industry to retail and worked as a cashier at Gap. I transferred to their store closest to Braxton until getting a job at Whiskey Joe's, a local bar near campus, last year. Blaire started working with me there last summer and while it is hard at times, we love working together and with our other coworkers.

"Part of me feels like you two are being wimps. How could waitressing be that hard? You just take orders and bring them back to the table when they're ready. The actual act of getting the drinks and food ready isn't even part of your tasks," Maddox rattles off.

I raise my eyebrow at him. "You're joking, right?"

He looks between Blaire, whose glare matches my own, and me. "With the looks on your faces, I want to say yes."

An evil smile comes across Blaire's face. "How about everyone at this table gives you a drink order and when we're finished, you tell each of us what they are?"

Maddox puffs his chest out. "Fine. Give me a notepad."

I shake my head. "Oh no, no, no, Maddy. Notepads are not allowed. In the middle of the hustle and bustle of a bar, you have to memorize your customers' orders."

Conrad leans back and laughs. "This should be good." His hand on the back of my chair begins playing with my hair, sending shivers down my arms.

Maddox glares at me. "Fine. Piece of cake." He looks toward

the end of the table to his right, where Levi is sitting. "You start, Mountain Man."

Levi's head jerks back at the nickname. "Um...an old-fashioned."

One by one, Maddox goes in a circle, taking everyone's drink order. He stops at Camden, who is tapping his finger against his chin. "Any fucking day now, princess."

Camden smiles. "Whiskey sour."

Maddox moves on and stops at Trazia. His eyes widen slightly as she bites her lip before answering. "Oh, um, a virgin strawberry daiquiri."

His nostrils flare. "Figures," he mutters under his breath.

She gasps slightly and looks over at her brother to see if he notices. His head is turned as he talks to Blaire and misses the interaction between the two.

Once Maddox gets to the last one—me—I decide to make it harder on him. "Peach margarita on the rocks with top-shelf tequila, sugar rim, a splash of lime, and a jalapeño slice in it."

With his jaw hanging open, he stares at me. "You're shitting me, right?"

"Nope." I shake my head. "Now go on. Repeat all the orders, starting with Levi." I point to the other end of the table.

Maddox looks down there and surprisingly gets the first drink right. He misses Jules's and Mateo's orders but gets Camden's and Blaire's right.

He looks at Trazia. "Liquor-free strawberry daiquiri for the virgin."

This time Camden hears what he says. "What the fuck, dude?"

Maddox shrugs. "Just messing, man."

Camden glares but lets it go. Trazia shrinks back into her seat.

Since we've gotten here and been able to get to know Camden's sister, I have noticed she is usually snappy and sarcastic, but when Maddox is around, she is quieter than shy Blaire.

Maddox gets Conrad's order wrong and curses. When he looks at me, there is clear frustration all over his face. His eyebrows pull together and he points a finger at me. "You know what, fuck you. You've been doing it for a long time."

We all laugh as Maddox mumbles, annoyed.

"Just admit what they do is hard. You've seen how busy that place gets on game days," Mateo tells him.

"Fine," Maddox reluctantly admits. He crosses his arms over his chest and sinks into his seat.

Warm lips touch my cold neck as everyone breaks off into hushed conversations. Our food has long been eaten and we have all been lounging around under the stars.

"You are so sexy when you're putting Mad in his place," Conrad whispers against my neck. I lean to the side, giving him better access as his lips explore.

"Hmm, it felt pretty good. He's always such a smart-ass and needed to be humbled."

Conrad nibbles on my earlobe, causing me to moan. "Let's go to our room."

The temptation is strong, especially when he's being sweet like this. "It's our last night here. Blaire and I got stuff to make s'mores. Why don't we hang out with our friends first and then I'm yours all night?"

He groans and drops his head onto my shoulder. "Fine, but I'm holding you to that 'all night' statement."

I laugh and push him off my shoulder. "S'mores time, ladies and gentlemen."

Blaire claps her hands together. "Oh yay, I've been waiting for this. My first s'more."

"Did you grow up under a rock, Blaire baby? Who's never had a s'more?" Maddox asks, shocked.

She rolls her eyes as she gets up and goes to get the s'mores supplies. "Shut up."

I help Levi and Jules clear the table as everyone else goes to claim chairs around the firepit. Conrad grabs a beer from the cooler and drops into one of the seats. With my hands filled with paper plates, I watch him as he takes a long pull from the neck of the bottle. Now without anyone around and with him thinking no one is watching, I can see the tension in his body. Something is going on with him and he hasn't talked to me about it at all. I'm afraid if I push him to tell me what is going on, he is going to close up.

After dumping the last of the plates and other trash into the bin outside, I head over to Conrad and join him in the seat next to his. Without looking, Conrad reaches over and links our fingers together. He squeezes my hand and rests it on my armrest. As he takes another sip of his beer, I study his face. His jaw is tense, eyes slightly squinted as he is deep in thought, not paying attention to our friends' conversations around us.

Asking him what's wrong is on the tip of my tongue, but I don't want to push Conrad. If he wanted me to know or my help, he would have asked. Conrad has never been an open individual and is more closed off than I would like. While I try to respect his need to keep things to himself, I'm someone who needs more communication. I want Conrad and me to have what my best friend and Camden have found. Never have I seen a couple more in love and open with each other.

After going through a hard part in their relationship last year when Blaire walked in on Camden in bed with another woman, only for it to not be what it looked like, the two of them have made it a point to always tell each other everything. Blaire had ended up leaving and none of us knew where she was for three days, and that entire time Camden was going insane with her out there thinking he cheated on her.

While I don't want Conrad and I to go through something

as horrible as that in our relationship, I would like to have him be more open with me. Not that I need to know his deepest, darkest secrets, but I would like for him to feel like I am someone he could come to when he has something sitting heavy on his mind like I can tell he does now.

Blaire comes around, passing out sticks and marshmallows. Everyone is smiling around the fire as they roast their marshmallows. Conrad stares at his burning white pillow of sugar at the end of the stick. I bump my shoulder into his.

"Hey, handsome," I say with a smile.

He looks down at me beside him and the sides of his mouth reach up. "You ready to ditch these guys?"

I laugh and shake my head. "We just got to the fun part. Look at how happy Blaire is burning her first marshmallow. How could you want to leave this?"

Blaire is currently blowing out the small fire on her marshmallow while Camden is laughing beside her.

Conrad looks over at our friends and then back at me. "Yeah, but it's our last night." The way he says it makes me think there is more meaning behind his words.

Rising on my toes, I kiss his neck, trailing my lips to his mouth. "We'll still have time tonight to be together. Plus, I'll see you back in Braxton, just not every night like here."

"Yeah," he says, kissing me back before turning toward the fire to pull his marshmallow out. "We'll have time back in Braxton."

CHAPTER SEVEN

CONRAD

With two s'mores already downed, I'm ready to take Emree upstairs and get lost in her one last time. Over the last couple of days, I have come up with what I am going to say to her when we get back and how I am going to end our relationship. After running it through my head several times, I decided not to tell her the truth about the arranged marriage. I don't want Emree to think less of me for marrying a stranger because my parents are making me. None of my friends, even Camden, who I tell almost everything, have any idea. It is not something any of them would understand because it sounds unbelievably insane when you really think about it. But this is the life I grew up in. The people in my life since I was young have all been through this kind of bullshit.

Maddox comes over and takes the seat Emree once occupied beside me. She moved to take pictures of Blaire roasting her first few marshmallows because the wonder on her face was something great to see.

"What's going on with you lately, man? You haven't been the most talkative or bubbly person, but you've been kind of...

closed off." Maddox's words make me realize I have done a shit job of hiding what has been going on with me.

Rubbing my hands down my face, I think of how to convince him everything is fine. "Nothing, Mad. Just the normal family bullshit. You know the kind." Luckily, Maddox comes from a family as fucking insane and rich as mine. Although his is new money and doesn't care about family name as much as mine, so he wouldn't ever have to go through something as senseless as an arranged marriage.

Maddox nods. "Yeah, man, I know what you mean. Anything I can help with?"

Bringing the beer bottle up to my mouth, I take a long pull before answering him. "Not much even I can do. Got some shitty family obligations I need to handle and my asshole father won't let me out of them."

Maddox laughs but not in a funny way. "Asshole fathers are my specialty. If you need anything at all, man, you know we're here for you." He slaps me on the shoulder before getting up and walking back to our group of friends standing by the fire.

Emree looks over and smiles at me. In the light of the fire, her blonde hair looks almost red and her tanned skin is glowing, highlighting her blue eyes. She ducks her head, breaking our eye contact, and the blush that graces her cheeks makes me wonder if she's thinking what I am. That I want us to be alone together in our room right now.

Tossing the rest of the beer back, I get up and dump it in the trash can. With my sights set on Emree, I head in that direction. Wrapping my arms around her waist, I can't help but notice how warm she feels after standing next to the fire for so long.

Pushing her hair to the side, I kiss her neck. "Let's go," I whisper into her ear. She shivers and nods.

Without saying a word, I grab her arm and pull her behind me toward the back door. Our departure doesn't go unnoticed.

THE HURT OF LETTING GO

"And where do you think you're taking Blondie?" Maddox asks, raising his eyebrow.

Emree giggles and tucks her face into my side.

"Going to bed with my girl, if you don't mind."

Maddox shakes his head and makes a tsking sound. "Ditching us on our last night. That's cold, Conny."

I roll my eyes and turn to head back through the sliding glass door. Our friends laugh from behind us and someone, I think Mateo, starts singing "Bow Chicka Wow Wow." Even though we're all in our early twenties, I swear this group of friends acts like immature teenagers sometimes.

Emree keeps up with my fast pace even though I'm basically dragging her up the stairs. Either she's just as eager as I am to get into our room, or my grip on her hand is too tight for her to let go. I'm not complaining either way. The faster we get up there, the faster I get inside her.

Pulling her into the room, I shut the door behind us and push her up against it. "Fuck, I was about five seconds from taking you down there in front of all our friends if you didn't agree to come up here with me."

Emree tilts her neck back as I drag my lips along her collarbone.

Her hands run through my hair, pulling it slightly at the base. "Spending time with our friends was the point of this week." She moans as I nip her earlobe before moving on to kissing her jaw.

My hands at her waist move up and cup her full breasts, massaging them through her shirt and bra. "Nope," I tell her. "The point of this weekend was to see you in as little clothing as possible each day. You wear too many layers at school."

She laughs, but it's cut short when I capture her lips with mine. Reaching for the hem of her shirt, I lift it up and over her head, only breaking our kiss for a second. After throwing the tie-dye material on the floor, Emree cages my face between her hands and brings my mouth back to hers. She kisses me with the same eagerness that I have.

Trying not to think about what is to come, I break our kiss and pull back, staring at her flushed face as she tries to catch her breath. Her eyes are filled with desire as she stares at me and licks her lips. Ever so slowly, Emree's hands slide down my chest to the bottom of my shirt and she runs her palms along my stomach, making my muscles tighten. As she holds eye contact with me, she grips my shirt and brings it up and over my head.

"You are so damn sexy," she purrs as she glides her fingers along my chest and up over my shoulders. "I don't think I'll ever get over how perfect your body is." Leaning forward, she kisses my right pec and then my left as she reaches for the waistband of my sweatpants.

Reaching behind her back with one hand while I cup her face with the other, I unclip her bra. Emree gives me a wicked smile as it slides down her arms, leaving her bare and beautiful from the waist up. She stands there, half-naked and not shy, in front of me. Sticking her thumbs into the waistband of her leggings, she brings them down to her ankles and kicks them away. Her lace underwear is the only thing covering her body.

Palming both of her bare breasts, I kiss her as she runs her hands through my short hair, tugging on the strands. She moans into my mouth, and that sets me off. Wrapping my hands around the outside of her thighs, I lift her and she wraps those beautiful legs around my waist. Walking across the room, I drop her onto the bed. She throws her arms above her head and stares up at me. Slowly, I glide my hands up her legs until I reach her underwear and begin dragging them down. After tossing the last piece of fabric covering her body, Emree lies on the bed, completely naked. Her long hair is fanned out and her glowing, smooth skin is a complete contrast to the white comforter with her new tan.

She bites her lip as she stares up at me. "You have me at a bit of a disadvantage here." One of her legs lifts and she rubs her calf against my hip.

Smirking down at her, I massage the leg that is hooked around me before letting it drop and pulling my sweats down, dragging my boxer briefs along with them. "This better?" I ask now that I'm standing completely naked.

She licks her lips as she takes me in and focuses on my painful erection. "Much. Now get down here and kiss me."

Not wanting to keep her waiting, I wrap my arm around her waist and lift Emree into the center of the bed so I can rest in between her waiting legs. She moans when our mouths connect, running her nails down my back. As our tongues mingle together, exploring each other's mouths, my hands run along the soft curves of her waist and hips. When we first started hooking up, I was worried my calloused hands were hurting her because of how smooth her skin was, but she said the rough feeling turned her on more.

Emree hooks her leg over my hip, bringing me closer. "Enough foreplay. I need you, Conrad," she whispers in my ear.

Using all my willpower, I push away from her and go to my suitcase to grab a condom from the box I brought. We made a nice dent in the brand-new box over the week we've been here, and I smile thinking about all the different ways I took her in this very room.

Once I rip the foiled package with my teeth and have myself suited up, I'm back between Emree's waiting legs. Pushing her hair back from her face, I stare into her crystal-blue eyes. Never have I ever felt a connection like this with another woman. So many times, I have come close to saying those three cursed words to Emree, but I stop myself before they can come out. I know she feels the same way, but with how I have treated her in the past, she holds back. Her beauty is unlike anything else out there, and Emree has a heart larger and more full of love than any other person I know. I think that made me fall in love with her. Seeing how good of a friend she is, not only to Blaire but even to my roommates, who have become her friends also, made my heart warm up to her. She is unapologetically herself and loves and cares deeply.

Cupping her face, I make sure she can't break our eye contact as I slowly push into her. Emree closes her eyes and her mouth falls open the farther I go in.

"Oh god," she moans.

I lift Emree's leg high on my hip as I thrust in and out of her, going faster and faster. She throws her hands out to the sides, gripping the comforter as her orgasm approaches. I know she's close because she begins to hold her breath and squeezes her eyes shut.

"Oh my god, Conrad!" she shouts as she explodes around me. Her hands leave the bed and reach for me. I drop her leg and they fall open on the mattress. She grips my shoulders, holding me close to her. My hips don't slow as I try to find my own release. After a few thrusts, I come, and my grunts and moans are muffled as I hold her close to me and bury my face in her neck.

As we both lie here, clutching each other and trying to catch our breaths, I know this moment is going to be burned into my brain for the rest of my life. Staring into this woman's eyes while I make love to her is something we have never done before, but what we just did was more than sex. Maybe it's because I know this is our last time, or maybe it's because I have finally admitted to myself my feelings for Emree. Whatever it is, I know tomorrow is going to be harder than anything I have had to do before because I am not only going to crush the first woman I have fallen in love with, but I know this is going to be difficult for me to recover from as well.

CHAPTER EIGHT

EMREE

Today is the day I've dreaded since the moment we arrived at the beach. Our time here has been relaxing and more incredible than I could have thought. Being able to let all the stress of classes and work out of my mind has been a blessing. Being with Conrad for seven days straight wasn't too bad either. Last night when we had sex, it was different than any other time before. It was as if he stared into my soul the entire time. While I have never made love with a man before, I can't help but wonder if that was what we did. It sure felt like it.

After we both came down from the high, we got ready for bed together. Brushed our teeth side by side in the bathroom, then he got dressed in a pair of boxer briefs and slid one of his T-shirts over my head to wear. When we got into bed, Conrad pulled me as close as possible to him and wrapped his arms tightly around me. I wondered if something was wrong, but figured he was just going to miss being at the beach house like I was.

While our long night left me tired this morning, I wouldn't give it up for anything. Levi wanted to leave early Saturday since it was over a nine-hour drive and we still had to load up all our suitcases into the cars. After changing and packing up the last of my stuff, Conrad comes over and kisses me on the lips before grabbing our bags and taking them downstairs to Mateo's SUV.

Once I have my shoes on and look around the room to make sure neither of us forgot anything, I grab my purse off the bench at the bottom of the bed and make my way downstairs to meet everyone in the kitchen. Maddox, Blaire, Trazia, Camden, and Jules are all in there eating breakfast.

"Hey, girl," Blaire greets me. "Jules and I made some eggs and bacon if you want any. I left the bread and butter out too." She smiles as she takes a bite of her toast.

"Thanks," I tell her as I grab a paper plate off the island and fill it with scrambled eggs and a couple pieces of bacon. Going to the fridge, I look for the ketchup and see they've already cleaned it out.

"You're damn right I made sure to pack that shit up. I couldn't handle another morning of you putting ketchup on your eggs like a serial killer," Maddox says from where he is sitting between Camden and Trazia at the island.

Shutting the fridge, I pop my hip out and rest my hand on it as I glare at him. "A serial killer? Really, Maddox? Putting ketchup on your eggs is very normal and common and does not make me a serial killer." I roll my eyes and walk over to where I left my plate. "I have no idea where you come up with the thoughts that go through your brain."

He points his fork at me, not realizing there is some egg hanging off the end. "You notice any of these *normal* people around us putting ketchup on their eggs? No, you don't. That makes you a freak and probably a serial killer. It's just a good thing we're leaving while we are before you kill one of us." He points his fork at all of our friends and ends up flinging bits of egg through the air.

THE HURT OF LETTING GO

"What the hell, Maddy," Trazia lectures him with a raised voice. The egg pieces flew through the air and ended up smacking her in the chest and falling down her shirt.

"Maddy?" Camden questions, but they ignore him.

"Shit. Sorry, peach. Here, let me get that out for you." He reaches toward the top of her tank top, but before he can get close enough to touch her, Camden pulls him back by his shirt.

"Touch my sister and I'll break your arm, Maddox." Camden's eyes are narrowed at his best friend.

Maddox looks to his right and then to his left at Trazia. "Apologies, my lady. Big brother over here has some issues with me helping clean up the mess I made in your cleavage."

She stares at him with her mouth slightly open. "Do you not have a filter?"

He shrugs his shoulders and begins shoveling his food into his mouth. "Why filter our most honest thoughts?"

Camden rolls his eyes. "Maybe because you make people uncomfortable."

Before Maddox can respond, Conrad, Levi, and Mateo walk in. They are slightly sweaty and just a little out of breath. "Cars are both loaded up," Levi informs us.

Taking the last bite of my eggs, I grab my trash and start collecting everyone else's empty plates and discard them in the trash can before pulling the bag out and tying the top off so we can put it in the dumpster outside. Blaire is already up and cleaning the few dishes she used to make breakfast and putting them away in the cabinets.

Conrad is talking with Maddox and Mateo in the foyer. I walk over to him and wrap my arms around his waist. "Hey, handsome."

He smiles down at me and wraps his arm around my shoulders. "Ready to go?"

I nod.

He kisses my temple and we all begin making our way

outside. Camden, Blaire, Conrad, and I end up riding in Mateo's SUV again. Camden grumbles and tries to get Conrad to switch with Trazia and says he has a weird feeling about leaving his sister with Maddox after what happened at breakfast, but Conrad convinces him everything is fine and there is nothing to worry about.

Since I didn't get much sleep last night, it isn't long before I pass out in the back seat. Camden said he was in charge of the radio since he was driving and knowing the type of music he would play, I popped my earphones in and put on some Taylor Swift to drown out his '90s rock. We jerk to a stop and the movement jolts me awake. My head hits the window when I'm thrown back.

"Damn, Camden, learn how to drive much?" I question as I rub the throbbing spot on my head.

He looks back and shrugs his shoulders. "Sorry. My girl had to pee and some guy cut me off trying to get the spot."

Looking around, I realize we're in the parking lot of a Publix. We must have made it to Florida already, so I've been sleeping for longer than I thought. The sun is high, so it must be the middle of the afternoon.

Blaire begins pushing on my shoulder from her seat in the middle. "Seriously, let's go. He is being strict about the pee breaks again and this is the first one I'm getting." After I get out, she takes off to the entrance, and I follow behind her at a normal pace. If this road trip has taught us anything, it's that Blaire has the bladder of a child.

After using the restroom, I walk around to try to find the guys. Conrad said he was going to grab a drink. Going up and down the aisles, I keep an eye out for them. I snag a bag of chips and ginger ale while walking around. Heading to the front, I catch up to Conrad, Camden, and Blaire in line. Blaire has an armful of candies and chips.

Approaching them, I laugh at her variety of sweet and

savory treats. "You think you have enough snacks for the rest of the drive?"

Blaire looks down and smiles. "I didn't get a chance to go to the store before we left, so I'm making up for the first few hours. It's not the same, reading a book on a road trip without snacking. Made the drive feel much slower."

We all stare at her with perplexed looks on our faces.

"You're really strange, you know that?" Conrad asks her with a small smile on his face, making it known he is not serious.

Blaire dumps her items on the conveyor belt. "Surprised you're just now realizing that."

Conrad laughs and grabs my drink and chips and places them on the belt along with his energy drink. He goes ahead of us and pays as the cashier scans the items. "You didn't have to do that," I tell him.

"Yeah, Con, I bought way too much for you to pay. Here, take some cash."

She tries to hand him a few ten-dollar bills, but he pushes her hand away. "Don't worry about it."

Camden thanks him as he grabs the bags of his and Blaire's sodas and snacks. Walking over, I wrap my arms around Conrad's waist from behind. He stiffens but loosens up right after.

"Thank you, babe," I tell him, placing a kiss between his shoulder blades before going to grab our one bag with our drinks and my chips.

We head back to the car and I take the middle seat this time, giving Blaire a chance to not be squished between a body and luggage. Instead of his usual rock music, Camden turns the radio to some sports station, and he and Conrad get to talking about a game that was playing today.

Blaire groans beside me. "Are we seriously having to listen

to this crap?" She tosses a few sour gummy worms into her mouth.

Camden glances over his shoulder and points at her. "You want to drive?"

She shakes her head.

"Then sit back, enjoy your snacks, and read whatever cheesy book you downloaded. No one else volunteered to drive, so that means the radio is under my control." He's right. Though Mateo said we could take his SUV on the trip since it's larger and better on gas, everyone got quiet after he said he wouldn't be driving. Camden stepped up and said he would. The only drawback is his lack of sharing the radio.

Blaire remains silent and goes back to snacking and reading on her Kindle. I laugh at the two of them because it is rare to see Camden get somewhat serious with her like that. To Camden, Blaire walks on water and can do no wrong. The driving must be getting to him.

I pop my earphones back in and decide to listen to my favorite fashion podcast. It talks about the history behind fashion, which has always been a favorite topic of mine. Getting a fashion management major with a minor in fashion design degree has always been my goal. My dream is to have my own fashion line, working for some of the greatest companies, like Chanel, Prada, or Hermès. While those are unrealistic companies to work for, I am making it my goal to at least work for one of the greatest and maybe even do Fashion Week.

Fashion has always been a passion of mine. Growing up with a single mom, we were stretched for money all my life. While the majority of my clothes were hand-me-downs or bought from thrift stores, my mom bought a sewing machine at the flea market, and together, we would spice up the used clothes we bought. I became obsessed with updating the clothes I had and then eventually was getting fabric at the store and creating my own outfits. My mom said I was a natural when it came to using the sewing machine and by high school, I was making almost all of my own clothes. Many of them were unique and very much me but still stylish. There were even some girls in my school who asked me to make dresses for them for homecoming and prom, and I was able to create a small business out of it.

Listening to fashion podcasts usually consists of me taking notes when the hosts talk about subjects I want to learn more about, but since I'm in a moving vehicle, I decide to lay my head back against the seat and absorb every word the hosts talk about.

Time goes by fast while I listen to my podcasts and before I know it, we are pulling into the guys' house. Blaire fell asleep after eating through half of her snacks, probably in a food coma. Maddox's truck is already in the driveway and the back looks empty from what I can see. Once the car comes to a stop, I nudge Blaire awake.

"What? What?" She looks around, frazzled. "We're home already? What time is it?"

I look down at my phone. "A little after six. You passed out after eating a crazy amount of junk food."

She looks down at the empty snack wrappers in her lap. "Damn, I really went a little crazy, didn't I?"

Laughing, I shake my head. "Move it, candy junkie. I need to stretch my legs."

Blaire stuffs all her candy and chips into the grocery bag, opens the door, and hops out of the car.

Following behind her, I moan when I'm able to extend my legs and reach my arms up toward the sky. "This was a much-needed and great vacation, but I am very happy with never sitting in a car ever again for more than an hour. My ass is killing me." Blaire laughs at me while she is bent over, doing some stretching of her own.

The guys head to the back of the SUV and begin unloading.

Between the four of us, we are able to get the car unloaded in no time. Camden and Conrad were sweethearts and made sure to grab the heaviest items, leaving Blaire and me with little to bring in.

Once the car is empty, we join everyone else in the living room. I plop down beside Conrad on the two-person sofa and snuggle up to his side. He takes a deep breath before wrapping his arm around my shoulders.

"Em, do you mind if Conrad drives you home and I take your car later? Camden and I are going to drive Trazia back home, so I'll be back at our apartment late."

Looking up at Conrad, I raise my eyebrow. "You okay with that?"

He nods.

I smile at my best friend. "No problem. Be nice to my baby, though. I'm sure she has missed me."

Blaire rolls her eyes. "Your obsession with that car is insane." She has always thought my love for Baby Blue, my car, was weird. I treasure that vehicle and make sure she is taken care of and loved.

"You ready to go now?" Conrad whispers in my ear.

"Oh, um, sure," I stutter. I don't want to leave, but he seems eager to drive me home. I'm sure he's tired from the drive like I am, so maybe he wants to go to bed early.

We go around saying goodbye to our friends, and I tell Trazia it was great to meet her. Camden had said she was considering coming to Braxton next year. It would be nice to add another girl to our group. The guys far outnumber us.

Conrad grabs my bags and we head to his car. He's quiet the entire ten-minute drive to my apartment and doesn't rest his hand on my thigh like he normally does. Maybe he didn't get to nap in the car and the lack of sleep last night is catching up to him.

In no time, we make it to my apartment, and he brings the

bags up the elevator for me. I thank him once we are inside my room, and he smiles at me.

We head out of my room, and Conrad stops in the living room, turning toward me. "Em…we need to talk."

My stomach sinks at those five words because nothing good comes after them.

CHAPTER NINE

CONRAD

I can't do this. I can't fucking do this.

The moment the smile drops from her face, I have to look away. She knows something is wrong, and her entire body tenses. Trying to find the right words to say, I look at my shoes. Everything I have thought up in my head over the last week disappears. Nothing seems right now that the moment is here.

"Wh-what do you mean?" Her voice is low and unsure. I hate that I've made this normally outgoing and confident woman quiet and nervous.

Running my hands down my face, I let out a groan. "This. I can't do it anymore. Our relationship needs to end."

A sob breaks out of her. When I finally look up, her eyes are filled with tears. "Did I...do something wrong? I-I thought we had a good week together. Why do you want to end us?"

I consider telling her the truth but know she will look down on me. All of our friends would. I have no backbone by allowing my dad to control my life this way. "You're perfect, Em. I swear, it has nothing to do with you. It's—"

"Don't you dare say, 'It's not you, it's me,'" she cuts me off. "I swear, Conrad, I will strangle you if you try pulling that on me." Taking a deep breath, she straightens her shoulders. "Tell me the truth. Right now. I want the honest-to-God truth from you on why you are breaking up with me."

Linking my hands behind my neck, I squeeze. Hard. "I can't do that, Em."

She stares at me. Like, really stares at me. It's like she is seeing me for the first time, and I feel naked under her scrutiny. "Then get the fuck out of my apartment."

"Em—"

"No!" she shouts. More tears are coming down her face as she comes forward and starts pushing on my chest. "Get the fuck out. Now. I hate you. I hate you, Conrad."

Grabbing her hands, I stop her assault. She sobs and tries to pull her hands away. "No, no, no. You…you made me fall in love with you, you bastard. I hate you. Let me go."

Love. She just said she fucking loves me.

"Em…"

"Don't," she whispers, tears falling freely from her eyes. "Just get out. Please."

Letting go of her hands, I stare at the tearstained face of the most beautiful woman. Those crystal-blue eyes I have grown to love are bloodshot.

I let this go on for too long. I'm a downright bastard for stringing her along for six months when I knew our relationship had an end date.

Her shoulders slump. Without another glance, I turn and head out her front door. Before shutting it, I can hear her sobs coming through the hallway. That sound breaks me and with every step away from her, I crack even more.

Getting into my car, I slam my fist against the steering wheel. The dam breaks and tears stream down my face. I can't even remember the last time I cried. Maybe my grandfather's funeral when I was in sixth grade?

My palm makes contact with the wheel once, twice, a third

time before I sit back, rubbing my eyes and trying to get the tears to stop coming. They flow and I realize how much it is hurting me to let her go. Never did I think a girl would affect me the way Emree has, yet here I am crying over losing her.

The thought of her sitting in that dark apartment alone pisses me off and part of me knows I should have waited to do this when Blaire would be home, but I also know that I could not put it off another day.

After controlling myself enough to drive, I head back to my house. The tears have since dried, but that ache in my chest is still there. When I pull into the driveway, I'm thankful that Camden's Jeep is gone, so I don't have to face him or Blaire. I know the two of them are going to give me shit when they learn about what I just did to Emree, and I'm not ready for that.

Walking in the front door, my roommates and Jules are all still sitting in the same spots from when I left. Maddox looks up and his eyebrows pinch together.

"What the hell is up with you?" he asks.

Ignoring him, I take the stairs two at a time to my room. On autopilot, I change into a pair of athletic shorts, a T-shirt, and tennis shoes, then grab my gym bag on the way out.

Once I am downstairs and at the front door, someone pauses the TV, and Levi is the one to ask me a question this time. "Seriously, man, you okay?"

Pausing with my hand on the doorknob, I don't look at him but answer. "Just ruined my future because of my fucked-up family." Without another word, I leave and get in my car.

The drive to our campus gym is short. Technically, the gym closes at seven, but upperclassman athletes get twenty-four-hour access with our key fobs. Once I park, I look around the parking lot and notice there is only one car there.

Inside, it's quiet, with only the sound of the air conditioning and a single treadmill making noise. Without looking around, I head straight to where a few punching bags are hanging in the corner. Grabbing the gloves from my bag, I begin taking my frustrations out one blow after another.

Emree's face, her beautiful fucking face, was crushed because of me. Her words keep running through my head.

She loves me. I let this woman fall in love with me when I knew nothing could come of this relationship. Who the fuck does that? There has to be something seriously wrong with me for me to have continued this relationship after I caught feelings for her when I knew we had an expiration date.

But that's just it. She was the reason I couldn't stop it. Being around Emree made me forget where I came from. She is so sweet and happy and filled with life. Being around her made it seem like I had this normal future that consisted of us being together. Not the one where I am destined to marry a complete stranger, all in the name of strengthening my family's business.

Several punches later, I am dripping with sweat. Even though the rule is you need to keep a shirt on while in here, I remove mine since the one guy who was on the treadmill earlier left, and I am alone. Pulling the gloves off, I head over to the fountain and guzzle down some water. As I'm walking back, my phone begins ringing from my bag.

Once in my hand, I pause at the caller ID. The man who is ruining me wants to talk. Knowing I can't let it ring any longer, or he will lash out, I answer. "Hello," I greet in a flat tone.

"I'm assuming you are back from your little trip away?" my father asks.

"Yes, sir."

"Good. It is time to get serious about your future, Conrad."

My nostrils flare at his mention of my future. The one he is dead set on destroying.

"I am sending Liliana out, and she will be staying at one of our hotels in Tampa. She will be there for the remainder of your semester. I expect you to treat this as if you were dating any other girl. Wine and dine her, even though she has already agreed to the marriage. We want it to look as organic as possible." Bile rises thinking about getting close to this girl when my heart belongs to the one I just had to leave. "We want the engagement to happen by the end of summer, so get to know her as much as possible."

"If she has already agreed to it, why do I have to basically date her?"

"Don't question me, boy. You will do as I say with no back talk. The merging of our families is going to be on the front pages, and we want you two to look as in love as possible." I can hear the squeak of his office chair as he leans back. "Between you and me, the girl is a looker. Your mother and I met her in person last weekend. You will be quite pleased with the choice. She is lean and has a body I am sure you will enjoy."

Hearing my own father talk like that is sickening. "Then you marry her." I knew those words were a mistake the moment they came out of my mouth.

"Talk back to me one more time, and I will fly to Braxton to knock some sense into you myself," he barks into the phone. "And marriage is more than good pussy, son. You will learn that when the time comes. Don't worry. You can always have more on the side, especially when you create an heir with this girl. Pregnant women are disgusting to fuck."

My breathing becomes heavy as I try to control myself and watch my words. "Are we done?"

He sighs. "She will be there tomorrow night. A car will pick her up and bring her to the hotel, but I expect you to greet her and take her to dinner."

"Of course."

"I'll have my secretary send you her flight and hotel details." He hangs up without a goodbye, as usual.

Sitting on the bench where I left my bag, I drop my head into my hands as I rest my elbows on my thighs. In two days, I am going to have to take a complete stranger on a date. No, not a complete stranger.

My future fucking wife.

CHAPTER TEN

EMREE

The house is dark by the time the front door opens again. I'm sitting on the floor, not having moved since I fell to the ground after Conrad left. After breaking up with me. The man I fell in love with and wanted nothing more than to tell him this weekend broke up with me. I could have sworn after last night, he felt the same way, yet here I am, crying on the floor of my apartment, experiencing the worst heartbreak I have ever felt.

"Em? You here? Why are all the lights off?" Blaire calls from down the hallway.

"B-Blaire?" I struggle to call out. My voice is hoarse from all the crying.

She comes around the corner and the moment she sees me, she drops her purse onto the floor. Once she is close enough, she drops down to the ground with me, sitting on her calves. "What's wrong? Are you hurt? What happened?" Her questions come out rushed as she looks me over, trying to find any evidence that I am injured.

A new wave of tears comes out, and I'm beginning to wonder if they will ever dry up. "C-Conrad…he…he…" Taking a deep breath, I try to get myself composed enough to talk. "Broke u-up with m-me."

Blaire leans back, her jaw dropped in shock. "No. There is no way. Em, there has to be a mistake."

Shaking my head, I wipe the tears away with the back of my hand. "Nope. He stood right there"—I point to the spot Conrad was when he broke my heart—"and told me he 'can't do this' anymore."

"Are you sure he didn't, like, hit his head or something?"

Staring into her eyes, I say the next words slowly, "He doesn't want me, Blaire. Even when I begged him to tell me what I did wrong, he couldn't give me a reason."

Her eyes fill with tears hearing the pain in my voice.

"He...he doesn't want me."

Lunging forward, Blaire wraps me in her arms and squeezes hard. "That man is an idiot, and I have no idea what is going through his big, dumb head." Sitting back, she releases me but holds on to my shoulders. "You are an amazing woman, Emree Anders. Not only are you absolutely stunning on the outside, but you have the kindest heart of anyone I know. He is a fool to do this to you, and I will make sure his death is slow, but you are strong. This will not tear you down."

Forcing a smile, I reassure her that I understand, yet doubt creeps in. "I know."

With a bounce, Blaire is up on her feet. "If there is one thing you taught me when Camden and I had issues, it is that there is no crying over men. They do not deserve our tears, and we do not need them." She walks over toward the kitchen, and I decide it is a good idea to get up off the floor.

Wiping my tears, I go to sit on the three-person couch. A place with a lot of memories I made with Conrad. Ones of us snuggling together and watching a movie that would eventually turn into us falling asleep in each other's arms.

Blaire comes in with my favorite ice cream, rocky road, and

THE HURT OF LETTING GO

hers, Ben & Jerry's Americone Dream. She hands me mine along with a spoon and takes a seat on the other end of the couch, tucking her legs underneath her. "We are going to drown ourselves in creamy goodness and have the night to be sad. Tomorrow, my badass friend, we are moving forward. Conrad has lost his marbles for letting you go, but he does not deserve your tears."

"But, Blaire—"

"No buts," she interrupts. "I am serious, Emmy. You are a catch and if he doesn't see that, we will find you someone who does. There are plenty of attractive men on campus. Or hey, what about that kickboxing instructor? He was hot, and you said he asked you out."

I hadn't even thought about Andres since we attended our class the Monday before our spring break trip. He did ask me out that first day and flirted some when we came to his class.

"Yeah, maybe you're right." Even I can hear the doubt in my own words.

The thought of jumping to someone else right after what just happened between Conrad and me doesn't feel right. While in the past, moving on with someone else was not uncommon, none of those relationships were as serious as mine and Conrad's. He was the first guy I called my boyfriend. The longest I had been with a guy before him was probably around two months. The sad fact is that the guys before were always the ones to end it. There must be some man repellent I have that makes them leave me.

Once she finishes her mouthful of ice cream, she points her spoon at me. "Of course I am right," she says in a stern tone. The longer she stares at me, the softer her eyes become. "This isn't you, Em. You're one of the most confident people I know, and you've dated before, but I've never seen you like this."

That's where she's wrong. I'm not a confident person. Blaire didn't know precollege Emree, the girl who felt like she wasn't desirable to men and was insecure about her body. Moving to Braxton and starting a new life helped me build that confidence, but those doubts are still lingering inside of me. The ones that tell me I'm not attractive enough or worthy of being loved.

The sad part is Conrad was bringing out a more self-assured Emree. The way he admired my body and the sweet, comforting words he would tell me made me think all my insecurities were blown out of proportion. I'm no longer the same girl I was in middle and high school. While I am still curvy, I have grown to love my body. No longer do I have a face filled with acne after finally seeking help from a dermatologist. I'm happier with myself in the years since leaving my small town in North Florida, but some of that self-doubt lingers. I must have been doing a hell of a job hiding it, though, since my best friend and roommate sees me as one of the most confident people she knows.

"I'll be okay, Blaire." Mustering up my best reassuring smile, I nudge her with my foot. "Maybe I'll take the hot kickboxing coach up on his offer."

She smiles. "He was pretty cute. Plus, I couldn't help but notice it took him a lot of self-control to keep his eyes off you during our class."

A laugh escapes me, and it feels good. "He was not."

Blaire nudges me with her foot. "He so was. You should have seen Jules on the other side of me. She was doing everything to get him to look at her. I swear, one of her boobs almost fell out of her sports bra because she was pushing them up so high."

"What?" I choke on some ice cream. "How could you not tell me that?"

She shrugs her shoulders. "Guess I kind of forgot about it until now. It was funny, though, but luckily, he didn't notice because he was too focused on the blonde bombshell beside me."

"Whatever." I roll my eyes at her. "Let's watch something mindless on TV to distract me from that asshole breaking my heart tonight."

Grabbing the remote, Blaire clicks the TV on. "Are we avoiding something sappy? Maybe some action? A comedy?" She begins flipping through Netflix movies.

"Definitely nothing sappy or romantic," I tell her. "What about *Wedding Crashers*? That always gets us laughing."

"*Wedding Crashers* it is then." Blaire turns the movie on and snuggles into her spot on the couch after grabbing the blanket behind her.

"Warning you right now, I'm going to finish this container of ice cream and make some popcorn and maybe even some brownies during the movie."

Junk food is a staple when your heart is broken.

Blaire looks over at me and smiles. "That is a beautiful warning, my friend."

We remain silent as the movie plays. I try not to get lost in my own thoughts, but I can't help it. Dating someone in your friend group is great until that couple breaks up. A lot is going to change. Blaire being in a relationship with Conrad's roommate/friend/teammate will become complicated. Then throw in that Jules (Mateo's childhood best friend), Blaire, and I have become close and are together regularly. Plus, Blaire and I would spend almost every weekend at the guys' house.

Part of me is worried that I'll be the one to fall off the friend group and not Conrad. It would make sense. The majority of our friends live with him and they were his first. I just hope I don't lose my girls. Not having them, especially after losing him, would make all of this so much more difficult and add even more heartbreak.

CHAPTER ELEVEN

CONRAD

There is a loud pounding coming from the other side of the room, making me jump out of bed. My door is locked, and now I'm glad I thought ahead before going to bed last night. Camden still wasn't home when I got back from the gym, but I knew the moment Blaire found out, she would tell him and he would kick my ass for hurting his girl's best friend.

"Open the fucking door. I know you're in there," Camden yells from the other side of the door.

Taking a deep breath, I square my shoulders. "As long as you agree to calm the hell down."

He stays quiet for a minute, but the pounding starts up again. "Nope. Thought about it, and you don't deserve that. Open the damn door, or I will break it down."

Deciding I would rather take the ass kicking than have to replace my bedroom door, I pull on a pair of shorts over my briefs and walk across the room. Flicking the lock, I swing the door open. The moment I see him, Camden's fist makes contact with my face.

"Motherfucker," I mutter as I stumble back.

Camden stalks toward me. "That's just the beginning, shithead."

I hold up my hands. "Can you just give me five fucking seconds to explain?"

He stops while towering over me. His nostrils flare as he takes in a breath. "Fine. Explain yourself."

Last night, I decided I was going to come clean to my roommates. At least as much as I felt was needed. No other explanation would make sense as to why I broke up with Emree the way I did, and they are going to find out about my almost fiancée soon enough. Liliana will be coming to town in the next week or so and they are bound to meet her.

Walking away from my angry roommate, I take a seat on the end of my bed and try to ignore the throbbing in my face. "There are these...family obligations I need to uphold and cutting ties with Emree now is for the best." Leaning forward, I rest my elbows on my thighs and put my head in my hands.

Camden is quiet. He is towering over me with his arms crossed over his chest. If it were possible, I am sure steam would be coming out of his ears based on how red his face is. "Going to need more of an explanation than that."

Groaning, I stand because sitting while he's glaring down at me like that is awkward. "I haven't exactly told you much about my family. You all know I come from a rich family and I've never hidden that, but it's more. The Dugrays are...old money. My great-great-great-grandparents came here from France or some shit. Didn't really interest me when my dad would talk to me about our family history."

Camden remains silent as I pause.

"My family's name is important, and who I, as their oldest son, marry has been planned basically since before my conception. It has to be someone that comes from an important family, generally one that benefits my father's business."

Camden's eyes widen. "Marriage? There's no way in hell you're getting married—"

"They've already picked someone," I cut him off.

"Like...a fucking arranged marriage? Dude, you cannot be serious." Camden's face is filled with shock and this is the exact reason I did not want to tell the guys about this. None of them would understand.

I nod. "Exactly like an arranged marriage. That's why I had to break it off with Emree." I kick the leg of my bed. "Fuck, man, I should have never dated her this long, but I couldn't stop. Now I've completely crushed her. You should have seen her face, Camden. I hate that I did that to her."

"Yeah, Blaire called me this morning to tell me what a fuckup you are. My girl's pissed, and I'm pissed at you for pissing her off."

Maddox walks into my room. "Hey, what's going on in here? You both have a little slumber party without me?" He comes over and lies down on my unmade bed. "I'm a little offended no one invited me for a cuddle last night."

"Shut up, man," Camden tells him, with an edge to his tone.

Maddox holds his hands up. "Whoa, hostile much?" He looks between the two of us. "What's going on here?"

Camden raises an eyebrow. "Conrad dumped Emree last night and was just giving me the bullshit excuse that he has some arranged marriage or some shit."

I roll my eyes. "It's not some excuse. You just don't understand because—"

"Oh, because I don't come from a rich family?"

I remain silent because clearly, anything I say isn't going to convince him what I'm saying is the truth.

Maddox's face turns serious. "Who'd they set you up with?"

Looking at Maddox, I try to gauge if he is joking or legitimately curious. "Liliana Hawthorne," I tell him.

His eyes widen. "The casino king's daughter?"

"You know her?" I ask.

Camden's head is going back and forth between our exchange. "What the hell are you two talking about?"

Maddox takes a deep breath and looks at Camden. "He's being serious, man. Dugrays are old money and this is the way things are in their world. I'm sure his dad picked Liliana after some business talk with her father. These rich pricks still live in the past of selling your daughter for a goat or some shit, except now it's selling them for the best business deal or merger."

"Wait, this is legit?" Camden asks in awe.

I groan. "I'm not trying to sound like a dick, man, but I do mean it when I say you won't understand because you didn't grow up in this pretentious world."

He rolls his eyes.

"Trust me, if I didn't grow up around these people, it would seem like a joke to me. Sometimes I still don't understand it, but it's what has been expected of me since I was born. There is no way out of it. My father had to do it, as did his father before him."

Camden narrows his eyes. "If you knew all of this, then why did you date Em? Why string her along all this time?"

Maddox chimes in, "Yeah, Con, that was a bitch move. That girl is damn near in love with you."

There is no excuse that I can come up with because what I did was wrong. I hate that I did it, but I don't regret the time I had with Emree. It was selfish and knowing I hurt her makes me sick.

"I know," I tell them. My shoulders drop. "It was fucked up, but you both know her. How could I not want to be around that woman? I tried, guys. I seriously did. You saw me dating other people and trying to keep her at arm's length in the beginning."

"Did you at least explain all that to her? Because from what

Blaire told me, you didn't give Em any indication you were going to be ending things or a reason why," Camden says. He seems calmer now, so maybe he believes the truth.

Shaking my head, I run my hands through my hair. "No, I couldn't. Telling you guys has been hard enough, and I don't want her to see me as pathetic. I already hate what I'm having to do and the more people who know, the worse it will be."

Camden steps forward and points a finger at my chest. "You better figure this shit out, and soon. I have an angry girlfriend who I had to talk out of driving over here this morning with the promise that I would rough up your pretty face. Her words, not mine." He starts to walk out of the room. "Now I'm going to their apartment with a long list of supplies Blaire gave me to get at the grocery store for their sulking day. I'll take money out of your wallet later as reimbursement."

Maddox laughs from the bed. "That's some funny shit. He's off to take care of your girl on your dime." He jumps off the bed and stretches.

"Yeah, hilarious," I grumble.

On his way out of the room, Maddox turns to me. "Listen, man, my family, while they are a group of rich assholes, is different than yours, but if you need any help or something, I'm here."

"Thanks, Mad, but there's nothing that can be done. My life was planned out from the beginning and there is no discussing it with my father."

He nods in understanding and leaves the room.

Walking over to the bed, I take a seat on the edge and feel my chest tighten. Part of me wants to text Camden and ask him to tell me how Emree is when he gets to her apartment, but I hold back. Going through Camden to get information about Emree isn't the way to go, and if she ever found out, she would kill me.

Not talking to or seeing her is going to get to me, though, but I need to find out how she is. If anything, I want to know she will be okay.

I *need* to know she will be okay.

CHAPTER TWELVE

EMREE

Today is the day I get my shit together. It has been almost a week since Conrad dropped the ball that he didn't want to be with me anymore. I have sulked. I have cried. I have been angry. I have wondered what I did wrong. I have almost called him several times.

Now, it is time to put on my big girl panties.

Conrad Dugray does not deserve another tear out of me. His lack of care for me after everything we shared the last six months shows me the kind of man he is. Blaire has made sure to tell me multiple times over the last six days that I deserve better, and I will be damned if I don't make sure I get better.

While I haven't seen Conrad since last Sunday night, Camden came by Monday morning before classes to let me know that he left Conrad with a nasty black eye. That information somewhat made me happy because maybe Conrad will feel some of the pain he put me through, but the thought of him being hurt makes me sad and part of me, the part that still loves him, wanted to go over and see how he was and if he needed anything.

Being in love with someone who has broken your heart is a

special kind of torture. Even though Conrad hurt me like he did, I can't stop the feelings I have for him, no matter how hard I have tried. I have attempted to keep myself busy between waitressing at Whiskey Joe's and working on my final project for my textiles class. Going nonstop has made me exhausted, but at least it has somewhat kept my mind off Conrad.

Luckily, we do not have classes together this semester, but as I stroll through the cafeteria and head toward the usual table where our group sits, my eyes make contact with Conrad sitting at the end beside Mateo. Levi, Blaire, and Camden are there too, but my best friend is sitting far away from Conrad and seems to be only talking to her boyfriend.

Blaire looks up and sees me, smiling. When she notices I'm not walking toward them, she looks down at the end of the table and glares at Conrad, then turns her head back toward me with a sad smile. She tells Camden something and goes to grab her bag, but I shake my head at her and hitch my thumb to the exit, telling her that I'm leaving. Her mouth drops in a frown and she releases her bag.

Outside, there are picnic tables scattered around the courtyard. There is a large three-tier water fountain in the center that a few students are sitting around and talking or reading. Circling the fountain, I look for an empty table with no success.

"Need somewhere to sit?" a voice comes from behind me.

I turn to see a guy sitting alone at a table big enough for four. He's smiling, flaunting a set of straight teeth. His eyes are shielded by a pair of aviator sunglasses and his dark hair is covered by a ball cap hanging low, but his hair is long enough that it is flipping out around the ends.

I return his smile and lift my tray of food. "Was hoping to not have to eat my lunch on the ground today."

He chuckles and waves a hand to the seat across from him. "You're free to join me."

THE HURT OF LETTING GO

Raising an eyebrow, I eye him suspiciously. "How do I know you aren't a murderer or something? You're giving off very Unabomber vibes."

A full belly laugh comes from him, and I have decided I really like that sound. It's loud and masculine. I imagine this stranger's stomach muscles contracting under his shirt like his arms are. "Oh, that was a good one. Can't say I have ever been compared to the Unabomber before." Reaching up, he removes his sunglasses, revealing a pair of dark-brown eyes that match his hair. "Better? I swear I'm not a murderer or something. Just a guy asking a beautiful woman if she would like to join him for lunch."

For the first time in almost a week, a genuine smile spreads across my face. Mystery Man is a charmer and knows it by the way he is smirking at me. "Fine, Mr. Not a Murderer or Something, I will sit with you."

Taking a few steps, I set my tray down first and then swing my legs over the bench to take a seat. I set my bright-pink backpack down on the empty seat to my right. The stranger from the other side of the table watches my every move with interest.

As I begin unwrapping my turkey sandwich, I ask, "You going to tell me your name or stare at me awkwardly?"

He gives me that award-winning smile again. "My name is Ian."

After taking a sip of my Diet Coke, I nod. "Nice to meet you, Ian. I'm Emree. And thank you for saving me from enjoying my lunch on the ground. That was very sweet of you."

Leaning forward, he rests his elbows on the table and smirks. In front of him is an open notebook and there is a Smoothie King cup to the side of it. "Not going to lie to you, but I may have had an ulterior motive."

I smile around my sandwich and take a bite, making sure to swallow it all before responding. "Is that so?"

"When someone sees a pretty woman in need of a place to sit, they would be a fool not to offer their table. Especially if that someone is free tomorrow night and wants to take said pretty woman out."

Oh, this guy is smooth and he knows it. He oozes confidence, and I've never been around someone like that. Well, until Conrad. Thinking of my ex is the last thing that should be on my mind right now, so I push all thoughts of him out.

"If someone were to ask said pretty woman out this Saturday, the pretty woman would be saddened to tell them that she has to work. But if that someone was free tonight, the pretty girl has the night off."

His dark-brown eyes light up. "Well, I have this thing tonight with my frat, but if you don't mind crashing that with me, I would love to hang out with you."

Am I ready for this? To date again? Ian is cute and clearly charming. Plus a bonus, he finds me attractive. Maybe Blaire is right, and I need to find a guy who actually wants to be with me and not end our relationship with no explanation. But is it too soon? Conrad still owns my heart, but maybe spending time with Ian is the quickest way to mend that.

Smiling at Ian, I nod. "I would like to crash your frat thing tonight."

He mirrors my smile, and I notice he has a little dimple on his clean-shaven left cheek. Ian has more boyish features, somewhat innocent. The complete opposite of someone who I would think is in a fraternity. His body, though, is far from boyish. With a wide chest and long arms, I can tell Ian is tall. His fingers are long and calloused. Maybe he plays an instrument like the guitar. With broad shoulders, his relaxed T-shirt fits him perfectly but is tight around his muscular biceps.

Ian is incredibly attractive, and I can see myself being with someone like him. He begins talking and from the corner of my eye, I catch sight of the tall, blond-haired man who broke

THE HURT OF LETTING GO

my heart not even a week ago. He is walking beside Levi and Mateo, laughing as he strolls across the courtyard without a care in the world.

Clearly, our breakup has not affected him at all. Just when I'm about to look away, a beautiful woman with long, black hair approaches him. She is tall—like a model—and beyond gorgeous, making it almost hard to look at her. She wraps her manicured hand around Conrad's forearm and kisses him on the cheek. He doesn't pull away, and she joins them as they walk toward the parking lot.

My heart clenches, thinking he has moved on. Did I mean nothing to him at all? Were the last six months just casual and fun for him? With how comfortable she is to approach him like that, maybe they have known each other, or he went back to one of his many hookups. I was clear with him all those months ago at my apartment that I needed more than casual sex, which is what he was used to. I had real feelings for Conrad and wanted to have a serious relationship. He was hesitant but agreed to make us official. Maybe I pushed him when he wasn't ready for something serious.

"Hey, you okay?" Ian asks, breaking me out of my thoughts.

Snapping my head away from Conrad and the Victoria's Secret model, I look at Ian. "Yeah, sorry. I thought I saw someone I know. What were you saying?"

Ian's smile falters some, but he answers anyway. "I was just asking what time you wanted me to pick you up. The party starts at eight, but we can grab dinner beforehand if you're interested?"

It's already three and I have one more class in half an hour that would end around four thirty.

"Dinner before sounds nice. How about you pick me up at six? Does that work?" I ask him.

He nods. "Perfect. How about I get your number and you can text me your address?"

We exchange numbers, and Ian stands, grabbing his empty smoothie cup and backpack. "I'll see you tonight." He winks and then walks away. Now that he is standing, I see that Ian is taller than I thought. Far bigger than my five foot four. His jeans hang low on his tapered waist and hug his generous behind, which is perfectly round.

Before I get caught staring at him, I look away and focus on finishing the rest of my sandwich and fruit bowl on my tray, thinking about what I am going to wear tonight. On my date. On my date with Ian.

My stomach grows queasy thinking about it. My Friday nights before were always spent with Conrad unless I was working. We would either go out with our friends or order in some food and end up watching some of the best comedies at either of our places. Going from all my time being occupied by a guy I was hopelessly falling in love with to now another man makes me sad, but clearly, I'm not the only one trying to move on.

BACK AT THE APARTMENT, I walk in on Blaire and Camden, horizontal on the couch. Camden's large body is covering my roommate's, and before shutting my eyes, I get a glimpse of his hand down her pants.

"Ah," I shout. "Why does this keep happening to me?" On multiple occasions, I have walked in on my best friend and her boyfriend getting freaky. The first time was completely my own fault, but in my defense, I did think she was alone in his room since it was before they started getting physical. Each time after that, though, it has been because these are two horny young adults who need to realize other people live with them.

"Em, I didn't know you would be home this early," Blaire says. I hear Camden make an *oof* sound from what I can only imagine is Blaire pushing him off.

With my hand still covering my eyes, I answer her, "Um, Blaire, it's almost five. My class ended almost half an hour ago."

"Shit, it's five," Camden says. "We're decent, Em. You can uncover your eyes."

Dropping my hand, I see both of them now standing. Blaire is adjusting her top and Camden is grabbing his phone.

"Do you have to go?" she asks him.

He nods. "Yeah. A few of us are going to support the freshmen tonight at some ceremony or something, not too sure. Coach just told me he thought it would be a good idea if the team captain and some of the guys were there for them."

"Aw, okay." Blaire pouts, but not in the annoying way some girls do it. She is genuinely sad he has plans tonight. "Guess I'll see you tomorrow? Emree and I are working the earlier night shift, so maybe you can stay over?"

"I'll be here, Gray Eyes," he says with a smile. Bending down, Camden kisses her hard on the lips. I look away, wanting to give them a private moment, but also sad because it is the little things like a goodbye kiss that I miss the most with Conrad.

Camden leaves, and I look at my phone, noting that I have less than an hour until Ian picks me up. I texted him my address, and he said he wasn't far since he lives in a house nearby. An hour is plenty of time to shower, do my hair and makeup, and put together a bomb outfit.

"Guess what, bestie?" I ask Blaire as I head to the bathroom and turn the shower on to the hottest setting.

She comes down the hall and stands in the doorway. "What's that?"

Smiling at her, I grab a fresh towel from the rack above the toilet. "I have a date tonight."

Blaire's jaw drops before a smile appears. "Emmy, I am so happy. Where is he taking you? What are you going to wear?"

Shrugging out of my bright-pink tank top, I toss it onto the counter. "Some event or something with his frat. He's taking me to dinner beforehand."

Blaire ducks her head while I remove the rest of my clothes, and I give her the okay that I am behind the shower curtain.

"You are going to have a great time, Em. Tell me about the guy."

While shampooing and conditioning my hair, I begin telling Blaire what little I can about Ian. Mainly that he is cute and seems nice and funny. She says the way we met is an adorable story, and I would have to agree with her.

Talking more about my lunch with Ian gets me excited for our date, and it helps me put Conrad out of my mind. I am hoping the hours I spend with Ian are the beginning of my progress to moving forward.

My heart needs this more than anything. Even if nothing comes of going out with Ian tonight, knowing that I'm able to take this step shows me that I am going to be okay. My heart may be broken, and I'm not sure how long it takes for something like that to heal, but I can't let that define my life. I allowed myself days to wallow, and now it is time to live.

CHAPTER THIRTEEN

CONRAD

The last six days have been absolute hell. First, because I miss the fuck out of Emree and not being able to talk to or see her has been torture. To top off the shitstorm that is my life, Liliana is the opposite of any woman I would want to be with, let alone marry. The moment I met her at the hotel for dinner, I knew we were not going to get along.

When I walked into the hotel lobby where we agreed to meet, Liliana was sitting on her phone with a nasty snarl on her face. Trying to be a nice guy, I brought her a bouquet of flowers and the first words out of her mouth were how cheap they were and that this better not be how our marriage was going to be since her dad promised her she was marrying someone rich.

The upside, I guess, is that she did say I was hot and she was glad she didn't have to marry some gross old man. While I thanked her for the compliment, it was the only one she gave me. When we had dinner, Liliana was rude to the waitstaff, complained about the food, and said the hotel was nothing like The Ritz-Carlton she usually stayed at. I remained quiet throughout dinner. She invited me up to her room afterward, and I politely declined.

The thought of having sex with my future wife made me sick.

Since we met on Monday, Liliana has been following me around like a little puppy. She showed up at the house, even after I told her it wasn't the best place for her to hang around since I have roommates. She even showed up on campus today, bouncing up to me as if we're a happy and in love couple. What's worse is that I am almost positive Emree saw our interaction.

While I have made sure that Camden keeps his mouth shut about Liliana to Blaire, I don't want Emree to think I have moved on so fast. As if she was nothing. Keeping Liliana hidden is going to be harder than I originally thought. Never did I think she would want us to spend time with each other every day and come around my friends and to campus. The more she is around, the more worried I get about Emree finding out.

While I know Em will eventually know about my impending marriage, I don't want her to think I was cheating on her because of how fast Liliana and I got together. On top of me being in a new relationship, I don't want Emree to see me being with someone like Liliana. While I have only known her for a few days, I can already tell she is an entitled and shallow person. It shouldn't come as a shock to me since that is the kind of people I grew up with, but being tied down to that kind of person was never what I saw for myself.

"Dude, you going to eat that bowl of cereal or just let it soak up all the milk?" Maddox asks as he walks into the kitchen. Looking down, I notice the bowl of cereal I am preparing to eat is now mush. I guess I zoned out longer than I thought.

He comes to stand at the counter on the other side of the

bar where I am sitting. "Guess not anymore," I say as I push the bowl of soggy cereal away.

Maddox opens the fridge and pulls out the orange juice, pouring it into a glass he grabbed from the top cabinet beside the sink. "You going with Camden to that ceremony thing tonight?" he asks as he leans against the counter, sipping his drink.

After getting up and moving from the barstool and into the kitchen, I dump the mush in my bowl down the sink and rinse it out. "Yeah. Coach basically told us it's mandatory."

Maddox rolls his eyes.

"Gotta support those freshmen."

"You bringing the bridezilla?"

Groaning, I drop my head back. "Hell no. It hasn't even been a week, and I'm already tired of Liliana being around."

Maddox laughs. "She's a handful, man. Mateo said she dropped by campus today."

"Acted like we were this happy, in-love couple. Not sure how much more of this I can take." I run my hands through my short hair. "When my dad told me about all this shit, I didn't think I would have to treat it like a real marriage, you know? I figured it would just be on paper, and we would know it was fake behind closed doors. But, dude, she grabbed my fucking dick last night when I dropped her off at her hotel after dinner."

Setting his cup down on the counter, Maddox looks at me with a raised eyebrow. "Wait a second, have you not been banging your fiancée?"

"Ugh, can we not call her that? And no, I'm not sleeping with Liliana," I tell him, an edge to my tone.

His eyes widen. "Why the hell not? Dude, you have easy-access pussy right there."

"Could you be any more crude?"

Maddox shrugs his shoulders. "Probably."

I can't help but roll my eyes. "Sleeping with Liliana isn't an option. At least not right now. I couldn't do that to Emree…or myself."

"You ever plan on telling her?" he asks in a serious tone.

This is something I have thought long and hard about and come up with no good response. While yes, I do plan on telling Emree, I don't know when or even how. Based on Camden's initial reaction, she probably will think I'm making it up. What I don't want is for her to find out from someone else or in the goddamn gossip reports.

"Of course I'm going to tell her. I just need to figure out how," I tell Maddox.

He shakes his head. "Better sort that shit out sooner rather than later. The longer you wait, the harder it's going to be on her."

Before I can respond to him, Camden walks into the kitchen, looking freshly showered and wearing a pair of dark jeans and a button-down black shirt with the sleeves rolled up on his forearms. "You guys ready to go?"

"Looking good, GQ," Maddox comments. He is dressed more casually in a pair of black cargo shorts and a white Henley short-sleeved shirt.

Camden shoves Maddox in the shoulder. "Shut up. Coach said this is an important event and that we should look our best. We're representing the team."

"I'll be representing our team in shorts and a T-shirt because it's hot as fuck," I tell our team captain. My light-blue cotton shorts and gray shirt are going to have to be good enough for our coach.

"Whatever," Camden mumbles. "Let's just go and get this thing over with. I hate this frat shit."

At the end of each year, the fraternities throw some massive parties. While we have never attended before, Coach likes for the upperclassmen to show up and support our freshmen frat teammates. The party part is going to be fun, but the beginning is filled with a ritual of new members taking the oath to join the frat.

Maddox drops his empty cup into the sink. "Mateo and Levi bailing tonight?"

"Levi has work, and Mateo is helping Jules move her roommate out. She and her boyfriend got a place off campus, so that freshman Piper, who's been bunking on their couch, is going to take over the lease," Camden answers.

Last year there was an incident with a ball chaser—that's what we call girls who try to sleep with soccer players for status alone—when she drugged and tried to take advantage of Camden. We would have never found out the truth of what happened if it weren't for her sorority sister Piper, who came forward and told us the truth because, with Camden not remembering what happened, it looked to everyone else that he had cheated on Blaire.

"Lucky bastards. I'd help move her shit to get out of this frat bullshit. These guys are the worst." Maddox is right. The frat guys are pricks, which is why we have always avoided their parties. We only have a couple players who join, and it's usually because their families have been members for generations.

Camden nods in agreement. "We don't have to stay long. No matter how big of an asshole these guys are, we're there to support our teammates."

"Better to leave early anyway. Their parties always get out of control. Jules said the Braxton Police Department shut down the Valentine's Day one, not even campus police. Shit was crazy. Had people jumping out of windows, for fuck's sake."

"Are you serious?" I ask Maddox.

He nods. "I was more surprised they were having a Valentine's Day party. Sigma Phi doesn't seem like the most *romantic* group of men."

"Let's just go and get this thing over with," Camden says as he starts walking out of the kitchen and toward the front door.

THIS FRAT PARTY is even worse than I thought it was going to be. While I'm not one who turns down a good party, this one is filled with some of the most egotistical and self-centered assholes I have ever come across. While hazing is not allowed, the upperclassmen in the frat get away with treating the pledges like shit.

The ceremony we attended before the party was for the freshmen, who had gone through months of bullshit to join the frat and were now becoming "brothers." Three of the ten guys are our teammates and watching them join the hypermasculinity and misogynistic brotherhood makes me wonder why anyone would want to be part of a society like this. Maybe it's because I grew up surrounded by these types of guys and made it my goal to never become like them.

The large, two-story house is shaking to the beat of the bass coming from the speakers strategically placed in each room. Bodies fill every area, some grinding against each other and more standing around with drinks in their hands. While my roommates and I have thrown our fair share of parties, they don't compare to what is going on here. There are girls in bikinis fighting in small pools filled with whipped cream, stripper poles placed throughout the open dining room, and guys high-fiving each other as they leave the bedrooms upstairs.

We have been here for all of half an hour, and I am already ready to leave. Camden and I are nursing a couple beers while taking in the various scenes around us.

"I've never felt more out of place at a college party," Camden tells me.

"I was thinking the same thing," I agree. "Were we ever like this? God, I hope not." While my freshman year, I do admit it was a wild time, I don't remember acting this foolish.

"Fuck no." Camden's tone is harsh. "These are privileged little pricks who know they can do no wrong because of Daddy's money."

Looking over, I smile at my friend. "Aw, thanks for not lumping me in with the group of privileged pricks."

Camden laughs. "While you may be privileged, you aren't a prick. Plus, the last thing you would want is your daddy's money."

"Guys, I have seen more tits tonight than I have ever before. Why don't our parties have this much toplessness?" Maddox shouts over the music as he strides over to us with a beer in hand.

"Maybe because we want to respect women and try not to objectify them?" Camden counters.

Maddox rolls his eyes. "You can still respect a lovely lady while admiring a nice pair of breasts."

I can't help but laugh because Maddox is dead serious. "Dude, I need you to get a girlfriend or something because you'll have a different thought about respect then."

Maddox clutches his chest in mock shock. "Me? A girlfriend? Absolutely not, and I am offended you would even suggest such a thing. No woman will be able to tie Maddox Stone down."

Camden and I chuckle. "It'll happen, man, just you wait. I never saw Blaire coming, yet she bulldozed right into me."

"Enough of this talk," Maddox announces as he waves a hand through the air. "This is depressing me, and I was on a tit high. Now I need to go back in and get my fill again." He leaves us and heads toward the dining room, where the women are still wrestling in the small pools.

"Should we be worried about him being off on his own?" I ask.

Camden stares off where Maddox went for a moment before answering. "You know, I'm not sure. Sometimes I feel like he needs supervision."

Flowing blonde hair flashes by in front of me, and my eyes instinctively follow it. My jaw loosens when I see Emree with her long hair perfectly curled and flowing down her shoulders, dressed in a short emerald-green wrap dress with thin straps holding it up. The fabric is molded to each of her curves, and the bust is clutching her full chest, dipping low and showing off a gracious amount of cleavage.

She looks fucking hot, and my pants tighten the longer I stare at her. Emree is the kind of woman who is unaware of her own beauty. While she doesn't try hard to be sexy, it comes naturally in the way her body moves and with her looks alone. Tonight her face is covered in minimal makeup, but her high cheekbones and naturally glowing skin make her the most stunning woman in the room.

Emree throws her head back and while she is too far for me to hear it, I know that laugh by memory and can hear it in my head. She is beautiful and unashamed when she laughs, not hiding it behind her hand like some girls do. Hers is loud and proud. I miss hearing it.

"Uh, Conrad?" Camden asks beside me.

"Yeah," I answer without looking away from Emree.

"You going to stop being a creep anytime soon?"

Tearing my eyes away from her, I look at him. "What are you talking about?"

He raises an eyebrow and lightly laughs. "You've been intensely staring at Em for, like, five minutes."

"Oh, shut the fuck up." Looking back at Emree, there is now

an arm hanging over her bare shoulders and a tall, dark-haired guy holds her against his side. She comfortably leans into him as if she has known this guy for a while.

Camden must have just seen what I've been looking at because he laughs even harder. "Oh shit."

Turning my head, I look over at him. "Who the hell is that douchebag?"

"No clue, but he and Em make a cute couple," he jokes.

I narrow my eyes at him. "You want to take that statement back?"

"Not really," he says while shrugging his shoulders. "You didn't expect her not to move on, did you?"

Truth be told, I never even considered Emree dating someone else. I have been too concerned with my fucked-up engagement and her finding out about Liliana. There has been too much going on for me to think about her moving on with someone else.

Looking back at Emree, I take in her relaxed posture beside this guy. She's looking up at him as he talks to someone else in front of them. She sips on a drink in a red cup as she hangs on to every word he says. Her eyes scan the room, passing over me. She freezes, and her head turns until she locks her gaze with mine. The relaxed posture she had before is now rigid as we stare at each other.

Fuck, I'm ready to snatch Em away from that piece of shit touching her and it's taking everything in me not to storm over there and get my girl.

CHAPTER FOURTEEN

EMREE

Ian is close to the picture-perfect date. He is sweet, attentive, handsome, and a great communicator. After picking me up at my apartment, where he brought me a beautiful bundle of flowers, we went to a local Mexican restaurant. There I learned that he is from Cleveland, Ohio, where he is the oldest of four sons and one sister. His parents are still together and very much in love. Growing up, he played hockey but wasn't good enough to make anything of it in college, so he is focusing on working toward an engineering technology degree and wants to work with an up-and-coming tech company in the future. I also learned he is a senior but plans to further his education at Braxton and work toward a master's degree.

He's sweet, and while I could see myself being with someone like Ian, I can't stop comparing him to Conrad. It's not fair, but I couldn't help the thoughts running through my head. Like the way Ian talks with food in his mouth while Conrad always makes sure to finish what he is eating before saying anything. Or how Ian talks with a lot of hand movements, whereas Conrad is less jerky when he speaks.

Comparing the two comes automatically, and I have tried my hardest to stop. Ian is a great date and a sweet guy. Plus, I need to get Conrad out of my mind. He shouldn't be living there, especially after the way he treated me. I deserve someone who wants me.

After dinner, Ian brought me to his fraternity's pledge ceremony. While I have never spent much time with the likes of Greek Row, the ceremony was not what I thought it would be. When I think of frats, my mind instantly goes to hazing and bullying. The swearing in of pledges seemed normal enough, and there were a lot of laughs shared as the guys told stories of what went on over the last year.

While that event was fun and light, the party here could not be any more opposite. The house is shaking and filled with sweaty bodies. While this is a large place, with the number of people here, it feels like I'm squished inside a sardine can. Ian has kept me held close to his body, but people still bump and rub up against me as they move around.

We made our way around the house, and he introduced me to friends and frat brothers of his as we passed by them on our way to get a drink from the kitchen. Ian stopped us in a noncrowded corner in the living room to talk to a couple friends of his, and they have been sharing stories of this year's pledges and what Hell Week was like for them versus Ian's freshman year.

Even though Ian has made sure to never exclude me from the conversation, I can't help but look away when I feel a set of eyes on me. As I scan the room, everyone seems to be lost in their own conversations or dancing to the beat of the music. There are a few people cheering on a group of girls in the whipped cream pools in the dining room, and I swear I see a flash of bare breasts. Just as I'm about to give Ian my full attention again, a pair of dark-brown eyes come into view.

Looking back, I'm staring into the eyes of the man I have

been trying to get out of my mind all night. The same man who owns my broken heart. My body goes rigid as he takes me in from head to toe. I feel naked under his stare, even though my dress and heels are on the modest side at this party. When he reaches my shoulders, his eyes narrow at Ian's arm that is lazily hanging there.

While my immediate reaction is to move out from under Ian's hold, I remain still. Conrad has no right to be angry that I am here with another guy. He is the one who made the decision to end our relationship out of the blue. He's the one who didn't want me anymore. He's the one who hurt me and let me go.

Breaking our eye contact, I focus on Ian and his friends as they talk about their upcoming graduation.

"I can't believe you're going to stay here for another two years," Ian's friend says. I have been introduced to too many people tonight, so all their names are running together. I think this one's starts with an S.

Ian laughs and the movement shakes my body. "Luckily, I won't be in the frat house anymore. Planning on getting an apartment off campus. I was able to get a TA job for Dr. Stewart, so that plus working at the Coffee Hut is enough for me to afford rent and expenses."

Looking up at Ian, I get close so I can whisper into his ear, "Where is the restroom?"

He smiles down at me. "Door under the stairs. Need me to show you?"

Shaking my head, I slide out from under his arm. "I'm good. Be back in a minute."

As I walk away, he continues his conversation with his friends. Making my way through the sea of bodies, I do my best to avoid the tall, brooding man in the corner. There is a short line outside of the bathroom, but thankfully it goes by quickly.

Just when it's my turn, as I enter the doorway, someone

shoves me from behind and slams the door shut. I'm about to turn around and give whoever this is a piece of my mind, when they grab my shoulders and turn me to face them. All the air exits my lungs as Conrad stands over me.

"What—" I'm cut off when his lips smash down on mine in a crushing kiss.

My brain and body are not communicating at this time. While my brain is telling me to break this kiss and shove him away, my body melts into his soft, warm lips and the feel of his strong body against mine.

As quickly as his lips are on mine, he removes them, but his body remains molded to my own. My back is against the wall, and his hands are on either side of my head, trapping me.

Conrad's eyes are closed and his breathing is harsh. "What are you doing to me?" he asks, but I'm not sure if the question is for me or himself.

"Why, Conrad?" I whisper. "You...you ended us. Why follow me?"

I hold my breath, waiting for his answer. Slowly, his eyes open and his gaze draws me in. "I don't know."

My chest tightens. I'm sick of his lack of communication. "No. That's not good enough this time. I'm tired of you not answering my questions." My voice is stern, and I try shoving against his chest, but he doesn't budge. "You don't get to come in here and kiss me when I'm on a date with someone else, then give me a bullshit nonanswer."

Pushing back, Conrad runs his hands through his hair. With the new distance, I'm able to breathe more easily. "I just... If I tell you what's going on, you won't even believe me."

"Try me."

We stare at each other for several seconds. Something snaps in him and before I have a chance to move, Conrad is grasping my face between his hands and crushing his mouth to mine once again. Everything around me becomes Conrad. He consumes me. His warm and cedar scent invades my senses as his tongue glides across my lips, seeking entrance.

One of the hands caging my face moves lower and grips my waist, pulling me close so every inch of my front is touching Conrad's. I gasp at the contact, and he uses this as an advantage to slip his tongue into my mouth. I moan, missing this familiar connection between us. He tastes like beer and Conrad. My body ignores my brain that's telling it to stop this and push him away as my hands glide up his chest and grip his neck, trying to bring him closer to me.

Conrad growls against my mouth, and before I can register what he's doing, his hands are on the back of my thighs and my feet are off the ground. My legs wrap around his waist on instinct, and his erection connects with my center through the thin material of my underwear.

Throwing my head back, I enjoy the feeling of Conrad against me and my hips begin to move, trying to find enough friction for release. Breaking the kiss doesn't stop Conrad as his lips move from my cheek to my jaw and stop at my neck. Moving my head to the side, I give him better access as he plants kiss after kiss along my neck and collarbone.

"Conrad," I whisper. This needs to stop. I'm here with someone else. He broke up with me.

Someone pounds on the door, shaking it with each blow from their fist. "Quit fucking in there. We have to piss," someone shouts.

Conrad ignores them and brings his mouth back to mine in a bruising kiss. I fight for breath as he devours me with every swipe of his lips. As his tongue battles with mine, Conrad's hips move in rhythm with the movements, and the friction causes that delicious feeling to build up inside me, and I come close to exploding.

The room shakes with more banging, and I pull away from

Conrad's aggressive mouth. "Conrad, we have to stop," I breathlessly tell him.

He growls and tries to kiss me again, but I dodge him this time. "Fuck, Em." He rests his forehead against my shoulder as he catches his breath.

The room fills with the sound of our breathing as whoever is on the other side of the door takes a break from hitting it.

"You have to let me go," I tell him, my voice barely above a whisper. Conrad sighs, hearing the double meaning behind my words. If he doesn't want to be with me, he has to let me move on.

"I know," he reluctantly admits. Squeezing my thighs one last time, Conrad drops me. As I steady myself on my feet, his hands rest on my waist. He stares down into my eyes as he lifts his hands off me, and my body goes cold with the loss of his touch. "It's harder than I thought it would be," he tells me.

"What is?"

Conrad's eyes soften as he lifts his hand and brushes his thumb across my cheek. "Letting you go." He removes his hand and turns around, unlocking and opening the door.

There are several angry faces on the other side, and their glares are directed at Conrad and me. I duck my head as I follow him out of the room, but I want nothing more than to ask him why he is letting me go if it's hard for him.

Before I can ask him what he meant, the brunette from earlier today comes bouncing down the hallway and into Conrad's arms, wrapping her long arms around his neck. She's smiling at him as if they have been friends for years, yet I have never seen her before.

"There's my hubby," she announces in her high-pitched voice right before pulling him into a forceful kiss.

Everything around me freezes. The voices and loud music around me disappear as I digest the words that just came out of this stranger's mouth.

Hubby. As in *husband*?

Surely she cannot mean what I think she means. But as Conrad pulls away from her and I see the regret on his face as he looks over at me, I know there has to be some truth to what she said. Bile rises in my throat, and I turn and run in the opposite direction before I do something stupid like projectile vomiting all over the happy couple.

CHAPTER FIFTEEN

CONRAD

Watching Emree as she fights her way through the sea of bodies down the hallway, away from me and toward her fucking date, about kills me. Following her into the bathroom was a dumb move, and practically dry-humping her was even worse, but my body moved of its own accord the moment I saw her step away from him and walk off into the crowd of people.

Having her body up against mine again and feeling her soft, plump lips molded against my own was pure heaven on earth until the realization that this was not the woman I was allowed to have hit me when she told me I needed to let her go. I heard the double meaning in her words, even though I didn't want to listen to them.

"What *the fuck* are you doing here?" I hiss at Liliana and try to pry her body off of mine.

Having the woman I am being forced to marry show up and call me *hubby* around everyone, especially Emree, is less than desirable. The moment I heard her voice, my stomach sank, and I could feel my heart pounding inside my chest. Of all the ways I thought of Emree finding out about Liliana, this is the worst. While I wasn't able to see her face since Liliana decided to maul me, I could only imagine the shock and pain that would be etched there.

Liliana pulls back but keeps her hands wrapped around my neck. "What are you talking about, sweetie?"

Clearly, the irritation in my voice goes unnoticed, or she chooses to ignore it. "Why are you here, Liliana?" I don't mean to sound like a dick, but my annoyance is at an all-time high at the moment.

She pouts. "We're supposed to be getting to know each other, silly. How do you expect us to be engaged by the end of summer if you're so resistant to being around me?"

This is not the conversation I want to be having in a jam-packed hallway filled with drunk college students. Detangling her arms from around my neck, I separate us but keep a firm grip on her upper arm. "This wasn't part of the plan," I hiss at her. "My school and family life are detached for a reason. I don't need people to be asking fucking questions, Liliana."

She tilts her head to the side, arching a perfectly sculpted eyebrow. "That isn't what I agreed to when I said I would do this. There is no way I'm going to be sitting in a hotel room, bored out of my mind, every day." Liliana's voice is low, and she maintains a perfect smile the entire time as if we are having a casual conversation. "I'm not even getting good sex out of this," she huffs.

This isn't the first time she has brought up sex, and it is starting to get on my nerves. "You came here to get to know me before our engagement, not the people around me. We will meet outside of my school life. They stay out of all this bullshit."

Liliana's hands slide down my chest and lower. She grips the waist of my shorts and tugs. "If you don't want me around your friends, then I'm going to need something to…occupy my time with."

My nostrils flare. "Get your hands *off* me." Gripping her wrists, I pull her away. "You're drawing attention. Attention I *do not* want. I'm leaving and I suggest you go back to your hotel. We can talk about your boredom in the morning."

Liliana's eyes widen as I tighten my grip, but she maintains her artificial smile. "Sounds like I'll be having a night in. Again."

Sliding out of my grip, Liliana turns without another word and disappears into the abyss of people.

Filling my lungs, I take my first deep breath since Emree ran off. My chest tightens at the thought of her. She probably ran into the arms of her fucking date, and I had to let her go. These stupid family obligations are starting to suffocate me, and I feel helpless when it comes to my life.

Sometimes I wish I were born into a different family. One that lets me lead my own life and make decisions that are best for myself, not them.

"You're in deep shit, man," someone says behind me. Looking over my shoulder, I see Camden leaning casually against the wall beside the bathroom door.

"How long have you been standing there?" I ask him after turning around.

He shrugs. "Long enough to see you fuck up even more than you already have."

Blowing out a breath, I rest my hands on my hips and try to calm myself down. "My life is messed up, man. I can't keep doing this."

Sympathy marks Camden's face for the first time since he found out about the arranged marriage. "Why don't you just tell your dad you can't do this?"

A laugh rumbles through my chest. "You've never met my parents, but the day I go against Howard Dugray is the day I can say goodbye to everything. He would disown me so fast."

"Would you rather have a life where you're free to do what you want or a life of more money than you could ever need?"

Never did I think I would be having a conversation about my fucked-up life while in a hallway full of tipsy students, with the smell of alcohol and a blend of perfume and cologne filling my senses. Songs from the Billboard Hot 100 spill from the speakers loud enough to make my head hurt, and I want nothing more than to escape here and drown myself in enough liquor to help me forget everything that has happened the last week.

"It's not that simple," I explain to Camden. "This is what is expected of me. Since I was a kid, I've known the path of my life: prepare to take over the family business and marry for status, not love. It's the way of the eldest Dugray."

Camden studies me for several seconds, and I can't help but feel the need to continue to defend my choices under his scrutiny. When he finally speaks, I'm surprised there is no judgment in his tone. "You're right. Nothing about this sounds simple, and I don't understand it. Never could I imagine making my kid choose anything other than their own happiness." Without another word, he turns and leaves the same way Emree and Liliana did before him.

My feet feel unusually heavy as I stand in the middle of the hallway, wanting nothing more than to leave, but I am grounded. My head is swirling with everything that has happened in the last half an hour. Moving past my feelings for Emree sounded easier said than done, and based on my inability to control myself tonight, I know I'm completely fucked.

CHAPTER SIXTEEN

EMREE

Hubby. The word is still ringing through my head the next day as I get ready for work. The beautiful supermodel-like woman so easily let that term of endearment spill from her lips, but consciously I know there is no way Conrad is actually her husband.

My body runs cold as the thought of him lying to me for six months crosses my mind. What if he really is married? Have I been dating a married man for half a year? While it seems crazy to me that a twenty-one-year-old college student would be married, I know it is not something that is uncommon. What would shock me would be if Conrad was *married* and not once in the six months we were together did I suspect another woman.

Since walking away from him last night and asking Ian to take me home, claiming a stomachache to end our date early, I haven't been able to get out of my own head. Thoughts of my being the other woman while I was falling in love for the first time had crossed my mind and kept me up most of the night until I finally drifted to sleep after being exhausted from crying.

Blaire was up and studying for a test she has on Monday when I entered our apartment after Ian dropped me off, and I was able to keep my composure long enough to tell her about the date, making sure to leave out the part about Conrad, the bathroom, and the stunning woman who wrapped herself around him. While I know Blaire has seen Conrad over the last week since her boyfriend is roommates and friends with my ex, she has made sure to keep our conversations exclusively Conrad-free. Explaining to her my lack of willpower the first time I'd seen him since he ended our relationship made me feel ashamed, especially since I was at that party with another man.

Ian was sweet about my request to head home. He said parties like this aren't his scene much anymore, but he wanted to hang out with me. On the ride back to my apartment, he asked if he could take me out again, and while I felt guilty for what happened in the bathroom with Conrad during my date with Ian, I told him I would love to see him again, and we made plans for next Friday. He promised it would involve no frat parties.

All day, I have thrown myself into my textiles final class project. This semester we have been learning about different materials and how they are made and work with each other. Our project is to create a piece using three different types of materials and blend them together flawlessly. The dress I have spent months on is floor length with a tight bust, almost Renaissance style, but more modern. The materials I have used are cotton, leather, and silk. While these would not conventionally work together, I have been able to blend the three from top to bottom without making them look out of place.

The skirt is a blush pink and flowy, the material a cotton and silk blend that I found at the flea market one town over. The woman there works for her family business, and they have a fabric company that her great-great-grandmother started. She likes to showcase their work at the flea market to target a different demographic and test out their new materials and designs before they go live.

The top half of the dress is my favorite. It is a corset style, except it looks more like something you would see a college student wearing rather than a woman from the fifteenth century. The mint-green leather top is cut right at the top of the breasts of my mannequin, and the straps are thick and fit snugly over the shoulders. The skirt is sewn into the bottom of the corset top in a lapped seam and the two materials meet just below the rib cage, giving the illusion that the mannequin is much taller than it really is.

As I stare at the dress I have put more work into than any other project, I can't help but feel proud. The last touch I will be adding is a jewel design across the top half of the corset with the most beautiful blush and mint jewels I found on a random shopping trip with my mom last month at the outlet mall in Orlando.

A loud knock echoes through my bedroom, startling me as I am lost in thought. "Yeah?" I yell through the room.

The doorknob turns, and Blaire peeks her head in. "You almost ready for work?" She is dressed in her usual jeans and loose T-shirt, with her dark-brown hair hanging in long waves down her shoulders. Blaire is a natural beauty, and with her staple look of little to no natural makeup, her face is glowing, and her unique gray eyes look bright and wide with her eyelashes darkened with a few swipes of mascara.

"Yes, ma'am," I tell her, keeping my tone chipper even though my mood does not match. Tonight I decided to keep my work attire simple with a pair of high-waisted black jean shorts that are slightly frayed at the bottom and a long-sleeved sage-green bodysuit that has a long cutout along the top of my breasts. Since I love color and the green shirt is not enough, I added a splash of pop with my yellow Converse.

Blaire and I have been able to persuade our boss, Garrett, to do his best to schedule us together. He is usually good about it, especially if we have a closing shift, like tonight. Last year, there was an incident between Blaire and an asshole drunk customer who thought it was okay to touch someone against their will. Since then, Garrett has convinced his dad, the owner, to do some renovations at the bar so that the bathrooms are not secluded down a dark hallway and there is now a new guy, Silas, who works as security on the weekends. We got lucky with a boss like Garrett, who cares about the well-being of his employees.

"I can drive tonight. Also, Camden said he was going to stop by but made sure to press that *thou who shall not be named* will not make an appearance." Her voice tenses at the mention of Conrad.

One of the worries I had about our breakup was what it would do to our friend group, and based on Blaire's inability to say Conrad's name, I don't see this going well.

Smiling at my friend, I do my best to assure her that I am, in fact, okay. "You can say his name, Blaire. I won't crumble if you do."

She eyes me with skepticism.

"Plus, I went on a date last night. I'm in the process of moving on, and hey, my date even ended with him asking me for a second one."

"Maybe I'm not saying his name because I think he is a jerk and don't want that energy in our home."

Laughing, I walk out of my bedroom and link my arm with Blaire's. "You aren't a spiritual kind of person, sweetie."

She rolls her eyes. "That's beside the point."

"Oh yes, of course it is. So sorry for pointing out the obvious. I don't know what I was thinking." The sarcasm is oozing from my tone.

Blaire grabs her keys and the two of us head out of the apartment toward her car. "You, of all people, should want to cleanse our place and get all the bad juju out. Isn't your mom a yoga instructor?"

We part and when we are both seated in the car, I answer her question. "She is, but that doesn't mean she is that far into all things spiritual." I pause, trying to find the right words. "My mom is more...eccentric if nothing else. She can't quite be put into a single category."

Pulling out of the parking spot, Blaire begins driving us in the direction of work. "Huh, I guess that makes more sense," she admits. "I still won't forget about that time we were over at her house for dinner and she tried to convince me a spirit was speaking to her."

We both laugh at the insanity that is Margret Anders. Growing up, it was just my mom and me. The sad story of how I was conceived can be shortened to my mom as a college sophomore, a dark walk home from campus to her dorm, and a terrible man who put my mom through something no person should ever have to experience.

While my mom made the difficult decision of keeping the child that resulted from her rape, she has never treated me as if I was unwanted. Growing up, I lived in a home filled with love and laughter. My mom was a young mother, only nineteen when I was born, and I think her age and the fact that it was just the two of us helped to create the bond we have. She is the best person in my life and while she only lives a couple hours away and we talk as much as possible, I miss having her around.

Whiskey Joe's comes into view with one of Florida's sunsets framing the one-story building in a pink-and-orange glow. It's almost seven thirty on a Saturday night and the parking lot is more than halfway filled with a variety of cars.

Blaire chooses a spot under one of the streetlights in the

unofficial employee area. I spot Garrett's old Ford truck a few rows down and smile, happy to be working with him tonight. Garrett is a nice guy and while he focuses on customer happiness, making sure his employees are taken care of is also a top priority for him.

Once inside, I welcome the familiar smell of mixed liquor and cigarette smoke. While some would be disgusted by that mixture, I have grown accustomed to it while working here. It has started to feel homey to me. Even though I have worked at Whiskey Joe's for only about two years, it has become a place that I perceive less as work and more as a comfort. Not only do we have the greatest boss, but the group of coworkers Garrett has put together mesh well. Everyone is helpful, and we always have a fun time working, even on stressful nights.

"Ladies," Garrett greets us from behind the bar on the left side of the room with a bright smile framed by his full beard. He is a large man, a former college football player, and has his long, dirty-blond hair pulled back in a bun tonight. If I didn't know him personally, his size and permanent scowl would be intimidating, but truthfully, he is a big softy, even if he would deny it.

Whiskey Joe's is the most popular bar in the college town for a few reasons. One is that we are lenient about ages here. As long as someone seems responsible enough to drink, we don't ask questions. From what I hear, the owner is on good terms with the police in town, and they turn a blind eye as long as no one gets sloppy and they don't find any patrons on the roads drunk driving. Another reason we are so popular is that not only do we serve a variety of alcoholic drinks and the best bar food you will find within thirty miles, but the atmosphere is top-notch. Inside, past the booths and tables on the right, are air hockey and foosball. Outside, there is a brick patio with mismatched furniture and a few cornhole games set up, as well as a giant Jenga. Since Garrett became the manager, he has turned his dad's outdated establishment into the most popular hangout area in town.

We both smile and nod at him on our way toward the employee-only area, where there is a wall of lockers and a couple tables meant to make up our break room. On the way back there, we pass the makeshift dance floor and stage where a local band is performing. Garrett likes to have live music on the weekends and Thursdays are reserved for karaoke night.

"I'm glad football season is over. Now we only have to deal with baseball, but they're at least a little less...rowdy than those Bucs fans," Blaire states as we load up our lockers.

Being mere miles from the Bucs stadium means we attract many of their fans. There have even been a few times players have come in for a drink and to hang out, and their jerseys are signed and framed, hanging on the walls.

Smiling at her, I wrap my black apron around my waist and tie it in the front. "Just be happy hockey season is about done and our town's team isn't in the playoffs. I'll never forget my first year working here when they won the Stanley Cup. I was covered in more beer and champagne than I liked."

Her eyes widen in horror. "While I'm happy for our town if the teams win, I am also content with them not winning and everyone remaining civil and calm and keeping me dry."

Laughing, I shut my locker after checking my apron is filled with my pens, bottle opener, and server pad. "Let's get to work, girlie. I'm ready to forget about my current life drama and focus on serving college kids alcohol and food that will take years off their lives."

While I love Whiskey Joe's and working here, this place will serve as a reminder of Conrad. More nights than not, he would show up while I was working and made sure to always sit in my section. Even on nights Blaire and I weren't working, all of us would come here to hang out. When I look at certain areas of the bar, I can't help but think of times we were together.

Nights that he and I would dance close on the dance floor. Moments of laughter we shared with our friends out on the patio when we would play Jenga or cornhole.

Coming to work, I thought I would be able to get lost in thought while waiting on tables, but when I look around, I wonder if that is going to be harder said than done.

CHAPTER SEVENTEEN

EMREE

The more than half-full parking lot turned into an overflowing one as the night went on. Apparently, everyone had the bright idea of coming to Whiskey Joe's tonight. Luckily, we had a full staff scheduled, so no one was overly stressed with tables and orders. Those nights are the worst, or if someone has to call out.

With how busy we have been, Conrad hasn't crossed my mind at all. A sadness did come over me when Camden, Maddox, and Levi came in about half an hour ago, but I pushed it aside and focused on my tables. Getting consumed by sadness is not what I need tonight. What I need to do is keep busy, and later, I can reflect on my messed-up love life.

After delivering a round of refills to my table with five guys and three girls who have made my night easy by ordering beer buckets and wings and checking in on my four other tables, I head over to the guys to say hello.

Maddox smiles and holds his arms out as I walk up to them. I lean against his side and wrap an arm around his neck. "Evening, gentlemen. How are we all doing?"

Three pairs of eyes make me their focus as they all grunt

out hellos. While I have seen Camden a few times since Conrad and I broke up, I haven't seen Levi or Maddox since the beach. I'm assuming they both know about what happened, but neither of them is acting differently toward me.

Maddox snakes his arm around my waist and gives me a squeeze. "Doing pretty well, beautiful. And yourself?"

Maddox is a notorious flirt and one of the best-looking men I have ever seen. With his long, dark-blond hair, tanned skin, and sparking light-green eyes, he knows others get mesmerized by his looks alone, but add in his charm and he is damn near irresistible to many women.

"Not many complaints from me," I tell him, hoping he can't see through the extra-wide smile I plaster on my face. My eyes automatically scan their drinks to make sure no one is running low, but they are in Blaire's section and she is always on top of her tables.

"Oh fuck," Levi, who is typically the quiet one of the group, mutters. He is looking toward the front entrance and his eyes are wide with concern.

We all turn our heads in the same direction, and my body freezes when I see who walks in. While I only saw her for a brief moment last night, I could never forget the woman who called the man I love *hubby*.

The stunning brunette waltzes through the double doors of Whiskey Joe's, turning almost every head in the room. Without even trying, she demands all the attention around her. She is looking even more captivating tonight than she was yesterday in a dark-blue dress that hugs each of her curves and hits midcalf. Her legs look impossibly long and she has added a few extra inches to her height with the black strappy heels she is wearing. Her face is perfectly contoured with the right amount of bronzer and concealer, and her eyelashes are fanned out around her light-brown eyes.

The mystery woman is dressed more for clubbing in downtown Tampa than she is for a college bar in Braxton.

"I'm assuming you all know who she is?" I ask no one in particular, not looking away.

None of the guys answer as I continue taking in the woman as she saunters up to the bar with a natural sway to her hips. She leans over the bar and even though her back is to me, I can tell by the smirk Dimitri, the bartender, gives her that she is displaying a generous amount of cleavage for him. He nods after listening to her and begins mixing a drink.

When my question is still met with silence, I turn to the three guys who are staring at me with pitiful eyes. "She...she called Conrad hubby last night," I tell them.

"Shit," Camden hisses under his breath.

"Please, guys, just tell me. Did he...did he cheat on me?"

"What? No," Camden answers automatically.

I eye him with skepticism. "Then how do you explain her? Who is she to him?"

Maddox looks between his teammates. "Listen, Blondie, we like you and what happened between you and Conrad is messed up, but we can't answer these questions. You have to ask him. It's more...complex than any answer we can give you."

"Well, if it isn't the little skank I found with my man in the bathroom last night," a voice comes from behind me. Even though April in Florida is filled with warmer weather, a shiver runs through me at the tone of the voice.

Turning, my blue eyes connect with a pair of brown ones that are searing through me. "Excuse me?" I ask.

With blatant judgment on her face, the woman drags her eyes from my head to my toes. She smirks before saying, "You heard every word I said, but don't worry. I have no concerns about someone like *you* when it comes to my relationship with Conrad."

While I have been on the receiving end of my fair share of bullying and scrutiny, most of that ended in high school. Never in my adult life have I had someone judge me when I don't even know their name.

Before I can respond to her hurtful comment, Maddox chimes in, "Listen, Liliana, I don't give a fuck about the arrangement between you and Con, but leave Blondie out of it. She's innocent in this."

Arrangement? What could Maddox mean by that?

"Innocent?" The woman who I now know as Liliana laughs. "She wasn't so innocent when I saw her coming out of the bathroom last night at a frat party looking freshly fucked."

"Back off, Liliana," Levi growls. His usually calm demeanor is altered into something defensive. His eyes are narrowed at Liliana, hands clenched on the tabletop.

She arches a perfectly sculpted eyebrow at him. "The day I take orders from a goddamn lumberjack will be a cold day in hell." She looks back at me with a sneer on her face. "Besides, the skank and I need to get this conversation over with sooner rather than later."

From the corner of my eye, I see Camden looking around and then down at his lap. Blaire is taking another table's orders behind him, but I can see her attention is split between them and us, clearly sensing some tension going on over here.

"Sweetie, I don't even know you. We have nothing to talk about because Conrad and I are not together and he is free to do what he pleases." The words taste bitter coming out of my mouth. Admitting to this woman that Conrad is not mine and she can have him feel wrong deep inside of me.

Over Liliana's shoulder, an angry Conrad storms through the door, fury evident on his face as he makes his way toward our table. Garrett is looking my way with an inquisitive look on his face, and I know I need to leave and get back to my job, but my feet feel as if they are cemented to the ground as I fight to catch my breath as Conrad approaches.

"Liliana, let's go," Conrad snarls.

Her eyes widen in shock at the sound of his voice, and she whirls around, coming face-to-face with him. "Conrad, what are you doing here? You said you were busy tonight."

He crosses his arms over his chest and stares down at her. "I am. Now you need to leave."

Being this close to him and hearing his deep voice reminds me of how he made my body feel last night, and my cheeks heat up thinking about how wonderful he felt against me.

"Oh, but you're not too busy to come rescue your little skank?"

"Liliana, please," he begs, sounding tired. The interaction is starting to attract attention, and I look over to see Garrett whispering something to the bartender Liliana ordered a drink from.

"We're getting fucking *married*, Conrad, and you're still fucking around with other women and barely even talk to me," Liliana screeches, her hands moving out to her sides with frustration.

Conrad looks over her at me, and I see the sorrow in his eyes. Bringing his eyes back to his *fiancée*, the look on his face changes to evident anger. "We'll fucking talk about this later, but you've created enough of a scene here tonight. Go back to your hotel, and I will come there tomorrow."

With an irritated huff, she storms off the way she came in, leaving behind a tense situation that she herself created.

Once she is gone, Conrad takes a step toward me, but before he can say anything, Garrett interrupts. "Not sure what has been going on here, but Em has tables to tend to." I'm grateful his tone is light and not stern like any other boss's would have been.

Ducking my head, I leave the guys without another word. Garrett walks beside me. "You okay?"

Replaying everything that has happened in the last twenty minutes, my head spins with more confusion than it ever has before. "I don't know."

CHAPTER EIGHTEEN

CONRAD

Getting a text from Camden letting me know that Liliana had walked into Whiskey Joe's and Emree was working tonight was the last thing I thought would happen today. When I got his message, I was in the middle of a gym session and letting out my built-up frustrations. At the rate my life is going, I'll have high blood pressure before I'm thirty.

After successfully getting Liliana to leave, I can breathe a sigh of relief that the situation didn't get more out of hand. If I had known she would go rogue like she has, I would have told my father I'd spend the summer in Boston to get to know her rather than have her close to my friends and Emree.

There is no leaving after the information Emree found out, so I take a seat beside Maddox at the table and lounge back. "Anyone want to trade lives with me?" I ask.

Camden laughs. "Not after seeing what a raging bitch Liliana is. Dude, how the hell is that the woman you have to marry? She is insufferable."

"Parents like his don't particularly give a shit if the spouse they're choosing is a good match or not. It's all about what their family can gain from it," Maddox answers. While I am grateful for the group of friends I have found during my time in college, I am even more appreciative that Maddox's family and life experiences are somewhat similar to mine in the sense that he can understand what I am going through.

Over at the end of the bar, Garrett and Emree are talking, their bodies close together as he rubs her upper arm. Something unsettling brews within me at the sight of his hand on her, and I have to restrain myself from storming across the room and pulling Em away from him. While I have never worried about Emree and another guy, especially Garrett, I've been feeling extra territorial over her since seeing her on a date last night.

"Dude, settle down. You're practically purring," Maddox tells me.

Levi looks at him with his eyebrows pinched together. "Purring? Like a cat?"

"Yeah, purring. You know, like his chest is rumbling." Maddox's tone is dead serious, as if stating that a grown man is purring is not unusual.

"Bud, I think you mean growling. Purring isn't manly enough," Camden states.

"Will you all shut up? I am not growling or purring. Just drink your fucking beers and stop talking about me."

Maddox laughs, with Camden and Levi following him. "Oh, you are too much, man. After the *Conrad's Love Life* show we were graced with tonight, you really think the subject of you is not the topic of interest?"

Resting my elbows on the table, I rub my hands down my face. "Jesus, you are worse than a bunch of teenage girls."

When I remove my hands, something catches my eye to the left, and I notice an angry Blaire glaring at me. Sitting at the high-top table makes us at eye level and those cloudy gray eyes of hers are storming with anger directed at me.

"Who was that woman and what did she say to my best

friend?" she questions me. Her hands are on her hips and her tone is stern. The usual quiet Blaire is gone, replaced with an assertive one that is protecting her friend.

"Blaire baby—"

"Don't you dare 'Blaire baby' me, Maddox Stone." She points a finger in the direction of his face. "I have a best friend who had her heart broken by this jerk"—her thumb is hitched toward me—"for no apparent reason, and now some random woman shows up, causing problems. While I love you all, I deserve answers, and apparently, my boyfriend feels some sort of loyalty toward Conrad and won't give me details."

Camden ducks his head and remains quiet to avoid his girlfriend's wrath.

"Blaire, before I give you an explanation, I need to talk to Emree. When are you both off tonight?"

She crosses her arms over her chest. "Not too sure she wants to speak with you."

"Not too sure I care."

"Hey, man," Camden chimes in, an edge to his voice. "Don't give a shit how pissed off you are. Watch how you talk to Blaire."

His girlfriend flashes him a sincere smile. "Thank you, sweetie. Still doesn't mean you're off the hook for not telling me what was going on when I asked yesterday after seeing Conrad and that girl together."

I let out a frustrated groan and look over at Emree. She has since ended her conversation with Garrett, who returned behind the bar and is back to tending to her customers. As she glides between the tables and bar, I can tell by her concentration she is forcing herself not to look in my direction. Little does she know I'm not leaving this bar until she and I talk.

Smiling over at Blaire, I lean back in my chair and get comfortable. "Blaire, sweets, could you please bring me whatever IPA you have on tap and a pulled pork quesadilla?"

Her eyes squint in my direction before she turns and makes her way toward the bar.

"What is the likelihood of her spitting in my drink or food?" I ask no one in particular.

My three friends laugh. "She's the sweetest woman I know, but I wouldn't look too closely when she brings your items back," Camden states with a smile on his face.

THE MUSIC HAS SHIFTED from a live band to late-night radio remixes of the Hot 100 over the last hour and a half that I have been sitting at this table. My ass has gone numb and Maddox, Camden, and Levi left about twenty minutes ago.

Blaire has put her focus on her other tables, giving me a questioning look twice to see if I needed anything. After my third beer, I switch to water to make sure I have a clear head when I talk to Emree. She has done a successful job of avoiding me, even though I haven't been able to take my eyes off her.

The bar has slowed down for the night, with it closing in about twenty minutes. Garrett has already shut down the patio since that was cleared out about half an hour ago. Blaire and Emree have four tables between the two of them and the other waitress working tonight has cashed out her last table and started wiping down the tabletops and stacking chairs.

"You done with that glass?" a deep voice asks from behind me.

Turning, I look up slightly and make eye contact with Garrett. His face is unfriendly as he stares at me and even though I am sitting at a high-top table, I feel like I am being towered over by his large frame.

"Yeah," I tell him, handing over the glass.

He takes it with a grunt but doesn't walk off. "What are you doing here, Conrad?"

Leaning back in my chair, I contemplate not answering because it is none of his damn business, but maybe it's because I'm tired or that my focus is off, but I answer. "Waiting to talk to Em."

His nostrils flare at my answer. "Not sure she wants to talk to you."

"Nothing personal, man, but what's going on between Em and me isn't any of your business," I tell him as I cross my arms over my chest.

"When I have an employee looking like someone kicked her puppy and a woman coming into my bar and causing a scene involving said employee, it becomes my business."

As much as I want to argue, he does have a point. "Listen, I'm sorry about that. Never did I think Liliana would come in here creating trouble. Em and I need to talk, though, so please just stop the big brother act and let me explain things to her."

We have a stare-off for several seconds, the tension between the two of us clear to anyone in the room. "Fine. But if any of the shit that happened tonight goes down again, you won't be welcome here anymore." He walks off without another word.

Over the next twenty minutes or so, as the bar comes to a close, I remain in my seat even as Blaire wipes down my table and flips the chairs apart from mine. Emree works on her own tables while Garrett cashes out the register and tips for the night. The four remaining front-house employees take their earnings after giving the cooks in the back their cut, and they all gather their belongings from the back locker rooms.

Since I know she will make an attempt at sneaking out of the building without seeing me, I get up from the table and flip my chair to match the rest before heading toward the front doors. One by one, Emree's coworkers make their way out of the building, making sure to stick to the buddy rule Garrett set in place.

When time runs out, Emree and Blaire finally make their way out of the back room. Em keeps her head down while Blaire is shooting daggers in my direction. While my focus is not on explaining myself to Blaire, I can't help but feel something unsettling in the pit of my stomach, knowing she probably hates my guts for how I have been treating her best friend.

"Em..." I trail off. Her head snaps up, and her eyes narrow at the sight of me.

Emree looks at Blaire, then back at me as they continue walking past me. "I have nothing to say to you, Conrad."

"Well, I have a lot to explain to you," I press.

They both stop before exiting the door. Blaire looks between the two of us before standing with her legs wide and arms crossed in a defensive stance. Having this conversation with Emree after midnight in the middle of a bar with her best friend beside us is not ideal, but I have put this off long enough and need to come out with the truth.

Emree visibly sighs, her shoulders moving with the action. "Conrad, I'm exhausted. I just spent the last five hours on my feet, serving drinks and food to tipsy coeds. I had to deal with whoever that woman was, and then a conversation with my boss about the drama I brought into the bar. I'm tired and cranky and sore." Her mask falls, and the exhaustion she tries to hide becomes evident. "Please just let me go home, shower, and crawl into my bed."

I think long and hard about my next words. "Fine. Let's go."

She stares at me with wide eyes. "What?"

"You heard me," I tell her.

Emree looks between Blaire and me. "But I drove here with Blaire."

"We'll follow her to the apartment. Now let's go." Without

another word, I turn and walk out of the building without checking that they're following.

Now is the time for me to step up and be honest with Emree, no matter how hard it is going to be. There is no more putting this off. She deserves the truth, especially after how I hurt her. My only worry is that the truth is going to cause more damage to her heart.

CHAPTER NINETEEN

EMREE

W hy am I following my ex-boyfriend through the dark parking lot and why am I going in the direction of his car?

Me being a pushover would be the simple answer. Letting people walk over me has been a problem of mine, and while I have worked on that, when it comes to Conrad, I seem to not be able to say no. Even though he broke my heart, I can't help but look at him and still be in love with the man in front of me.

"We'll meet you back at the apartment, Blaire," Conrad tells her as he watches her walking to her car a few spots away.

She glares at him and turns her head to me. I give her a reassuring nod, even though I feel anything but assured at the moment. Being alone with Conrad has shown to bring out the poor decision-making part of my brain. For example, what happened in the bathroom last night at the party.

Yeah, being alone with each other is not smart.

The only reason I am silently following Conrad and not putting up a fight is that while I know whatever he says is going to hurt, I need answers. The last week, I have felt lost, not knowing what went wrong with our relationship. If I had done something wrong, I couldn't think of what that could have been to result in our breakup.

After Blaire is safely in her car, Conrad rounds to the passenger side, where I am, and opens the door for me. His shoulder brushes against mine and at this close distance, I can smell leather and sandalwood, two scents I have grown to recognize as his cologne. Without a word or glance in his direction, I lower myself into the seat.

The drive to my apartment is met with silence. Conrad didn't turn the radio on, so the only sound is the town's nightlife as it passes by. Even Conrad's car is quiet besides the low hum of the engine. With no sound and neither of us talking, I get lost in my own thoughts. Being surrounded by Conrad's smell and the familiarity of being in his car is messing with my head.

What happens if he admits he was cheating on me with the woman in the bar? What if I was "the other woman"? If he didn't cheat, how could he jump from being in a relationship with me for six months to bypass even dating her and apparently having a *fiancée*?

Guilt washes over me when I think about how I was trying to move on so quickly after our relationship. While I don't see Ian becoming a life partner, maybe going on a date may have been too soon and not fair to myself or him. Conrad has my thoughts far too jumbled, and I need to get my head on straight before I say or do something I know I will regret.

Too lost in my mess of a mind, I barely register the drive, and all too soon, my building comes into view through the windshield and the car stops. The tall, four-story building is cloaked in darkness besides the faint and flickering lights in the entryway that leads to the front.

"Just say the word, and I'll walk you to the door and leave, Em. I don't want to force you into anything, but I need to explain what's going on," Conrad says, breaking the silence.

In front of us, I watch Blaire cross the parking lot toward the door that leads to the elevator to our apartment. Her head moves back and forth as she checks her surroundings. I wait to answer him until I see our living room window light up, letting me know that Blaire made it inside.

"I need answers, Conrad," I whisper to him. "No." My voice is harder. More stern. "I *deserve* answers. What you did was fucked up."

From the corner of my eye, I see Conrad staring at my profile. "You're right," he admits. "And I wish I didn't have to do what I did. You have no fucking idea how badly I wish things could be different."

None of what he says makes sense because I feel as though I walked in in the middle of a conversation. "Let's just go and get this over with." I open my door and step out of the car.

Conrad follows me into the building, and we ride up the elevator. The silence from earlier is back as we make our way through my apartment. He passes me and goes into the living room while I hang up my purse on the hook by the door.

Taking a deep breath, I head down the hallway and enter the living room. Conrad is standing awkwardly at the back of one of the two sofas with his hands in his pockets. His shoulders are slumped, and I can tell by the worry on his face that he is unsure of what to do right now.

He and I both.

"I need to shower," I announce and go to my room to grab something to change into and then head in the direction of the bathroom Blaire and I share.

If we're going to do this tonight, we are doing it on my terms. That means I want to get the smell of bar food off me and wash away the sweat and grime from the night.

Once in the shower, I spend extra time scrubbing my body with the new vanilla scrub I got from Bath & Body Works. When too much time passes and I need to stop stalling, I exit the shower and towel dry. Standing in front of the mirror, I apply my nighttime moisturizer with shaky hands.

Once I have my hair brushed, apply my lotion evenly, and change into a pair of sleep shorts and a T-shirt, I leave the bathroom and make my way past Blaire's closed door and to the living room.

Conrad has moved from standing behind the couch to sitting on the middle seat of the sofa. Entering the room, I take my place on the two-person couch across from him. With his eyes closed and head resting against the cushion, I take in his strong jaw with a light dusting of hair and his perfectly straight nose. Conrad's hair is disheveled, something that is not his typical look. He is almost always well put together, but given that it is the middle of the night and he spent the last few hours waiting for me at the bar, I wouldn't expect him to be his put-together self. His face is relaxed as he rests, and I can't help but feel happy seeing that. Conrad has always carried tension within him, and while he would tell me he was okay, I saw he was struggling with something.

"Okay, talk."

His head comes up, and his eyes pop open to look at me.

"Hey," he says lazily. "Sorry I dozed off."

"It's okay. You're tired and it's late." When he continues looking at me and not saying anything, I speak up. "Tell me what the hell is going on, Conrad."

He sighs. "Not really sure where to even begin."

"How about from the beginning?"

CHAPTER TWENTY

CONRAD

My body is fighting sleep with the late hour, and I want nothing more than to collapse into bed and never get out. With the team getting a week off from practice for spring break, starting up daily sessions in the last five days has taken a toll on my body.

"Well, you know how my last name is Dugray?" I ask Emree after she tells me to start from the beginning.

She raises an eyebrow with a muddled look. "Yeah…what about it?"

"One of the many things I liked about you from the moment we met was that my last name meant nothing to you. When I told you what it was, there was no reaction, and I knew you didn't know who my family was."

"Conrad, you're starting to make me nervous." Her voice is more alert.

"Baby, my family is rich. Old money rich. My dad's family started a small hospitality company over a hundred years ago, and since then, it has spiraled out. Now my father is the CEO of several companies, but the most notorious one is The Dugray Group. It includes hotel chains, clubs, and—"

"Oh my god, hotels," she cuts me off with a shocked gasp. By the look in her eyes, I can tell it is all clicking together. "Your family is *the* Dugray family? Like they own the Dugray Hotels that are across the nation?"

Nodding, I continue. "Yes. They're the most pretentious and selfish people you will ever meet, but that is my family."

Emree leans back against the cushion, watching me. "Why did you never tell me?"

Resting my elbows on my knees, I rub my eyes with my palms. "Because, Em, I didn't want to be a Dugray for five fucking seconds." I stand, frustrated with my family name. "It's exhausting living with a family name like that. Moving here, meeting you and the guys, it was nice to finally not be recognized because of where I come from. Everyone in my life up north treats me differently, thinking they can get something from me because of my father."

"Wow...just wow. I'm not sure what to say right now." Emree is staring at her lap as she fiddles with her fingers. "Basically, you're saying that you come from this millionaire family that is well known, and I've been blind to it for the last six months?"

Billionaire, but I won't correct her. She doesn't need to know just how much money my family is worth.

"Basically," I agree. "There is more to it than that, though."

"Jeez, I can't wait," she expresses with an eye roll.

Ignoring the sarcasm, I take a deep breath and prepare to tell her the part I'm even more ashamed of. "I'm the oldest of two sons and a daughter. In my family, there are expectations that come with being the eldest son."

Emree bites her full bottom lip as she takes in what I am telling her.

"From a young age, I've been taught the family business and have been told I needed to get a proper education at only one of the best schools and the moment I graduate college, I'm to join my father to prepare to take over when he retires. Part of all this means marrying a woman who comes from our way of life, preferably someone whose family has something for the family business to gain." The words taste like metal as they come out of my mouth.

"That someone not being a poor girl from a small town and a single mom," she states, her voice small, and her shoulders drop. Emree's expression has shifted from the hardened protective shell she created at the beginning of the conversation to something softer. Sadder. Her eyes are cast down as she nervously bites her bottom lip.

"Unfortunately," I tell her honestly. "I wish it didn't have to be this way, but this was the hand I was dealt when I was born a Dugray. My life has been mapped out since before I was born, and none of it has been my choice."

Emree's eyes darken and her nostrils flare just the slightest. "That's bullshit, Conrad. Everyone has a choice in their life."

Pinching the bridge of my nose with my fingers, I struggle with an oncoming headache from exhaustion. "Em, if it were that simple, do you think I would even be entertaining the idea of having a fucking *arranged marriage*? It's not. Nothing in my life has ever been simple. The only time I have felt like a normal goddamn human being has been the last three years at this school with the guys and...and you."

She stands and begins pacing as if she can't handle sitting still. "Listen, I may not know all about rich families and obligations, but I do know what free will is, and you have that. Tell your dad there is no way you're marrying a complete stranger. Tell him you'll take over the family business, whatever that means, but your life is your life, Conrad." Her eyes soften as she looks at me. "You should be able to fall in love with whoever you want."

While a laugh fights its way out of me, I control it. "Baby, that's not how it works with Howard Dugray. If I ever went against him, he would cut me off from everything. I'd no longer be a Dugray."

We stand there, mere inches between us, staring at each other. Emree's chest heaves with each heavy breath she takes. Looking at her, I know for a fact that this is the woman I love, not only for her exterior beauty but for what is inside her as well. Even after I hurt her only a week ago, Emree was willing to listen to me explain myself. Not all women would do that after being burned, especially with how many times I've fucked up when it comes to us.

"I hate your dad," Emree whispers.

While I try to stop the smile that springs up, it wins the fight. "Me too, baby."

Crossing the short distance between us, I take calculated steps and try to gauge if she doesn't want me to come near her. When she doesn't say anything after the first two steps, I close the distance and cup her face with my hands, and she grabs my wrists. Brushing her cheek with one thumb, Emree leans into my touch and nuzzles her head against my hand and shuts her eyes.

After a moment of quietness with us standing together, crystal-blue eyes meet mine. "Is that who Liliana is? The woman your parents…chose for you?"

A lump forms in my throat. I nod, and Emree tenses and pulls back from me, but I maintain my hold on her. "She is. I've barely spoken a couple sentences to her before this week."

Her eyes widen, shocked at my announcement. "You didn't even know this woman? How can your parents expect you to marry someone who is a stranger?"

"It's how the Dugrays do things." I laugh, but there is no humor behind it. "They expect us to date, be engaged by the end of summer, and get married after graduation. My father wants me back up in Boston working under him the moment the wedding is over."

"Ugh." Emree lets out an exhausted breath. "I hate this. Your family sucks. Liliana sucks. This entire relationship sucks."

Frustrated, Em backs away, breaking my hold on her, and storms into the kitchen. "I need a drink." She pulls down a bottle of Patrón and a shot glass from the top cabinet beside the oven. Filling the glass, she tips her head back and downs the shot.

"I'm sorry, Em," I admit to her as I come up to the kitchen entrance, making sure to keep my distance. With all the shit I just dropped on her, I wouldn't be surprised if she got the urge to smack me across the face. Not that it wouldn't be justified.

Emree fills the glass one more time before shooting the shot. "I just have one question, and I really need you to leave after that," she whispers, her back still to me as she faces the cabinet.

"Okay."

Turning, Emree's face comes into view and her jaw is clenched. "Why, Conrad? Why did you date me and let me fall for you these last six months? You knew nothing could ever come of this, yet you strung me along for half a year, all while lying to me."

This is the one question I haven't wanted to answer because I have been lying to myself about the real answer. But while I can lie to myself, I could never do that to Emree. The last six months weren't a lie to me because what I felt for her was real, and in another life, it would have been a different ending for us.

Being sure that she is looking me in the eyes so that she can see there is nothing but truth in my words, I answer her. "Because I was falling in love with you, and the thought of leaving you made it hard for me to breathe."

CHAPTER TWENTY-ONE

EMREE

B*ecause I was falling in love with you, and the thought of leaving you made it hard for me to breathe.*

Two days ago, I asked Conrad to leave my apartment at two in the morning after his answer to my question. Without another word, he nodded and walked out the door. The moment I heard the click, my defensive walls broke. I cried like I never cried before while standing in my kitchen in the middle of the night.

The next morning, I woke up to a steaming cup of coffee beside me, the smell wafting into my senses and Blaire's smiling face looking down on me. Even though I was exhausted from the emotional night and getting to sleep late, I knew I would never get rid of her without going into detail about what happened with Conrad. After an emotional morning, where Blaire, the sweetest person I have ever met, threatened Conrad with bodily harm if he tried to come near me again, we decided to order a large breakfast to be delivered and spent the morning in our pajamas watching reruns of *Gossip Girl*.

While the threat was delivered via text in our "friends"

group chat, which I left the day after he dumped me, her message was met with approval from Camden and Maddox. Conrad did not reply, but she knew he had heard her loud and clear.

After a TV marathon, Blaire and I decided to pamper ourselves with mani-pedis, and I can't help but admire my new pale-pink nails with tiny daisies on the ring fingers. Nothing helps to get over a broken heart like treating yourself to luxuries.

The sun is beating down on my skin, and I soak in the vitamin D and sip on my green juice while reviewing the notes I took during my last class. While my head has been spacy the last couple of days, I did not want what was going on with my personal life to affect my schoolwork. Having a partial scholarship means I must maintain a certain grade point average.

"Well, well, well. Hello, gorgeous," a deep voice breaks my concentration. Gazing up, Ian comes into view. His face bright with the glow from the midday sunlight and his shining smile on full display.

While I hadn't talked to Ian since Friday night when he dropped me off at my apartment, he did text me Sunday afternoon to make sure we were still on for a second date. Guilt fills me, remembering that I haven't replied to his question. That is one of my biggest pet peeves, and I don't want him to think I am ignoring him.

"Hey, how are you?" I ask him, matching his smile with my own. Gesturing with my hands, I invite him to sit across from me. He drops his backpack and lowers himself into the seat.

Resting his elbows on the table, Ian leans forward. "Not so good, if we're being honest. Kind of digging this girl I met a few days ago, and it seems she may not be feeling the same way about me." He smiles the entire time he is talking, and I'm glad he doesn't seem like the type who would be angry with being ghosted. Ian reaches forward and grasps my hand in his rough one.

"Yeah, I suck. I'm so sorry, Ian," I tell him honestly. "There has been a lot of drama in my life the last few days, and my head has been swimming since Saturday."

Leaning in close enough that I can smell the minty scent of his breath, Ian nudges his head over my shoulder. "The drama have anything to do with the guy who is currently ready to come over here and pound my face in for talking to you?"

Without looking in the direction Ian is indicating, I know who he is talking about. While I didn't see him when I took up occupancy at this table, it doesn't take a genius to know there is only one man who wouldn't like me sitting here with another guy.

"Dark-blond hair and brown eyes?" I inquire.

"That's the one." His eyes are dancing between me and Conrad.

Sighing, I peek over my shoulder. Conrad is standing with Mateo and Jules, and he is looking this way exactly like Ian described. Breaking his stare-down with Ian, Conrad turns to me and raises an eyebrow. That single motion alone sets off a fury inside me. The fact that even after everything he told me Saturday night, he thinks he has the right to be angry that I am talking to another guy is laughable.

Turning back to Ian, I roll my eyes. "My ex. And yes, he was the drama."

Ian studies me for several seconds. "Something still going on there?" He releases my hand but doesn't move his too far.

The question catches me off guard. While our breakup was only a little over a week ago, I am struggling with my feelings for Conrad and how I need to try to move on from those feelings I have because of his *family obligations*. Telling Ian there is nothing going on between Conrad and me feels like a lie after what happened Friday night. Clearly, there are still going to be feelings and attraction between us, and dismissing that makes my throat tighten.

"I'm sorry, Ian," I admit, trying hard not to make eye contact. "Our breakup was recent, and I think I was trying so hard to move on from him by going on that date with you."

He sits back and nods, observing me. "I see."

"Going out on our date wasn't fair to you, Ian. You're sweet and I had a good time, but I don't think I'm anywhere near ready to start dating right now," I tell him honestly. Being in love with a man while going on a date with another isn't fair to either of us.

Ian's eyes soften. "I get that. Before coming to Braxton, I was in a long-term relationship. It sucks."

I laugh at our bonding over broken hearts. "'Sucks' is a pretty perfect way to put it."

"To heartbreak," Ian announces, holding up his water bottle. Smiling, I tap my juice against his drink.

"Incoming," he mutters and before I can ask him what he is talking about, a shadow casts over our table.

"Em, a word?" Conrad is standing to my right with his arms crossed and his lips pursed. His tone is stern and while he asked it as a question, the way he spoke left little room to tell him no.

Looking between the two men, I feel like I'm in the middle of a "whose junk is bigger?" testosterone duel. "Um, sure."

"I'll catch you later, Emree." Ian smiles at me as he stands and leaves.

Once we're alone, besides the dozen or so other coeds sitting around us, Conrad grips my arm as he takes a seat beside me. "What the hell was that?"

Pulling my arm from his tight grasp, I glare at him. "Get your hand off me, Conrad."

His nostrils flare. "That's the guy you were out with Friday night. You dating him now? Moving on that fast?"

The condescending tone infuriates me more than I have ever felt before. "Fairly certain you gave up the right to ask me questions like that the moment you ended things," I grit out through clenched teeth.

Conrad takes a deep breath and lets it out through his nose. "Just fucking tell me, Emree. Are you dating that prick?"

Standing, I square my shoulders and narrow my eyes at him. "Maybe I am, or maybe I'm not. Being broken up means I don't have to explain a single thing to you." I hitch my backpack over my shoulder. "Have fun with your *fiancée*, Conrad."

Without another word, I storm off and pass Liliana as she bounces her way through the courtyard, pinning me with a death glare.

CHAPTER TWENTY-TWO

CONRAD

Slick with sweat, I wrap my arms around Emree's shoulders as she snuggles into my side. We're both out of breath and trying to come down from the high of such explosive sex. She kisses my jaw and I look down and stare into her wild blue eyes.

Cuddling after having sex with a girl has never been something I wanted to do, but I find myself enjoying this part of my time with Emree. It's intimate and I feel this connection to her that I have never felt before.

"I'll never get tired of this," she whispers to me.

"What, great sex?"

She laughs and I feel it through my body being this close to her. "No, not just that. But seeing you like this. You're always so tense. I love being able to see you at your most relaxed."

She tucks her head back against me and I close my eyes, taking in her words. If she only knew what was causing all this tension...

My eyes shoot open, taking me away from the dream I was having that was more of a memory. It was the last night I stayed at Emree's house before our spring break vacation, and we spent the night wrapped around each other for hours.

Groaning, I look down at the tent the memory created

under the blankets and curse the beautiful woman for remaining a constant fixation in my head. It has been three weeks since our breakup and almost two since the last time I talked to her. The semester's end is approaching and that means I will be moving into an apartment in Boston with Liliana and announcing our engagement in mere months.

While I wish I could do my best to avoid her, Liliana has made it her mission to become the doting girlfriend. I reminded her last week that this is a business arrangement and I don't expect her, and in return me, to act like this is a real relationship, but she insists on showing up everywhere I am and bringing me food after practice. Never home cooked since she admitted she knows nothing about cooking.

The guys all hate her, even Maddox, who I don't think has ever disliked a person in his life. Levi says he always carries headphones around with him now because he cannot stand her high-pitched laugh, and I can't blame him. It's fake and forced, much like her personality. Even though we met three weeks ago and I truly have been putting in effort this last week, I feel as though I don't know who the real Liliana is. She puts on a mask in public, but the way she talks to me in private is controlling and demanding.

Part of me wonders if maybe I'm not seeing the true her because my head is wrapped around another woman. One I can't have and who refuses to even look in my direction since I became a jealous asshole, seeing her with that dickwad in the courtyard. His hand holding hers and her smiling at him with ease. That should be me. Only I should be allowed to touch her. Her laugh and smiles should only be directed at me, not some douchebag who doesn't even know her.

The pain from my hard-on becomes too much, and I throw the covers back and push my boxer briefs down, exposing myself. Wrapping my hand around my dick, I begin stroking it while bringing up the memory from my dream. My hand is nothing compared to Emree's soft body and her moans filling the room, but it will have to do at the moment.

"Hey, Con, you awake? I don't know how to put this tie together and you're an uppity guy." My door swings open and a suit-covered Levi barges into the room. "Dude, fuck." He covers his eyes. "Do you not lock the door when your dick is out?"

Grabbing the sheet, I throw it over to cover myself and wiggle my briefs back up. "What the fuck are you doing coming into my room without knocking?"

"What the hell is all the yelling about?" Maddox asks from the hallway. When he comes into the room, his eyes immediately focus on the tented sheet. "Hey, buddy, you want to simmer Little Conny down? Don't want to hurt someone with that thing."

Groaning, I throw my arm over my eyes. "Please, for the love of God, get the hell out of my room."

"Just me, or Levi too? And why is the lumberjack in a suit? What is going on here?"

"I came in to see if fancy pants here could help me with my tie, but apparently, he has nothing better to do at ten in the morning than stroke one out with the door unlocked," Levi answers.

With my hard-on officially deflated, I sit up and look at the two of them. "If you leave my room, I'll fix your goddamn tie when I come out."

Levi's mouth falls open. "You think I want that hand coming near me after seeing it on your junk?"

"Whose hand was on their junk?" Camden comes into the doorway and joins the party.

"For God's sake, are we having a roommate meeting or something? What the fuck are you all doing just hanging around outside my room?"

"In my defense, I was coming out of the bathroom and heard raised voices," Camden responds.

"Lumberjack came into Conny's room and caught him stroking the salami." Maddox shivers, probably with a visual.

"Oh my god," I groan.

Camden looks at me with disappointment. "Dude, why don't you lock your door?"

"Seriously?" I ask, dumbfounded. "This is *my room*. He shouldn't be coming in without knocking."

Maddox comes forward and sits on the edge of my bed, being sure to keep a good distance between us. "Buddy, we're all besties. We shouldn't have to knock. There is an unspoken no-knock rule around here. Unless, of course, the door is locked. Then we know funny business is going on."

I rub my hands down my face.

"You going to wash that hand? Because that's just gross." Maddox's eyebrows are drawn together as he looks at my right hand with disgust.

"That's it," I say as I stand. "Get the fuck out. Now. And there isn't a no-knock rule here. It's an invasion of privacy and fucking stupid." Luckily, the conversation had helped to simmer down my erection completely.

Maddox stands with his hands held up. "Whoa, man, don't come any closer with that thing."

"Get. Out."

"We're going. We're going. I can tell when I'm not wanted somewhere."

Levi and Camden chuckle as they turn to leave. Before I can close the door, Levi turns around. "But for real, my tie?" His face disappears as I slam the door in his face. And lock it.

THE HURT OF LETTING GO

THIRTY MINUTES LATER, after I have showered and changed into a pair of gym shorts and a T-shirt, I join my roommates in the living room. Levi is still in his suit with a now knotted tie, and Maddox and Camden have changed from their sleepwear to more casual attire of relaxed jeans and shirts.

"Oh, good morning. Nice to see you," Maddox greets me.

Camden smiles. "How has your day been?"

Flipping them the bird, I take a seat beside Levi. "You're all assholes."

Levi leans away from me just a bit. "You did wash your hand, right?"

Turning my head, I glare at him. "Fuck you." Today may be the day I decide I need new roommates and friends because this group is becoming too much with their nonsense.

The front door swings open, and Mateo comes in with a smiling Jules.

"Hello, boys," Jules greets. Her sultry voice is effortless, as well as the sway of her hips as she stalks through the room.

Mateo walks behind the couch, and I hold out my hand to high-five him as he passes behind me.

"Don't touch him!" Camden, Maddox, and Levi shout before we come into contact, and Mateo's hand freezes in midair.

"Um, why?"

Maddox clears his voice. "Since there is a lady present, I will keep this classy. Levi walked in on Conrad...charming the snake if you will."

A crease forms between Mateo's eyebrows. "What?"

"You know," Maddox continues. "Making the bald man cry."

"What the hell are you talking about?"

"Oh jeez, Mateo," Jules jumps in. "He was jerking off and Levi walked in."

His eyes widen in shock. "Why the hell didn't you knock?"

Smiling, I look at Mateo. "Thank you. Seems our roommates believe if your door is unlocked, it means there is an open-door policy."

"That's weird," he says as he takes a seat on the arm of the sofa. "Also, not touching your hand after getting that visual."

Groaning, I drop my head back onto the couch. "You all are the worst. I took a damn shower. Can we please move on from this?"

"As uncomfortable as the topic of your masturbation is, I agree." Jules truly is a lifesaver. "We actually ran into your girl coming into Broken Yolk after our brunch."

My ears perk up at the mention of Emree. "Yeah? She alone?" I try to keep my tone neutral, but I'm dying inside to know if she was there with a particular guy.

Levi chuckles, but I ignore him.

"She was with a rather handsome guy if I do say so myself," Jules answers.

Irritation pricks at me, knowing she is out there with that little fuckface. "You don't say."

"Think before doing something stupid, man," Camden warns me.

Getting up, I wipe my hands on the front of my shorts. "Nothing to worry about. I got plans today anyway. Got to meet Liliana for a conference with our parents." The lie rolls off the tip of my tongue. Guess it's not a full lie since tomorrow after practice, I do have that meeting, but they don't need to know that.

Grabbing my keys and wallet from the hook and entryway table, I wave the guys and Jules goodbye and head out the door.

Knowing where Emree is and who she is with was information that came to me without inquiry. It isn't like I was actively seeking to know if she was with that guy, but now that I know, I can't *not* show up to see what is going on.

Broken Yolk isn't far from our house, thanks to Braxton being a small town. Unfortunately, it is the most popular spot for breakfast and brunch, so the parking lot is overflowing with cars.

Finding a spot, I hop out of my car and make my way into the restaurant, determined to make this the most casual run-in possible.

CHAPTER TWENTY-THREE

EMREE

Sitting in a booth with Ian with the hustle and bustle of a busy morning brunch rush around us makes me smile. After my altercation with Conrad a couple weeks ago, Ian texted that he couldn't stop thinking about me even when he was trying to and asked if he could take me on another date. While I went back and forth about if I should or should not go, I came to the realization that I needed to take these opportunities as part of my moving-on process. Since then, Ian and I have been on one date and this morning is our third.

While I don't know him all that well, I can tell Ian is someone I like. He is kind and I love when he talks about his family back in Cleveland, especially his grandma, who he shared fond stories of, and I can tell by the look in his eyes that he misses her.

With the semester coming to an end and finals week approaching, our schedules have been hectic. Finding time to go out and get to know each other has been harder than I thought it would be, but we are taking advantage of our free mornings, like today.

"Would it make me the most basic young person if I ordered avocado toast?" Ian laughs as he scans the menu.

Smiling, I look at him over the top of my own. "Personally, I wouldn't judge you. Even though I despise avocados."

My hair blows back at the sudden gust of wind from his hand flowing through the space between us and landing on his chest. "Excuse me? How can you not like avocados? No guacamole? In salads? Nothing?"

I shake my head. "No. They're gross and mushy."

"Not sure we are going to make it to date four, Em. You not liking my favorite food may be a deal breaker. What if we make it to marriage and now I have a wife who won't enjoy some guac with me? That's divorce waiting to happen." His tone is light, and the smile on his face reassures me that he is not being serious, but I play along.

Shaking my head, I try to hide my own smile. "Guess we will have to end it here. Sorry we only made it to three dates, but you need an avocado wife, and I'm too far against the vegetable."

"Aren't they a fruit?" he questions.

Shrugging my shoulders, I answer, "How should I know? You're the avocado lover."

His deep chuckle mixes with the multiple conversations around us and the sound makes me feel warm all over. Ian has a welcoming laugh that has you feeling comforted around him. "Avocados aside, I'm getting the country breakfast since you said you're paying, and it comes with a side of fluffy pancakes that is making my stomach growl just thinking about them."

Our waiter approaches with his pad and pen in hand, ready to take our order. Ian goes with the avocado toast and a side of eggs and bacon, and we both get a cappuccino. The waiter warns us that our meals may take a while, especially with a table of fourteen that came in before us. I'm grateful that Ian is calm and understanding when he responds because how someone treats waitstaff means a lot to me in a relationship, as it shows their character.

Ian leans back against the booth and takes a sip of his water. "Need to be honest with you about something."

My stomach becomes uneasy. No one likes when a guy starts off with a sentence like this. "What's that?"

His grin shows off his small dimple. "I really like you, Emree Anders."

The uneasiness turns into butterfly flutters at his sweet words. "That so?"

Nodding, Ian leans forward and rests his forearms on the table. "What's not to like? You're sweet, drop-dead gorgeous, and make me laugh. And that's only from being on three dates with you. Imagine if this ends up going longer and I get to see more of that? Damn, girl, you'll have me falling for you faster than I ever have before."

My smile fades just slightly at his words because they make me think of Conrad and what he told me only weeks ago about falling in love with me. Apparently, loving someone isn't enough to stay with them. Not when you have *family obligations* and a shit ton of money and power as a promise to follow through with the life your family wants you to live.

Pushing past the thoughts of my ex, who needs to remain out of my head, I smile over at Ian. "You're too sweet and not a hard guy to fall for either." My words are honest because Ian is an easy man to fall for...if you aren't already in love with another.

Our food is delivered faster than we thought, and Ian and I dive into our hot, flavorful breakfast. Broken Yolk is known for having the best brunch in town, so our conversation is limited, with our mouths full of deliciousness. Ian tries to get me to try his avocado toast, going so far as to bribe me, but I hold strong with my aversion to the foul vegetable (or fruit).

Brunch is over too soon and after enjoying a final cup of

coffee, Ian takes the check from our waiter, refusing to let me pay when I offer, even though he told me brunch was on me, and we head out of the restaurant. On the way out, I can't help but look around when I feel eyes on me. With how many people are occupying the restaurant, it's hard to tell if someone is looking at me specifically.

Once we walk outside, Ian grabs my hand and interlocks our fingers. His hand is rough and feels nice against mine. I lean into his side as we make our way to my car around the building. The parking lot has only gotten more busy since I arrived an hour ago, and it was full then. The Florida spring weather has created a nice day today. The humidity isn't too high, and the cluster of clouds in the sky has created a barrier between us and the sun, helping to keep the temperature lower.

As we round my car to the driver's side, Ian releases my hand and repositions it on my hip, guiding me so my back is against the door. He brings his body in front of mine so that we are close but not touching.

The hand that was on my waist comes up to caress my face. "While I'm not a guy to push a girl into anything she doesn't want, I need to be honest with you, Emree." He pauses, his eyes dancing between mine and my lips. "Don't think I've ever wanted to kiss someone as badly as I want to kiss you."

The smile on my face is hard to contain. "You wouldn't be pushing me if I wanted you to kiss me."

Ian's hand on my face moves to the back of my neck as he brings his head forward and lightly touches his lips to mine, testing the waters before deepening the kiss. The hand on my neck tightens as he moves my head to where he wants it, and at the new angle, Ian presses his lips harder against my own.

He brings his other hand to my waist and pulls my soft body flush against his hard one. My hands leave the spot against my car, where they had lain limply, and glide up Ian's chest, clutching his T-shirt and pulling him closer to me.

A car horn blares and a middle-aged woman yells out her window for us to get a room. Burying my face in Ian's chest, my laugh is muffled against his shirt. "Pretty sure my face is as red as a tomato right now," I tell him.

Wrapping his arms around my shoulders, Ian pulls me closer to him and kisses the top of my head. "Got a little carried away there."

I nod in agreement. Pulling back, I look up at him. "That sure was some kiss."

He smiles and bends down to softly kiss my lips but pulls back after just a second. "I have to get to my professor's office for a meeting. I'll text you later?"

Smiling, I nod again and reach up on my tiptoes to kiss his cheek. He grips my waist before backing away and heading toward his car at the front of the restaurant. I stand there smiling as I touch my fingertips to my lips. They still feel tingly from Ian's kiss.

"Guess I don't need to ask if you're dating him this time," a familiar voice states from somewhere around me. Turning my head toward the front of my car, a clearly fuming Conrad is leaning against a pillar with his arms crossed.

Squaring my shoulders, I prepare myself for a fight. "What are you doing here, Conrad?"

He shrugs his shoulders. "Was in the mood for some brunch. Didn't know I'd be getting a meal and a show while I was here."

If he thinks shaming me for kissing the guy I have been on a few dates with will hurt me, he couldn't be more wrong. "Hope you enjoyed it."

Turning, I unlock my car and open the door. Not even five seconds later, a large hand smacks against my window and pushes the door closed. His body cages me in as he brings his other hand up to rest against my car on the other side of my head.

Hot breath glides across my neck as Conrad leans in to whisper in my ear, "You happier with him, baby? Don't need me anymore?" My body shivers and he notices. "Ah, seems maybe you do still need me. He make your body feel this way, Em?"

"Fuck you, Conrad." My tone is harsh as I spit the words out through clenched teeth.

He laughs, and that deep tone does something to me. "You already have, baby."

Whipping around, I come face-to-face with him. This close, I notice that his usually clean-shaven face is scruffy from days of not shaving, and his hair, which he always made a point to flawlessly style, is more disheveled. While he looks like the Conrad I know and love, there is something…different about him. There is a hint of dark circles under his eyes, and I reach up, lightly tracing them with the tips of my fingers.

"What's going on, Conrad?" I whisper. "You've never been cruel like this before, and you look as if you haven't slept in days."

Something changes in his face. Before, his eyes were hard and his lips tight, but he softens at my words. He leans forward, resting his forehead against mine. "I can't fucking do this anymore, Em."

Already knowing the answer, I ask anyway, "Do what?"

"Stay away from you," he admits just before crashing his lips against mine in a kiss that steals my breath.

Conrad's arms that are caging me into my car move to grip my face, his thumbs going beneath my chin to tilt my head up. His hands are warm from resting on the car and the calluses he has gotten over years of lifting weights in the gym are rough against my skin. Something that I love about Conrad is his coarse hands. While he is always put together and not a hair is out of place, his hands are a different story. An imperfection in an otherwise perfect man.

The smell of sandalwood and leather invades my senses as Conrad fights with my mouth in a ruthless kiss. His tongue battles its way through my lips, and the moment the taste of coffee and mint enters, my head spins. Conrad's familiar scent and taste cause a moan to escape from me, and he moves one of his hands to the side of my neck, holding me in a tight grip.

Kissing Conrad feels completely different than my kiss with Ian. Not only because Conrad knows my body better than anyone, but my feelings for him make every touch, every kiss more meaningful. Kissing someone you love involves not only your body but also your heart. Conrad owns that organ, and I'm afraid he will never give it back.

Pulling back, I try to catch my breath. Breaking our connection doesn't stop him, though. Conrad moves his lips to my jaw and then my neck, sucking a trail as he descends. My hands move to his neck and then up, running through the strands of his thick hair. Conrad's hot mouth is nipping and trailing kisses along my neck, jaw, and collarbone, and the sensation is making my head foggy. Each time his mouth makes contact with my skin, it feels as though he is leaving a burn behind.

Struggling to stand up straight, I muster up the strength to push Conrad away at the shoulders, though my body wants nothing more than to pull him closer to me. My efforts to get him off go unnoticed as Conrad's grip on my neck tightens and he brings his lips back up to mine, cutting off the words I was getting ready to let out. His mouth is ruthless against mine as he takes what he wants, and this kiss is different than the first. More forceful. Angry. He bites my bottom lip, and I squeak in surprise.

Turning my head to the side, I gasp for breath. "Conrad, stop." His lips don't leave me as he fights to get my mouth back to his. "I said *stop*." My tone is more forceful and he notices this time.

Conrad pulls his head away from me but keeps his body close. "What? What's wrong?"

Staring at him, I'm trying to gauge if he is serious or playing dumb. "What's wrong? You're really asking me that?"

"Yeah, why wouldn't I? We were having a hell of a kiss, baby. Figured we could go back to your place."

My nostrils flare. "So I'm good enough to fuck but not good enough to tell your family about?"

He blows out a frustrated breath and takes a step away from me. "You know that's not what this is about."

A laugh escapes me. "That is exactly what it's about, Conrad. You *broke up with me* because of some fucked-up family obligations to marry for status, and I am clearly not near the same ranking as the Dugrays." His shoulders slump. "But hey, the girl from the wrong side of the tracks is perfect for keeping behind closed doors for a good fuck here and there."

Conrad's brows pinch together. "Stop fucking saying that," he seethes. "You know I care about you, Em. I can't change who I am, though. Just because I have to follow the path my parents created for me doesn't mean I don't care about you."

My heart clenches at his admission. "What does that mean then? You're going to marry Liliana and what? I'll be your mistress? A secret where I can only have you if it's behind a bedroom door?"

He stares at me with a complex look. Like he is absorbing the questions I asked him because they are not easy for him to answer. This should be a yes or no question, but I know Conrad is fighting with the choices he must make. My biggest issue is that his struggles with the choices he has made are affecting my heart, and I'm not sure how much more it can handle this back and forth.

"It means I care about you, and I don't know what else," he whispers.

My heart clenches at his words. I love this man, even when I shouldn't. He owns my heart, and I wish more than anything for him to give it back. "If you care about me, Conrad, you need to let me go. It hurts too much to hang on to a fantasy that will never be."

Without another word, I open my car door and start the engine. Conrad remains in the same spot as I switch the gearshift to reverse and back away from him. Away from the man I wish I could move on from. The man who made me fall in love with him under false pretenses.

CHAPTER TWENTY-FOUR

CONRAD

For the last four days, I have barely slept. My brain has been running through how this scenario is going to play out, and all conclusions end badly. Each night, when my body is too exhausted from practice to do anything besides lie in bed, I think of ways to alter the current path of my life. Emree is right when she says that I need to live my life for myself.

It took me almost a week to build up the courage to book a flight and head back to my hometown to have a conversation with the most nonunderstanding man I have ever met. Almost a week of my roommates telling me I am the biggest dumbass they have ever met. Day after day of having to see Emree and that dickhead she is now seeing, having lunch and smiling at each other. Luckily, I haven't had to see them kiss again because that one time was enough to set me off.

Not sure if it was Emree telling me I was hurting her and that I needed to let her go last Sunday or realizing how much I love the fuck out of this woman when I saw her each day with another man, but whatever the reason, it has helped me muster up enough balls to confront my father about what I want in life, and that is not marrying Liliana.

The Uber ride from Boston Logan Airport seems longer than ever before as I make my way to my hometown, Blackburn. The driver is playing a current hits station and, luckily, has kept conversation to a minimum since we drove away from the airport. The lack of talking is helping me play out everything I plan to say to my father the moment I confront him in his office. I've come to terms with the fact that marrying Liliana, or anyone my parents choose for me, is out of the question. Just because they made these plans for me before I was born doesn't mean I should have to give my life up and do as they say. My parents have never been warm or loving, but some parts of them must care about their kids' happiness. While I don't fully believe that, I need to keep a positive thought that they can't be that heartless.

Too lost in thought, I don't notice that we have made our way through Boston and into Blackburn. The neighborhood I grew up in passes by as I stare out the window. The houses are larger than anyone would ever need. At the end of the gated neighborhood is my family's home, secured by its own private gates. The house looks as if you took two typical New England homes and put them together to create a mansion. The house is colonial style, with its stark white coating and off-gray shutters on each of the windows in the front, which is a shit ton of windows now that I'm taking it all in. The long driveway is made of perfectly paved brick and leads straight up to the front of the house.

Nothing has changed since I visited home over the winter break other than the lack of professionally installed Christmas decorations. It is still cold and unwelcoming, much like it was during my childhood.

The driver rolls to a stop in front of the porch that leads to large double-entry doors. After telling me the amount owed, I pay through the app on my phone and exit his sedan with only my backpack with an extra change of clothes in case this conversation leads to an overnight stay.

Looking up at the front door, I take a deep breath before climbing the four steps onto the porch and heading inside the house. The moment I'm in the entryway, the familiar scent of fresh lilies and jasmine invades my senses. My mother has always made sure our home was overflowing with flowers and sent whichever maid she had at the time out to buy them at least once a week from a local florist. The small touch of color in an otherwise hospital-like house is welcoming.

Deciding to bypass seeing my mother and having her question why I'm here, I head to my father's office. It's after seven at night, and I know by this time he is home from work but not done working. When I was in middle school, she made him promise to be home by dinnertime, but that never stopped him from retreating into his private cave until exhaustion took over and he eventually went to bed.

Approaching the thick, white door, I knock once and step back, waiting for a response from the man I know is on the other side.

"I'm busy, Annie. Just go watch your reality shows." His tone is short, and I can't imagine how any woman would want to be married to a man like him, not that my mom is much warmer.

Rather than walking in or yelling back at him, I knock again. Through the door, I hear a huff and the sound of a chair rolling against the hardwood floor. The door flies open, and my father's face changes from annoyed to one of surprise.

"What the hell are you doing here?" he snaps.

Plastering on the fakest smile I can muster, I resist the urge to match his harsh words and decide to take the higher route. "Here to speak with you, if that's okay?"

His eyebrow stretches up in curiosity. "Must be important if this needs to be in person." Stepping back, he holds the door open for me to come in.

Walking in, I take in the smell of old cigars and wood. My father's office is what I would think a mafia leader's office would look like, a complete contrast to the rest of the house. It's dark, with every inch being made of deep wood. His desk sits in the middle of the circular room, and by the size of it, you would think this man was the president. I'm sure he feels as important; his ego is that large. Behind his desk is a wall made of bookshelves filled with antique books, which I am sure he has never read, and decor that my mother picked out.

There are two oversized leather seats in front of his desk, angled toward the center of the desk. I take a seat in one of the chairs as my father rounds his desk and sits down. He's still in his suit from work, but the tie is now lying on the chaise lounge in the corner and the top two buttons of his white shirt are undone.

Leaning back in his chair, my father locks his hands together over his chest. "Well? Out with it. I don't have all night." Ever the conversationalist Howard Dugray is.

Inhaling a much-needed breath for strength, I mentally run through what I plan on saying to him before letting it all out. "Father, I understand that there are certain…obligations I am to meet as the oldest of your sons. I fully intend to follow through with my duties like you expect of me, except for one."

His eyebrow arches at my admission.

"While I am sure Liliana is a lovely woman, I cannot in good conscience marry her. It would be a loveless marriage, and neither of us would be happy."

My father stares at me for several seconds without saying a word. After an awkward amount of time has gone by, he throws his head back and lets out a laugh unlike any I have ever heard from him before. His usual laugh is forced, like when he is making some business acquaintance happy after they tell a poor joke. But this laugh? It's not forced at all and his entire body shakes.

After composing himself, my father looks back at me. "Oh, you had me going there, Conrad. You flew all this way to play a joke on me? We don't have that kind of relationship, son, but I appreciate the humor. Haven't laughed like that in a long time."

Clearly, he thinks I'm joking, and telling him I am more than serious makes me nervous. Growing up, my father was a strict and serious man. While he was never abusive to my mother, siblings, or me, he did instill fear in us by making sure we knew the power he had. We knew to never go against him or break his rules, or there would be major consequences. Not once did one of us make it to the major consequences, and luckily, when we broke his superficial rules, he was never home, like when I was creeping out of the house, getting drunk at a party, or when I would sneak a girl into my room.

Clearing my throat, I continue with our conversation. "Glad I could give you that good laugh, but I'm being serious, sir."

He sobers, and the vein that always appears on his forehead when he's angry makes itself present. "What do you mean, Conrad?"

"Liliana was a good choice, and you are right; she is a beautiful woman, but I can't make her my wife. All the other obligations I will uphold, as expected of me, but this is one of your rulings I can't follow through with."

The vein makes a stronger appearance. "You speak to me as if you have a choice."

A lump forms in my throat. Howard Dugray can be a ruthless businessman, but he usually saves the harshness for work-related conversations. His family would be on the receiving end of a curt tone. But at this moment? I'm getting the ruthless Howard and for the first time, I'm becoming scared around my own father.

"Sir—"

"Shut the fuck up this moment, Conrad," he cuts me off.

Leaning forward, he rests his forearms on the thick wood of his desk and takes a deep breath, releasing it through his flared nostrils. "I'm going to give you the benefit of the doubt and just assume you're a goddamn moron for coming into my office and making demands like you just did. If you think there is even a chance of taking over my business and not marrying Liliana, you are in for a rude awakening of what the real world is like, boy."

Sitting upright, I square my shoulders. "Like I said, sir, I will still uphold my other obligations as expected of me. There is someone else in my life, and it would not be fair to Liliana or myself to follow through with your plans."

He barks out a laugh once again. "A woman? You're going against your obligations for some pussy? Boy, I told you once you're married, you can have any sidepiece you want. Liliana is good for breeding, but a man has needs. Marry the girl and keep your other one on the side." He gives me a pointed look. "Just as long as you always wrap it up with other women. Don't need any bastards running around, and God knows how hard it is to get these whores to get rid of the thing when you have money."

My blood boils anytime he mentions side chicks and just the way my father speaks about women. My mother is no saint and has had her own affairs, but she would never speak about the people she has been with the way my father does.

"Respectfully, you're wrong. Emree is more than that, and I won't keep her as a sidepiece. She means more to me than that, and I plan to marry that woman, whether you accept that decision or not." It takes every bit of strength in me to say this to him, but it needs to be done. I'm tired of living the life he wants me to and feeling shackled when it comes to what I want.

My father stands, using his over-six-foot height as a power advantage over me in my seated position. "It seems you have become stupid since the last time I saw you, so I'm going to make this very clear." He rounds the table to stand in front of me. "You have two choices here, Conrad. You either marry Liliana Hawthorne after graduation and move here to learn the business and eventually take over, or you go with this woman, but you're cut off. Nothing from me from this point on."

My jaw slackens, but I manage not to let it fall. "You would really disown your own son because he fell in love and wants to be with that woman?"

An evil grin appears on his face. "Don't act like we have this close father-son relationship. It wouldn't be a loss on either of our ends." He stares off into the distance, pondering a thought. "I will say it'll have been a waste of time with all the effort I put into you all these years. Luckily, I trained Archer enough."

My nineteen-year-old brother is not only the spitting image of my father, but he acts like him as well. For a teenager, he is the most serious young adult I have ever met. While my sister and I had more of a social life, including hobbies and friends, my brother's idea of a good time was reading the business section of a newspaper or attending a seminar on business fundamentals.

Standing so that my father and I are on equal ground, I look him in the eyes when I ask my next question. "You're telling me I'm disposable?"

"I gave you your options. Decide and get out."

The realization that my father is crueler than I believed he was hits me. This man has never cared about his own son a single day of my life. I am a means to an end for him. He needed an heir, and I was born first, making me his project. He may have taken care of me growing up with basic needs and extras that any kid would want, but I owe him nothing. Giving up my life, the woman I can't get out of my head or heart is not something a father should make their son do.

Deciding to take my life into my own hands, I turn and

head toward the door. "Have a nice life, Dad. I'm making my own decisions from here on out."

Without another word, I leave my childhood home that holds no sentimental feelings. Leaving Emree that day in her apartment after I broke her heart was harder than leaving my family, and that tells me I'm making the right decision.

CHAPTER TWENTY-FIVE

EMREE

CONRAD
> We need to talk.

The text has been sitting on my phone unanswered since last night. I haven't talked to Conrad since the parking lot of Broken Yolk, and if I'm being honest with myself, I've wondered why he hasn't reached out to me. Basically, I'm a glutton for punishment for having that thought. All week I've been hanging out with Ian and having a wonderful time partaking in lunch with him. He's sweet and good company. He's safe, unlike Conrad, who can destroy my heart in an instant.

The biggest struggle is while I find Ian attractive and we have a good time together, there isn't that spark I've been looking for. When he kisses me, which hasn't been more than a couple times, it's nice, but I'm missing that tingly feeling that consumes my body. The butterflies that settle in my stomach whenever I'm around Conrad. And that's my issue. Conrad Dugray. It's hard to move on when I so clearly want someone else.

Blaire and I have this weekend off and made plans to spend Saturday at the beach with some of the guys. I went back and forth on whether or not it would be a good idea to invite Ian but went with not mentioning it. We haven't been on many dates, and I'm not ready to have him meet the guys yet. Camden said it wouldn't be a problem, especially since Conrad left yesterday morning for his hometown and they didn't know when he would be back.

After slipping on my sandals, a knock fills the silence in my room. "Come in," I call out.

Blaire enters wearing a white sundress over her bikini and a pair of brown Birkenstocks. Her long, dark-honey hair is sectioned into two braids that fall over her chest. "Aw, you look cute, Emmy."

I look down at my loose jean shorts and neon-green tank top that is covering my tie-dye bathing two-piece. My hair is tossed up in a messy bun, and my face is void of any makeup.

"Thanks," I tell her with a smile. "You're looking hot as ever in that little number. You know you're going to have to fight Camden off the entire time we're at the beach, right?"

She blushes and the color is clear as day, even from across the room with how fair her skin is. "Stop. Don't give him any ideas either." She smiles and I know she's thinking about her hot-as-hell boyfriend. "You ready to go? The boys are going to meet us at the pier."

Grabbing my tote off the bed, I slide the sunglasses I have sitting next to it onto my face and smile at my best friend. "Let's go get some fresh sea air and show off these hot bods."

As we make our way out of the apartment and to Blaire's car, I check that my phone is on silent and continue to ignore the text message from the one man I want out of my mind but who seems to remain a permanent resident.

Growing up in Florida, I'm no stranger to the beach scene. The smell of salt water, sunscreen, and sunshine surrounds me while the sound of seagulls, waves, and people's chatter breaks through my own music playing through a small speaker I brought. It feels like home, and I think back to all the times my mom would drive us out to the beach on the weekends because it was one of the free activities to take a young kid to.

We've been at the beach for over an hour now, and I've been baking in the sun since we set up our spot. Camden brought a large umbrella for Blaire since that girl can't even be saved by the highest SPF sunscreen. She's been reading one of her books under there, oblivious to anything going on around her. The guys have gone back and forth from kicking a soccer ball around to playing a makeshift game of volleyball in the water.

Flipping over onto my back, I apply a light layer of tanning oil to my front and lie out in a position to make sure all my parts are tanned evenly. The sun has been in my favor today and there have been minimum clouds covering the sky, providing me with a perfect amount of sunshine for an even tan.

With my glasses protecting my eyes, I inhale a deep breath and savor the fresh, salty air. A shadow casts over my face, and I snap my eyes open, wondering where this obstruction is coming from since there hasn't been a cloud in the sky.

Lifting my sunglasses up, my line of sight trails up a tall, tanned boy. When I get to the face, my stomach clenches at who is above me. He was supposed to be out of town and nowhere near this beach.

"You didn't answer my text," Conrad states, his tone void of all pleasantries. He crosses his arms over his chest, stretching out the sleeves of his shirt.

I reposition my eyewear and close my eyes. "Not in the mood to talk to you today."

Conrad's shadow moves from my face to my torso and I imagine him walking around so that he isn't looking at me from upside down. Even though I'm trying to ignore him, my body hums, knowing the man it so dreadfully wants is near.

"Listen, Em, it's been a long fucking twenty-four hours for me. I've dealt with conversations that were less than pleasant, had a few realizations about people who should love you unconditionally, and had the worst journey back with three layovers on what should have been a four-hour flight." He rests his hands on his hips and lets out an exhausted breath. "Please, just talk to me. I have some important things I need to tell you."

Sitting up, I lift my sunglasses to rest on my head and look up at Conrad. This time I notice the dark circles under his eyes, the unkempt hair, and the clothes that are so wrinkled they look like they've been on his body for days. He's wearing jeans, a dark-gray T-shirt, and white sneakers, which makes me wonder if he came here straight after his flight since he isn't dressed for the beach in the least bit.

"Fine." Waving my hand out, I gesture to the towel beside mine. "Have a seat."

Conrad looks at the towel and then at me. "Can we go for a drive? Or back to my place? I'm exhausted, Em, and it's too damn hot here to sit around in jeans."

Being alone with him is never a good idea, seeing as how I have no restraint the moment he touches me. Conrad looks enormously uncomfortable and while I know I shouldn't go off alone with him, I don't want him to sit here with how he feels.

Sighing, I make my decision. "You have one hour."

Conrad stands in the same spot, wordlessly watching me pull on my clothes and gather my belongings in the tote I

THE HURT OF LETTING GO

brought. Blaire still hasn't looked up from her book to notice that Conrad is here and the guys are down in the water.

Walking over to my best friend, I clear my throat loud enough to get her attention.

"Oh, hey. Everything okay?"

Turning my head over my shoulder, I look at Conrad, who is standing about fifteen feet away, and then back at my best friend. "Okay is a relative term at this point. He's insisting we need to talk and by the looks of him, I don't think he's going to make it sitting out in the sun that long."

Blaire worries her lip as she looks between the two of us. "Will you text me if anything happens? And don't let him smooth-talk you, Emmy. He's too good at that, and you deserve someone who chooses you. Remember that."

Smiling, I lean down and hug her before following Conrad to his car. The walk through the sand is quiet, neither of us saying a word and me making sure that we don't touch. Even just the brush of a shoulder is enough to ignite something in me.

Conrad's car is at the far end of the parking lot at the pier, and we pass several cars doing laps around, looking for a spot and people cleaning off sand as they get into their cars. Conrad's BMW comes into view, and I worry about sitting in the expensive leather seat with my oiled-up body and sandy feet.

He goes to the passenger side of his car and opens the door for me. I stand by the back, looking down at my sandy feet, then back up at him. "Are you sure you want me in your fancy car? I'm kind of oily and sandy."

The side of his mouth perks up, and his tired eyes are brighter than they have been since he arrived at the beach. "Don't give a shit about the car, Em. Come get your ass in."

I scoff but get into the car. He laughs as he shuts the door and goes to his side.

Conrad smoothly slides into his car, looking like a model as he does it, and starts the engine. He doesn't back out right away, and I can tell by the few honks that there is someone waiting for the spot.

"Listen, I know I told you we could go for a drive, but honestly, baby, I think I'm too tired to be behind the wheel for too long. Can I just take you to my place? I'll make some coffee and we can talk."

Even his voice sounds exhausted. Reaching forward, I do something I shouldn't and place my hand on his forearm in a comforting gesture. "That's okay. I'll make some coffee and you shower before we have this conversation. You look like a mess, Conrad."

He smiles over at me and puts the car in reverse, making those waiting in their cars happy. We drive the thirty minutes from Treasure Island Beach to Braxton, the sounds of a playlist on Conrad's phone filling the car. I keep my hands in my lap, resisting the urge to lace my fingers with his like we used to do when driving together.

The house is quiet as we enter. With the rest of the guys at the beach, we are alone and that realization makes me nervous.

Conrad stands awkwardly at the bottom of the stairs. "I'm going to shower real quick. You want a drink or anything? The living room is all yours, and we can talk there since no one is home."

Giving him a small smile, I head toward the oversized leather sofa and make myself comfortable. He seems to relax some now that we're here and without another word, he heads up the stairs. I notice he moves slower than usual as he takes one step at a time.

Worry overcomes me. Each time Conrad has had to talk to me in the past month, it has left me heartbroken. Telling him no should be my go-to answer anytime Conrad asks for something, but the seriousness that came off him when he asked to talk and the fact that he hasn't tried to put a move on me like the times before tell me something is wrong.

While he's up in the shower, I put a pot of coffee on to brew and head back into the living room to wait.

The walls whine as the pipes push water to the bathroom. With the quietness, I can hear the shower running from downstairs. Opting to sit in silence and wait for him, I lean back into the cushion and get comfortable as I get lost in my own thoughts.

Less than five minutes later, Conrad strolls down the steps. His hair is still damp, and he has changed into a pair of gym shorts and a faded blue T-shirt. His feet are bare, and for some reason, I find this look more attractive than when he is dressed in his best for postgame questions when their coach makes the guys wear slacks and button-down shirts.

"Hey." He gives me a soft smile but looks unsure of himself as he comes to stand behind the large sofa beside me. "Do you want a drink or anything? I think we have that diet soda you like."

My heart clenches. Conrad always made sure to keep their fridge stocked for me at all times with my favorite drink, Diet Coke. "Sure. Thank you."

He walks through the archway that leads into the kitchen, and I hear him moving items around in the fridge. He comes back into the living room with a cup of coffee and my can of soda. After handing me my drink, he takes a seat on the larger sofa beside the one I'm sitting on.

Neither of us says anything for a solid minute, and I start to worry. Just before I break the silence, Conrad speaks up. "I'm not marrying Liliana…and my father disowned me."

My jaw slackens. This was not what I thought he brought me here to talk about.

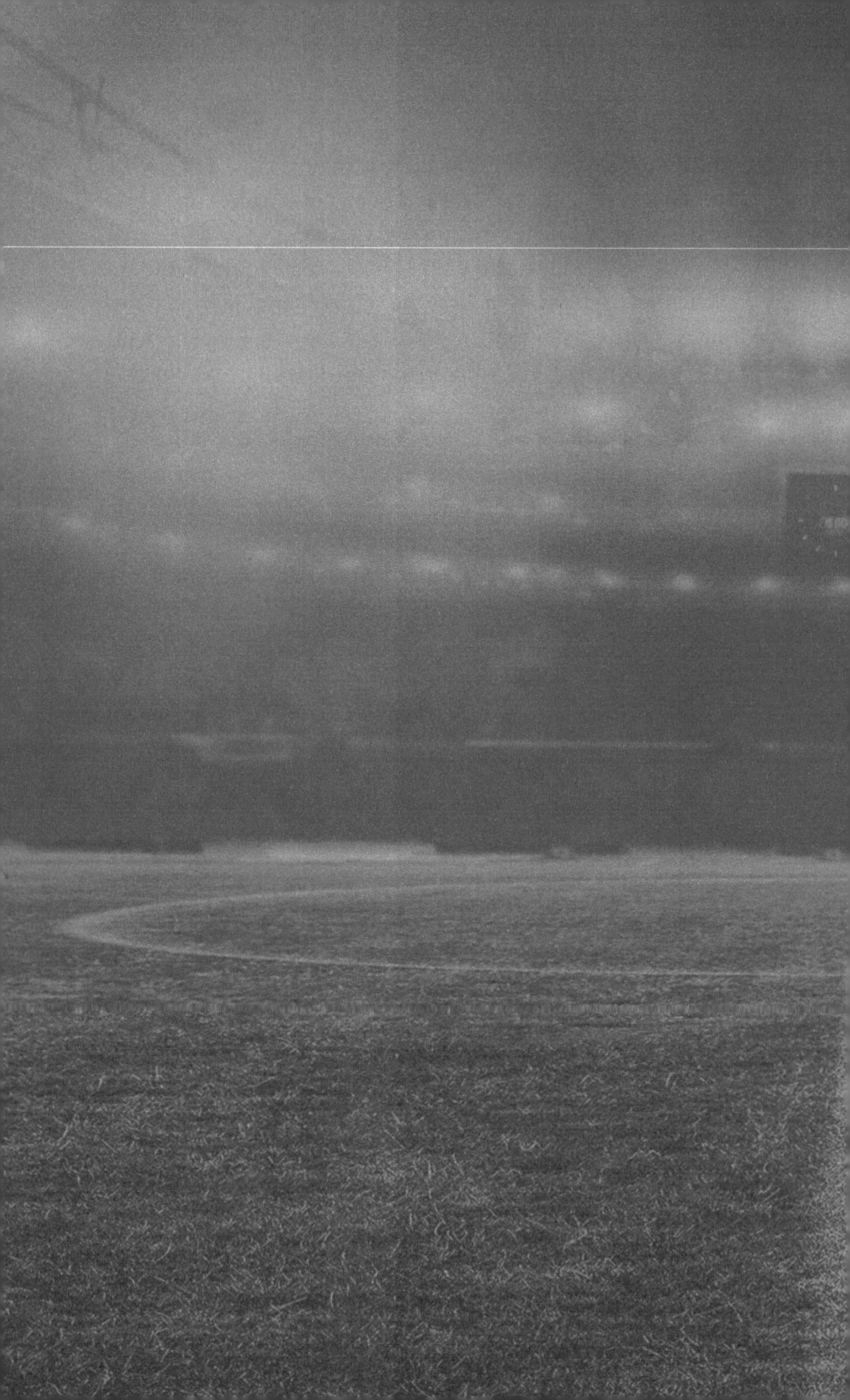

CHAPTER TWENTY-SIX

EMREE

The Publix sub I ate for lunch over an hour ago weighs heavy in my stomach at Conrad's confession. Never did I think he would be telling me that the arranged marriage his parents set up for him would not be happening, let alone that his father disowned him. I can't imagine a parent disowning their child for any reason other than maybe committing a heinous crime.

Neither of us has said a word and truthfully, I'm not sure what to respond with. Conrad looks nervous. It is a look I have never seen on him before. Since we met, I have only been around a self-assured and collected Conrad, and the man sitting across from me is neither of those.

"Can you explain to me what this means?" I ask, breaking the silence.

Conrad is toying with the bottom of his shorts, not looking in my direction. He keeps his head down for several beats before meeting my eyes. "Well, for one, it means I'm single. Hopefully not for long." That cocky smirk I have grown to love appears, and his joke breaks the tension that has been stewing in the air.

Smiling, I offer a light laugh. "Cute, but I'll need more from you."

His smirk fades away and serious Conrad is back. "For starters, I went to visit my father in Massachusetts. He wasn't too happy with me when I told him I couldn't marry Liliana."

Genuinely shocked that he would confront his father like this, I ask the only question that comes to mind. "Why would you do that? Wasn't marrying her the only option he gave you?"

"Yes, but I couldn't marry her when I went and fell in love with someone else."

My breath catches in my throat, and I gape at him. No words come out as I open and close my mouth several times. Conrad watches me with uncertainty sketched across his features. How could he tell his father no to an arranged marriage he'd planned since before his son was born?

"Wh-why would you do that? Conrad, he disowned you because you wouldn't marry Liliana?" I'm not ready to process the "in love with someone else" statement, so I exclude it from my question.

His shoulders shrug. "Not all that surprising, if I'm being honest. Howard Dugray has never been the warmest or most caring father. I think having kids was more of a necessity for him. There was no love in my house and little to no father-son time unless it was about the family business and me attending board meetings when I entered high school."

Thinking of a young Conrad who was deprived of love and affection and felt unwanted by his parents makes my heart clench. While he was a kid who grew up with everything someone could dream of in a material sense, he was missing one of the most important provisions a kid needs: their parents around.

"What did he say to you when you went to see him?"

Conrad sighs and sinks back into the sofa. "I went there prepared, Em, but it threw me off when he started laughing after I told him I plan to uphold all of what is expected of me, except marrying Liliana. While I tried coming to terms with having to live a loveless marriage, I couldn't do it. Not only to myself but to you."

Frustrated, I stand and begin pacing the area between the boys' TV and coffee table before facing Conrad. "How can your father be that big of a jackass? His son says that he wants to live his life as he pleases, and the automatic response is to disown him? The boy he raised? His own flesh and blood?"

Conrad offers up a humorless laugh. "Not sure I would say my father raised me."

Rolling my eyes, I let out a huff. "Beside the point. You are his son. He should want you to be happy. It isn't like you said you would be walking away from the family business as well. You still wanted to hold up that end of the stupid obligation."

Leaning forward, Conrad rests his forearms on his thighs. "You need to get it out of your head that my family is meant to be a normal one. They're the furthest thing from that, and if you keep trying to figure out why my father treats his kids the way he does, you will make yourself mad."

Feeling defeated, I make my way around the coffee table and plop down on the seat beside him. For some reason, the urge to be closer to Conrad is high right now. To comfort and reassure him that, while he broke my heart trying to uphold his duties, he is a wonderful man and doesn't deserve a father who cares so little about him.

Resting my hand on his warm forearm, I give him a gentle squeeze. "Have I mentioned I hate your father?"

Offering up a soft smile, Conrad places his hand on top of mine. "Think you've mentioned that once or twice before."

We sit there in silence, with Conrad caressing my hand with his thumb and me staring at the side of his face as he watches where we are touching. While I know he is trying to make light of his father's treatment of him, I can see the stiffness in his shoulders and know this is weighing on him.

"Father aside, do you want to circle around to the subject of me being single now?"

While I was hoping to avoid this conversation since he brought up the *L* word and "someone," I know it is inevitable that we talk about it, seeing as how he most likely just walked away from his family, his fortune, and his future for me.

"Almost missed that part," I whisper, avoiding looking at him.

The movement on my hand halts, and I can feel Conrad's blazing stare on the side of my face.

"I meant what I told him."

My head snaps up at his confession.

"I love you, Emree."

The words I have desperately wanted to tell him get caught in my throat. While I still love this man and probably always will, giving my heart over to him again is dangerous. Since the moment he broke it all those weeks ago, I've tried to mend the cracks he's created. Could I easily give it back to him again?

Removing my hand from touching him, I scoot back enough to turn and square my shoulders. "My heart belonged to you, Conrad, but you put me last and that one decision shattered every bit of me. I've never been in love before, and quite frankly, I don't let many people close enough to hurt me."

The sides of his mouth turn down.

"You *hurt* me, Conrad. Hurt me more than anyone has before, and while I still love you, I don't know if I can put myself through that again."

Conrad leans forward and grasps my hands in his. "Em, I swear you will always be first. I'm choosing you. I love *you*."

Looking at the face of the man who holds my heart, I can't help but wonder if he is telling the truth. Before the breakup, Conrad made me feel like I was his love and he cared for me, but then he seemingly left everything we had so easily. What if he does it again?

"I believe you love me, Conrad. My worry is that loving me is not enough for you. What happens after graduation when the life you had planned has changed? When you lose the safety net of your dad's income? Are you going to be okay getting a regular old job and living the life of an average person?"

He doesn't answer right away, and I can see the tables turning in his head. This isn't something he has considered yet. "I can do it, Em. I promise, there is no way I will turn my back on you again."

"I want to believe that, but getting my heart broken twice? I don't know if I can handle that."

His eyebrows push together at my confession.

Reaching forward, Conrad caresses my jaw with his rough hand and runs the pad of his thumb along my cheekbone. On instinct, I lean into the comforting touch. "You're not worth letting go twice. I'd be an idiot of a man to not realize that."

Staring into his eyes, I see the honesty in what he tells me. "Then prove it."

CHAPTER TWENTY-SEVEN
CONRAD

P*rove it.*
Those were the last words Emree spoke to me before Blaire and the guys came barreling into the house. The audience effectively ended our conversation. Blaire pulled Emree aside while Maddox and Camden went upstairs to shower, followed by Mateo and Levi and then Jules. Everyone ended up agreeing to order pizza for dinner, and since I had been up for over twenty-four hours, I opted to crash rather than fall asleep in a plate of food.

Yesterday, Em was working a double shift, and Maddox and I showed up at Whiskey Joe's to enjoy a beer and be near my girl. The place was packed, so I didn't get to talk to her other than saying hello and goodbye, but just being around and shamelessly looking at her was enough. Gone were the dirty looks she would justifiably cast my way, replaced with shy side-eyes and the sweetest pink tint on her cheeks when our eyes met. I gave her a wink.

"Dude, how hungry are you?" Levi asks as he looks at my tray of food. Usually, I don't eat basically two lunches, but I have plans for the extra food I've collected.

Shrugging, I try to brush off his question. "Just wanted a little extra."

Levi drops the conversation when we reach the cashier, and he hands her his credit card. Sliding my wallet out of the back pocket of my jeans, I grab my black Amex and wait my turn. After ringing up the items I have, the cashier gives me the total, and I swipe my card. An obnoxious sound comes from the machine, and the screen reads, "Card declined."

Curious because this has never happened, I give the cashier a questioning look. She chews her lower lip as she presses buttons on the machine. "Go ahead and swipe it again. Maybe there was something wrong with how it was done the first time."

Swiping once more, the same insufferable sound rings through my ears. "What the fuck?"

The elderly cashier lifts her glasses that are hanging around her neck and takes a closer look at the keypad. "Sorry, darling. Declined again. You have another card?"

While I don't want to sound like a dick and tell her there is no way an Amex Black Card can be declined, I'm confused because this is a first. Deciding to let it go, I hand her cash, and she gives me the change back.

Shaking off the confusion of why my card isn't working, I nod to my friends at our usual table and head outside. From what I've noticed in the past, Emree is usually at the table first before the little dickhead shows up. I want to be there before he shows up in the courtyard. Not sure if Emree ended whatever she had going on with him, but I want to make my intentions with her clear. He needs to stay away from what's mine.

Making my way through the cafeteria doors, I'm hit with the heat of Florida's springtime. While the humidity hasn't hit its highest like it does in the summer, it's starting to get there. It has made practices brutal, and Coach hasn't let up at all, even though it's the off-season. I'll be glad when summer is here, and we will have a couple months off from the drills he puts us through.

Scanning the courtyard, I spot Emree's golden-blonde hair piled high on top of her head in a messy bun with a clip holding it together. From the side, I can see a few strands have fallen into her face as she looks down at her laptop with determination.

And she's alone.

Passing the few tables in my way, I approach her. She is so distracted by what she is working on that she doesn't look up when I'm standing beside her. Setting the tray down, Emree's head snaps up at the sound.

"What are you doing here?" she asks as I sink down into the seat diagonal from hers.

Unwrapping the burger I got for myself, I give her my ever-winning smile. "Having lunch with my girl since she insists on eating outside."

She studies my movements as I bring the burger toward my mouth and take a generous bite. "I feel as though I should remind you that I am no longer your girl and also, I have lunch with someone else." She looks around, most likely searching for that guy.

Ignoring her, I continue enjoying my food. "Then I feel as though I should remind you that you told me to 'prove it' when I said I loved you, and here I am. Proving it to you."

Emree physically relaxes and her eyes go soft. "And sitting with me at lunch is proving your love for me?"

I'm glad she finally asks. "Not at all. Getting your favorite foods for lunch since I know you most likely forgot to pack something today since you were working all day yesterday is part of my proving-it plan."

"How did you know I would forget to bring something?"

Shrugging, I hand her the chicken sandwich I know she likes so much and a Diet Coke. "You have a history of doing it."

She accepts the items with a bright smile, displaying her perfectly straight teeth. "You're sweet. Thank you."

As she begins to unwrap her food, someone approaches the table. "Hey, Em..."

Looking up from my mediocre cafeteria food, I see none other than the douche who has been trying to take my girl. He's standing across from Emree with his backpack slung lazily over his shoulder and a fast-food bag in his hand.

"Ian. Hi," she greets him with uncertainty.

He offers up a tight smile but looks uncomfortable with my presence. "Guessing the ex is no longer an ex?"

She looks at me, and I see the conflict in her eyes before she turns back to him. "I'm not sure yet."

He nods, and his eyes soften in understanding. "I get it. Let me know when you figure that out." He squeezes her upper arm.

Emree watches his retreating form as he leaves the courtyard. I study her face to see if there is any longing or regret evident, and when I see neither, I feel relieved. From the display I saw in the parking lot at Broken Yolk, I was worried their dating was leading somewhere serious.

"Well, that was awkward," Emree announces with a soft laugh. "I feel bad, though. That's not the way I would want to end things with someone."

"Was that serious?" I ask, nodding in the direction where he disappeared.

Em looks off into the distance and then over at me, a small smile placed on her face. "No, but I wish it could have been. My heart couldn't let you go."

Unable to control myself, I reach forward and wrap my hand around the back of her neck. Bringing our faces closer, I brush my mouth against hers, testing the waters. When she doesn't pull away, I press harder and savor the feeling of her lips. Emree melts into the kiss, and I use that to my advantage.

Her lips are slightly parted, and I make my way in, claiming what's mine.

Emree moans and cages my face between her hands as we make out in the middle of the courtyard. The feel of her soft lips against mine and having her kiss me like this gives me the reassurance that I haven't royally ruined us and there still may be a chance.

"This is a school, not a whorehouse. Keep it appropriate when you're here, please." The sound of someone's voice nearby has me breaking away from the sweetness that is Emree Anders. A woman, who I assume is a teacher, in a dark-blue pantsuit, graying hair that is cut above her shoulders, and a briefcase clutched in her hands has approached our table. Her face tells me that she is less than impressed with us right now.

"Sorry. Was trying to win my girl back." I offer up an apology, but the teacher doesn't fall for it.

"Keep it behind closed doors," she warns us, then walks away toward the science building.

Emree's cheeks redden, and she hides her face in my chest. "That was embarrassing."

Our bodies shake with my chuckle. "Hey, I got to touch you again, so I'm not upset about it."

Pulling back, Em gives me a stern look. "As if you breaking up with me stopped you from touching me. Your jealousy knows no end, Conrad Dugray."

She has that right. Even when I was trying to let her go, the moment I would see her, my body would gravitate toward her.

"Wasn't a fan of that guy being around you."

Emree looks into my eyes and rubs my cheek with the palm of her hand. "I like this," she whispers as she feels the scruff on my face.

Smirking, I turn my head to the side and kiss her palm. "You like a beard, baby?"

A soft smile comes out of her. "I guess I do."

While I didn't forgo shaving on purpose, I haven't had the energy to keep up with the clean shave I have had since I started growing facial hair. My father taught me that only bums and criminals did not have themselves put together, and that includes always having a clean face.

"What in the hell are you two doing sitting out in the heat?" Maddox calls to us from a few tables away. Behind him are Blaire, Camden, Jules, Levi, and one of my other teammates, Rodrick.

The six of them approach our table. Maddox takes the empty spot on Em's bench while Camden and Blaire occupy the vacant one across from me, and Jules, Levi, and Rodrick take the remaining seats.

Maddox swings his arm over Emree's shoulders and pulls her close to him. "What're you doing hanging out with this loser, Blondie?"

She giggles while nudging him with her elbow. "He is trying to win me over."

Camden blows out a whistle. "That is a mighty high feat." They all laugh, with the exception of Rodrick since he doesn't know what happened between Em and me.

"Yeah, well, my girl knows I love her, and I'll make it all right again."

She smiles at me, and I pull her closer, away from Maddox, to give her a chaste kiss.

Maddox laughs and removes his arm from her shoulders. "Our boy has a lot of ass-kissing to do."

"Are we going to start eating lunch outside now or something? It's hot as hell out here." Levi changes the subject.

Maddox groans. "Fuck that. Love you and all, Blondie, but my balls are sweating already."

Blaire's face scrunches up in disgust. "Ew, Mad, no one wants to hear about that."

He points at her. "Don't think that your boyfriend doesn't have swamp ass right now, too."

She looks at Camden and he shrugs, not denying it.

"But for real, we're not moving the lunch table out here, are we? Because there's barely any room," Levi asks again.

Resting my hand on Emree's thigh, I answer him, "Well, that's up to Em. You going to join us again, baby?"

She taps her finger against her pointed chin. "Hmm, I may have to think about that. I mean, it is nice and peaceful out here."

"And hot," Levi protests.

"Oh, Emmy, don't act like this is even a choice. You're texting me almost every day how much you hate sitting out here," Blaire chimes in.

Emree's mouth gapes open. "What the hell, Blaire? What happened to girl code?"

"Don't think that pertains to something like this, but also, it really is gross out here. I have back sweat, Emmy."

My girl rolls her eyes. "You are all babies."

Levi stands and hooks his bag over his shoulder. "As much fun as it's been sitting in my own sweat, Jules and I have class in ten minutes."

"Oh shit," Jules hisses as she grabs her own messenger bag. "We need to hurry, or that little brownnoser is going to steal my spot in the front."

They run off after waving goodbye.

"What a fucking nerd," Maddox announces to the table, and we all let out laughs.

This is what I have missed the last month. While I love my friends, something felt off each day we were together. My missing puzzle piece is back and even though the relationship with my family is complete chaos, I feel more complete.

CHAPTER TWENTY-EIGHT

EMREE

Staring at my face on the screen of my phone through the camera, I play around with the different filters on Snapchat. From a fox to a devil, they are all fun. I stop at one that interested me a few minutes ago and an idea pops into my head.

"I think we should go get our noses pierced," I tell Blaire.

She looks up from the book she has had her head stuck in while I watched the latest episode of *RuPaul's Drag Race*. Having a roommate that is more in favor of reading than watching TV means I usually have the freedom to put on whatever I want unless Camden is here and they're watching a movie.

"Where in the world would you get an idea like that?"

"A Snapchat filter," I answer with a smile.

Blaire rolls her eyes. "Emmy, really? You're going to poke a hole in your nose because it looked good on a filter?"

Shrugging my shoulders, I close the app and open my messages. "Thinking I am. I'm going to text Levi and see if the tattoo shop he goes to has a piercer." My fingers are tapping away to ask the question to our tattooed, lumberjack-looking friend.

Blaire places the bookmark into her spot in the book and sets it on the seat beside her. "Are you thinking one of those cute little studs or those bull rings people are getting all over campus now?"

I roll my eyes. "Of course not the bull ring one. I like those hoop things. Maybe a gold one?"

She studies my face for a moment. "Okay, I think that would look cute then." My phone buzzes in my lap. "What did Levi say?"

Smiling, I look up. "He said to meet him at the house in twenty and he'll bring us."

Blaire's eyes widen. "Us? When did this become a group activity?"

Jumping up, I smile at my best friend. "Since I need a support system to hold my hand."

After we change and I fix up my hair, we head to my car and drive toward the guys' house. Their driveway is full, so I know they must all be home. Conrad and I have been texting almost all day since Monday when he sat with me at lunch. His coach has been rough on him since he missed practice Friday. He told me his coach lightened up today, but for the last two days, he was running extra drills.

We exit my car and now that we're getting closer to it happening, my heart races with anticipation of adding a hole in my nostril. I've never gotten a piercing—besides my ears when I was a baby—or tattoo before, but I have wanted to. My friend from high school got her tongue pierced after we graduated and there was so much blood I ended up backing out even though we made a pact to do it together.

Bypassing knocking, we enter the house and the living room is littered with hot soccer players. Maddox and Mateo are relaxed on the three-seat sofa with a bowl of popcorn between them, Camden is lying across the single-seater with his legs dangling off the end, and Conrad is on the two-seater with his feet resting on the coffee table.

"Hey, what are you two doing here?" Camden asks, his head hanging upside down as he looks at us.

Blaire skips over and sits on his lap, bending down to kiss his lips. "I was kidnapped."

Rolling my eyes, I head toward the only empty spot and sit beside Conrad. He snakes his arm around my waist and pulls me closer, kissing the side of my head. "Did you kidnap my roommate's girlfriend?"

I shrug him off me. "I did not kidnap anyone. She needed to come with me for moral support."

"Moral support for what, Blondie?" Maddox asks.

Smiling at the boys, I tell them what my plan is. "I'm getting a piercing."

"No shit?" Camden asks, surprised at my announcement. "What're you getting done?"

Maddox leans forward in his seat. "Please tell me you're getting your nipples pierced. And if you are, I will totally be there for moral support or any kind of support you need."

I can't help but laugh because while Maddox may say some of the most inappropriate things, they can be funny. "Thank you for the offer, but I will not be getting my nipples pierced."

"Well, could you?" he pleads, giving me those puppy-dog eyes I know work on many women.

"How about you stop looking at and talking about my girl's tits?" Conrad growls out.

Maddox holds his hands up. "Hey now, no need to get feisty on me. Was an innocent question to ask a *single* woman."

Conrad's hands clench on his thighs, and I reach over, rubbing his forearm.

"Single or not, my boobs are none of your business, Mad."

A wicked smile spreads across Maddox's face. "We could rectify that. Let me take you out. We'd have a good time. I'll treat you like a queen, and then we could come back here where I'd throw you onto my bed and do every possible nasty thing you could think of—"

"You son of a bitch," Conrad cuts him off and jumps out of his seat, but my grip on his arm stops him. His nostrils flare, his face turning several shades of red.

"How about we all calm down?" I say, using the most soothing voice I can muster. "Conrad, you know how Maddox is. He was just trying to get under your skin."

Maddox raises his hands. "Um, I'd like to clarify that while I was trying to get a rise out of Conny, I would very much like to bang you, so that is always on the table."

"Oh, fuck off." Conrad is back on his feet, and I grip him with both hands now. With one hard pull, he falls back beside me.

Mateo, Maddox, and Camden are all laughing as Levi makes his way down the stairs. He slows to a stop as he takes in the scene in front of him. My iron grip on Conrad's arm, Blaire's red face, and the other guys laughing.

"Um, what's going on here?" Levi asks.

After controlling himself, Mateo starts to tell him. "Well, Maddox—"

Levi holds his hand up. "Enough said." He looks at me. "You ready?"

Conrad looks between Levi and me. "Whoa, what the hell? Lumberjack is taking you?"

Levi rolls his eyes. "Can we stop with the lumberjack comments?"

"We can when you stop looking like a lumberjack," Maddox chimes in. "For real, dude, you look like you should be guarding a mountain or something, not a college student. I swear you're really a thirty-year-old man with that beard."

"We're moving on." Levi looks at me. "I told Axel we'd be there in twenty. You ready?"

THE HURT OF LETTING GO

Jumping up, I grab my bag and smile at him. "Ready to get poked."

Maddox offers a low chuckle at my choice of words, but I ignore him.

Conrad is beside me within a second. "Fuck that. I'm coming too." He's pulling on his sneakers by the front door before I have a chance to say anything.

"Bye, baby." Blaire kisses Camden and then is on her feet, heading toward me.

Camden is right behind her. "Yeah, no way, Gray Eyes. I'm coming too."

Blaire loops her arm through Camden's. "Aw, are you going to get a tattoo for me?"

His face pales. "Oh, um. You want that?"

She lifts her shoulders. "I don't know. It's kind of hot."

"Is that so?" Camden asks, his eyebrow raised in interest.

Maddox slaps his knee. "Are you that pussy-whipped you're going to ink yourself, man?"

Camden keeps his eyes connected to Blaire's. "Fall in love, Mad. It'll change you."

That sobers Maddox. "Never going to happen," he says through clenched teeth. Thinking back, I've never seen Maddox with a girl more than a couple times and never on a date, usually at a party or hanging on to him after a game.

Grabbing Conrad's arm, I pull him close to me. "You really don't have to go. Levi set it all up with his friend, and I'm just getting a quick nose piercing."

He shakes his head before I even finish my sentence. "Not going to have some guy touching you while I'm not there." Conrad snags his keys off the hook by the door and pockets his wallet. "Em and I will drive in my car." He grabs my hand and shuffles us out the front door.

"What the hell, Conrad?" I try to rip my hand from his hold, but he's got a good grip on it, so I dig my heels into the ground and stop us. "You can't take over like this. Going to the tattoo shop was my idea, and you can't just swoop in and act like this."

With a firm pull, I'm now flush against Conrad's chest. "Make no mistake, baby, there will never be a moment that I am okay with another man touching you, especially when I'm not there." His face is close enough that I can feel his breath against my cheek. "You getting some jewelry jammed into your nose? I'll be there."

My heart flutters. Conrad has never been jealous or possessive, and I wonder if all that has changed now that he has the freedom to be with the person he truly wants. Me.

Lifting my hand, I caress his fuzzy cheek. "Let's go before I lose my courage."

THE SOUND of buzzing fills the room, and my body feels hot as my adrenaline spikes. I've filled out all the necessary paperwork and am now sitting in one of the waiting chairs with Blaire by my side. Conrad and Camden are looking through one of the books scattered on the glass countertop. Levi has been talking with the beautiful receptionist with bright-red hair and tattoos covering every part of her body besides her face.

Conrad points at something in one of the books and calls Levi's friend and tattoo artist over. He nods after Conrad asks him something and takes the book away.

The guys come back over to us, and Conrad sits beside me, taking my sweaty hand in his. "How you feeling, baby?"

"Like shit," I confess. "Why the hell am I doing this? Poking a hole in my nose is stupid."

He leans in and kisses my neck. "I think it's going to look

hot." His hot breath against my skin makes my body shiver, despite it feeling like it's on fire with the anticipation of getting my first piercing.

"Anders?" someone calls out, and I look up to see the piercer I met earlier standing there with a clipboard in his hand. He smiles when I begin to stand, and his eyes rake down my body, blatantly checking me out.

Conrad is by my side and his arm snakes around my waist, hugging me tight against him while glaring at the piercer. I roll my eyes at his absurd newfound jealousy. What Conrad doesn't realize is that while yes, I did go on a few dates with Ian, I don't have eyes for anyone else. Not even the hot tattoo artists in here.

While I know he has nothing to worry about, I allow him to continue his claiming. If he feels better making sure that every guy in the room knows I'm his, I won't stop him. Even though I told Conrad that I needed him to prove his feelings to me, I like the possessiveness he has shown lately. He's lost me once and I think knowing what that has felt like changed something in him.

We follow the piercer into a small room that smells sterile, like a hospital. There is a black chair that reclines, a rolling stool, and a counter that has drawers with a variety of piercings. A metal rolling tray sits beside the leather chair with a needle, a clamp, an alcohol wipe, a piece of jewelry, and a cork. The cork confuses me, but I'm new to piercings, so maybe that's normal.

"Take a seat and pull your hair back from your face," the piercer instructs. There is a license on the wall that says his name is Drew.

Taking a deep breath, I hop up on the chair, my feet now dangling several inches above the ground. Conrad comes behind me and gathers my hair in his hands, being sure that it is out of my face like Drew instructed. He kisses my shoulder as Drew washes his hands at the counter and gloves up.

"I can feel your pulse on my hands," Conrad whispers in my ear. His hands remain against my neck as I sit and wait. I'm sure he can feel my rapid pulse because I can sure hear it.

Turning toward him, I whisper, "Maybe I'm a little nervous."

Drew turns to me with the alcohol wipe in hand. "Ready?"

I nod. He approaches and stands between my legs, the outer part of his thigh touching my inner ones.

"I need to clean the area, then I'll just poke the hole and put the stud in. No need to worry. It's a fairly fast process." As he cleans my left nostril, he moves in close enough that I can feel his body heat.

Conrad's hands on my shoulders tense, and I know he is having an issue with how close Drew is. "You need to stand that close to her?" he asks through clenched teeth.

Drew continues his task. "I'm happily married, dude. Trust me, I've never been inappropriate with a client and don't plan to. I see enough tits and pussies in this line of business. Your girl's nose piercing isn't going to have me break my vows."

My shoulders shake with a silent laugh. Reaching up, I pat Conrad's hand. "No need to worry, sweetie," I comfort him with a soothing voice as if he were a child.

Once Drew is satisfied with his cleaning of my nose, he grabs the needle and clamp. "Okay, I'm going to have you take a deep breath but don't release it until I say so." After I nod, he positions the clamp on my nostril. It stings a little from the pressure, but nothing like what I think the needle going through my nose is going to feel like. "All right, inhale." I do as he says. "Now release it." As I let go of the breath, he pushes the needle through my cartilage. The motion is fast enough that I barely register what happened.

"Wait, was that it?" I ask as he removes the clamp and picks the small cork up.

Drew nods. "Yeah, but don't move. You have a needle through your nose and I need to put the jewelry in." He focuses on his task as I try to remain calm after he tells me there is a needle sticking through my nose.

Once he is finished, Drew hands me a mirror to check it out. I smile when I see the small diamond stud that now resides on my face. While I thought it looked good on the Snapchat filter, that doesn't do the piercing justice. It's dainty and feminine, adding a certain shift to my look.

"Fuck, that's hot, baby," Conrad lets out from behind me. Tilting my head to the side, I have to agree with him. It is hot.

Turning so we're face to face, I smile at him. "Do I look badass now?"

Conrad laughs and wraps his arm around my shoulder, kissing the side of my head. "For sure, a badass. Now all we have to do is get you a leather jacket and motorcycle."

Drew puts together a care package for me with instructions, soap, his business card, and a coupon. After he dismisses us and begins cleaning his station, Conrad stops before crossing the threshold.

"Hey, you have time for another piercing?" he asks Drew. My eyebrows shoot up.

Drew pauses his task and looks at the clock. "Yeah, I can fit you in. What're you looking to get?"

Conrad thinks for a second. "Just my ears."

Wrapping my hand around his upper arm, I squeeze. "You're joking, right? Why would you want your ears pierced?" Never once in the more than seven months I have known him has Conrad said he wanted any kind of piercing. Although I could say the same about me with my new nose stud.

Conrad lifts his shoulders. "Dunno. Now that I'm not under

my dad's control, seems like a good idea to do something rebellious that he would hate."

My heart clenches thinking about Conrad not being able to live his life as freely as he would want to because of a controlling father who is there to throw in his opinions and rules. "I think you'd look hot with a couple studs in your ears." Reaching up on my tiptoes, I kiss his stubbled cheek, being sure not to smoosh my nose.

"All right, come have a seat," Drew instructs, and I position myself behind Conrad the same way he was there for me.

CHAPTER TWENTY-NINE

CONRAD

My impulse control is nonexistent apparently. Never have I thought about getting a piercing or a tattoo, yet here I am in a tattoo shop, having a man poke a hole into each of my ears. The spontaneous decision could be a result of the news I received this morning about why my Amex card was declined not only at the cafeteria but also at the grocery store last night. My fucking father already removed me as a user.

While I did stress for a moment about the loss of unlimited funds, I remembered that part of my trust fund kicked in when I graduated from high school, so I have enough to remain comfortable at the moment. Howard already paid my school in full, which I am sure he is kicking himself about right now, and my car was a high school graduation present, so the only monthly payment I have to deal with for that is the insurance.

My father may have thought he could control me by taking away his money, but the trust fund my grandfather—his father—set up for each of us grandkids made sure that neither of our parents would ever be able to control it. I haven't touched a penny of that money and never planned to, so I had put half of it in different stocks to accrue interest. The other half I had planned to invest once I graduated and started making my way into the business world.

Getting a piercing would be a great "fuck you" to Howard Dugray. Potentially getting a tattoo would be an even bigger "fuck you," which is why I was debating it while looking through Levi's artist's portfolio. Camden and I are the only ones of our roommates who don't have tattoos, and while I haven't exactly considered getting one, the guy's work interested me.

Drew marks my lobes with a black pen and has me approve that they are even. I nod and he gets to work setting up a fresh clamp and needles.

Emree kisses my neck, being sure not to touch my sterilized ear. "Not going to lie, you're going to look very sexy with a couple piercings," she whispers.

I smile. "You want your boyfriend all pierced and tatted up, baby? Should I get us matching leather jackets?"

She lets out a breathy laugh. "You haven't earned boyfriend status back yet, mister. You still haven't made up for all the bullshit you put me through."

My heart clenches at the thought of everything I put Emree through the last month. I hurt her over and over and left her with several unanswered questions. While I would love nothing more than to move forward and leave the past behind, that is not fair to her, and I have some serious making up to do.

Turning my head to the side, I kiss her softly on the lips. "I know. Love you, baby." She smiles but doesn't say it back, and I understand her not being ready to give her heart to me completely yet.

Ten minutes later, after having filled out the necessary paperwork, I now have two new holes punched through my ears. It didn't sting as bad as I thought it would, but the pulsing that hasn't gone away is uncomfortable. Drew goes through all the same aftercare instructions he talked to Em about and gives me the bag filled with supplies. He dismisses us once again and tells me I can pay at the front desk.

"Dude, you got your ears pierced?" Camden asks when he, Levi, and Blaire come up to us as I hand over my debit card to the receptionist to pay for Emree's and my piercings.

"Em! Your nose piercing looks so cute," Blaire raves as she looks at Emree's new jewelry. The two of them start walking toward the exit as Blaire snaps pictures of Emree.

The tatted-up woman hands me back my card and receipt.

"First, you're booking a tattoo session with Axel, and now you have your ears pierced? What's going on, man?" Camden asks.

We follow the girls out of the shop as they gush over how cute Em's new look is.

"I have lived under my father's thumb for as long as I can remember and I'm tired of it. Besides soccer, I've never done anything for myself, especially on impulse. This seems like fun and a nice way to celebrate being free."

Camden nods and a sympathetic look comes across Levi's face.

"Your dad's a dick, and I'm glad you're away from that. The tattoo you picked out is going to be badass." Levi has been covered in tattoos since we have known him. He convinced Maddox and Mateo to get one too, though they have far less than he does.

"Maybe I'll try and catch up to you with the body art," I joke with Levi and punch his jacket-covered arm.

He laughs and runs a hand over his full beard. "Yeah, you can try."

Blaire turns around and bounces over to us. "Boys, how do you feel about heading over to the hibachi restaurant that just opened?"

Camden wraps his arms around her waist and buries his face in her neck. "I'm down for some food."

"I'm taking Em out, so unless she wants to ditch my surprise, we're out."

Emree's eyebrows shoot up. "A surprise?"

Smiling, I reach for her hand. "Yeah, baby. You in for a drive?"

She smiles and nods.

Pulling her closer to me, I kiss the side of her head. "Sorry, guys. Rain check on the hibachi, but you may want to ask Maddox because I know he was dying to try that place and would get his feelings hurt if you went without him."

Emree and I walk toward my car hand in hand as the afternoon heat pelts down on us. One of the reasons I wanted to drive my own car here was to be alone with her, and I was also planning on convincing Emree to spend the rest of the day with me. She is holding her heart protectively from me until I earn it back.

We drive to Publix, where I can get the supplies for our day. I tell Em to stay in the car while I run inside. She protests and I eventually win. My plan is to get all of her favorite snacks, drinks, and sandwiches for an afternoon picnic on the beach. Emree deserves to be spoiled, and I hadn't done enough of that in the time we were together. While she is holding back in our relationship now, I did that for the six months we were together because I knew what was coming. I understand more than anyone why she is choosing to protect herself first.

Luckily, the Publix I stop at is near the water, and there is a wall full of everything you need for a good beach day, including picnic blankets. After ordering our sandwiches, grabbing a water for myself and a Diet Coke for Em, and our favorite snacks, I pick out a nice white-and-blue blanket I think she would like and head to the checkout.

After packing the trunk with all of the supplies, we're heading in the direction of St. Pete Beach. It's one of the places Mateo lifeguards at during the summer, and the guys and I like to come out here. It usually has a good crowd, but nowhere near as packed as Clearwater Beach. That place is tourist central.

With my hand resting on her bare thigh and the windows down with Emree's variety playlist—which has everything from Eminem to Taylor Swift—blasting around us, we drive through the busy streets until you can start smelling the saltwater air. Even though I'm driving, I try to catch glances at the girl at my side. Her long, blonde hair is floating through the air, and she doesn't give a shit about it. When Emree put the windows down, she never bothered to tie her hair back like most women would do and opted to let it fly freely through the wind, most likely getting tangled in the process. She has a bright smile on her face as she watches her hand float through the air outside the window.

She is the most gorgeous creature I have ever laid eyes on and I'm a fool to ever have let her go.

The realization that I almost lost her has hit me hard these last couple days because the time without her in my life, when she probably hated me, was miserable. Not only because I had to spend my free time with Liliana but also because losing the person you love is a special kind of hell. One where your chest constantly aches and you feel off balance like a piece of you is missing.

Emree was the missing puzzle piece and since coming back to her, I feel whole again.

The air changes as we reach the coast. It becomes cooler and smells fresher. With Mateo working out here the last couple summers, he knows all the secret parking lot spots that are less crowded. I follow the flow of traffic on Gulf Blvd until I see the small, one-way street that leads to a tucked-away parking lot. Not only is it unknown to many, but it is free, unlike most of the parking areas around here.

I pull into a spot and put the car in park. Emree looks over at me with her brows pinched together. "If you were planning a beach afternoon, it would have been nice to know. I could have packed a bathing suit."

Shrugging, I turn the car off. "Was kind of last minute. Plus, I brought you here for a picnic. We'll come back the next weekend you have off because seeing you in a tiny bikini all day is at the top of my best days list."

She blushes at my honesty and hides her face from me.

"You remembered me telling you I've always wanted a picnic date?" she whispers.

Gripping her chin between my finger and thumb, I lift her face so I can look into those clear blue eyes. "Yeah, baby. And this date is long overdue. I'm sorry about that."

She smiles. "It doesn't matter how long it took. All I care about is that you got there."

While I don't deserve her heart or her forgiveness, I'm claiming both and not letting go.

We exit the car and as I open the trunk, Emree laughs at the amount of junk food. "I thought I was dating an athlete."

Smirking, I address the words she chose to use. "Dating, huh?"

Emree rolls her eyes and grabs the picnic blanket. "We can officially move on to dating status. I think you've earned that, at least. We'll discuss an official title later."

With an armful of grocery bags, I shut the trunk and we walk toward the beach. "You won't be able to resist me, baby."

While she would usually laugh at my overconfidence, Emree gives me a sober look. "I'm beginning to see that I truly can't."

This area of the beach is fairly deserted. There are a few people walking along the shore and some families set up with every single item you could need for the beach. There are stragglers swimming in the ocean and a volleyball game going on at one of the three nets set up far from the shore. This time of year is perfect for the beach because it's not as sweltering as in the summer, but the water is warm enough to swim in.

We find a spot far enough away from other groups but with a clear view of the ocean. I'm hoping Em will want to stay out here long enough to watch the sunset because holding her in my arms as daylight fades away sounds like the perfect end to the night.

"I can't believe you got all my favorites. Or that you even remembered." Emree smiles as she unloads the chips, candies, drinks, and sandwiches from the bags. I made sure to grab those spicy red candies she likes so much and Pringles, which are basically a food group for her by how much she eats them.

We fall into a comfortable silence as we enjoy our lunch and absorb the fresh air and cloudy sun. As Emree eats her sandwich, she stops every few minutes to close her eyes and enjoy the breeze.

There is something I have been wanting to ask her the last couple days, and I feel now is the perfect time. "Are you working next Saturday night?"

Emree turns to me with a mouthful of turkey sandwich. She shakes her head in response since I asked her at the most inconvenient time.

"We have the end-of-year sports banquet. How do you feel about being my date?"

Her eyes widen, and a smile graces her face. "To a banquet? Hell yeah. Is there a dress code, or can I make my own dress?"

Knowing Emree can create the most beautiful and sexiest outfit, I try to hide the grin on my face from her. "Baby, I don't give a shit what the dress code is. Whatever you wear is going to look hotter than hell. But the invitation does say it is cocktail themed."

Her lips glide up. "I have just the material to make the perfect outfit."

Leaning in close, I brush my lips along the shell of her ear. "You going to tell me about this dress?"

Despite the heat, Emree shivers. "Nope, I'm keeping it a surprise."

Groaning, I lie back on the blanket. "Ugh, you and your surprise outfits. That Halloween one nearly killed me, woman." Last Halloween, Emree decided to make hers and Blaire's costumes for our party. She ended up making some sexy, low-cut jerseys with Camden's and my numbers and names on them. Emree paired her top with some short shorts that had her ass hanging out. It took everything in me not to haul her off to my room the moment she got there.

With a sexy smirk, Emree comes down on top of me so we are face to face. "Don't worry. I promise you are going to love it." She drops her lips to mine, and I run my hand through her hair, deepening our kiss and earning a moan out of her.

Next Saturday can't come soon enough. Not because our team did incredible this year and they will be singing our praises at the banquet, but because the most beautiful woman in the room will be on my arm.

CHAPTER THIRTY

EMREE

My hometown is nothing to brag about. Westford is home to around two thousand people, and it is one of those places where everyone knows everyone. My mom's great-grandparents first moved to the same house her parents live in now and her grandparents lived in before. Westford is a generational place, and while some may love the small-town charm and how everyone knows your past, it has never been a place for me.

My mom was the first in her family to leave Westford and go off to college. Her parents were nervous because my mom had never stayed in a big city before and Miami was as big as they get in Florida. Their nerves turned out to be true because my mother was raped her sophomore year, resulting in my life.

While my mom never resented me for her assault and for dropping out of college, some part of me wonders if she regrets keeping the child who was created in such a violent way. She always assured me that I was loved more than anything by our family, and I never felt anything less than unconditional love growing up. My grandparents were an active part of my life and were always there to help my mom when she needed someone to watch me. They tried to get my mother to go back to college, but she decided to take health and wellness classes at the local community college and now has her own studio outside of town. She offers everything from yoga and boot camp classes to nutritional help.

The house I grew up in is modest. It has three bedrooms, two bathrooms, a small kitchen with a dining area connected, and a living room that is big enough to fit two oversized couches and a TV stand. My mom has always been a more 'one with nature' kind of person and that is reflected in our house. There are plants in every room, on tables and hanging from plant holders. The colors are earthy tones: greens, browns, and rich oranges. Even if you didn't grow up here like I did, the moment you walk into our house, you feel like you are at home. My mom also always has a candle burning, creating a warm ambience.

Even though my mom has been through the unimaginable, she is one of the most positive and uplifting people I know. On top of running her own business, she volunteers at the crisis center and helps women who have been through something similar to what she experienced. She is the most amazing woman, and I hope to be half as incredible as she is when I'm her age.

Since I could only bring so much material with me when I moved into the apartment, I'm now at my mom's house to get the turquoise silk fabric that I know will make the perfect cocktail dress for Conrad's banquet in five days.

"Tell me more about this event," my mom gushes from the spot on my bed where she is lying on her stomach.

Even though she is in her early forties now, Margret Anders is still the definition of beauty. Her blonde hair sits at her collarbones, and there isn't a gray hair in sight. While she has a few crow's-feet around her eyes and some laugh lines framing her mouth, her skin is devoid of wrinkles or many signs of aging. With years of fitness and yoga, my mom has kept a body any twentysomething would be envious of.

Searching through the stacks of fabric, I smile, thinking about Conrad. "He said it's some kind of banquet for the sports teams, but the men's soccer team did the best this season by far, so they're going to be spotlighted during the night."

While my mom has known about Conrad, she has not officially met him yet. Between his soccer schedule, my work, our classes, and my mom running her own business, there never seems to be the right time. The two of them talked during one of my mom's several FaceTime chats. He won her over with his charm, as he does with anyone who meets Conrad Dugray.

What I have failed to tell her is about our breakup, Conrad's arranged marriage, him being disowned by his family, and then him confessing his love for me and trying to win me back. I felt as though my mom didn't need to know all those details.

Finally finding the silk I've been looking for, I pull it out. "Aha, here it is." Holding the fabric up, I inspect it, making sure there is enough material for me to make an outfit out of it.

"Oh, honey, that is going to look beautiful on you. The color is very flattering to your skin tone."

Holding up the material against my arm and inspecting it, I happen to agree with her. My skin is now a shade darker, thanks to my last two beach visits, and the shimmering turquoise color makes my skin glow. While I have never made an outfit out of this material, I have had ideas playing around in my head for it. Conrad's event seems like the perfect time to bring one of those ideas alive.

After carefully stuffing the fabric into my tote bag, I join my mom on my full-size bed. She hasn't changed my room since I moved out for college almost three years ago. The walls are still the light blue I was obsessed with in high school, which reminds me of the sky. My comforter is a dusty-pink color and the bed, nightstand, and dresser are all an off-white.

My mom clasps my hand in hers. "How are you holding up, baby girl?"

One of the good things about living a few hours away from my mom is that it is easier to hide things from her when we communicate through the phone versus in person. She has always been able to tell when something is wrong. Each time I was bullied in school, I would try to compose myself before coming home and act as if nothing was wrong, but she knew after spending just a few minutes around me. Her favorite saying is, "A mother knows."

Plastering on a smile, I squeeze my mom's hand. "Everything is gravy, Mama."

She arches a perfectly sculpted blonde eyebrow. "You know, lying to your mother is frowned upon in the eyes of the Lord."

A laugh escapes me. "Mama, that would work if we were a religious family."

"That's beside the point," she answers as she waves me off. "Tell your mom what's going on in that head of yours."

With a huff, I flop onto my back. "Why do you make it so hard to lie to you?"

"Because I'm your mom, and it's a mom thing. Now tell me what's been bothering you. Is it classes? Work? Conrad?"

"Conrad," I groan. "We went through sort of a breakup the last month, and it's been a roller coaster ever since."

"Emmy, why didn't you tell me?" She sounds genuinely hurt.

"Because I felt stupid. What he did and how he did it hurt me, and then when I found out the reasoning behind why he ended our relationship, it made me feel less than."

My mom studies me. I'm sure what I just told her is confusing, with zero context of what happened. "Why don't I put a pot of tea on and you tell me what has been going on?"

Half an hour and two cups of tea later, my mom knows everything that has happened in the last few weeks. From

Conrad breaking up with me after spring break to seeing him with another woman and then finding out that their families had arranged for him to marry that woman until he went against his father and is now disowned.

"That is a lot to take in, baby girl." My mom sips her tea, clearly in thought. "He really flew to his father and told him he couldn't marry that girl because he was in love with you?"

When she says it like that, it sounds like a Hallmark-worthy romantic gesture. "I guess so."

"Emmy, that boy clearly loves you. How long are you going to keep yourself closed off from him?"

What she doesn't realize is that holding my heart from him has been harder than I imagined. Conrad makes it easy to fall for him with his charm, sweet words, and thoughtful gestures.

"I'm afraid to get hurt again," I whisper.

"True love isn't worth it unless there are some ups and downs and struggles throughout."

Do I think what Conrad and I have is true love? I know my heart aches for him. When he is near, my body is in tune with his presence and yearns for him. While love is not something I have experienced before, I also have never felt as much love for another like I do for Conrad.

"What if he shatters my heart again after I give it to him?"

My mom looks at me with a small smile. "Sometimes that's a risk you are going to have to take for the one you love."

While I know what she is saying holds true, I wonder if I would be able to recover after another heartbreak from Conrad. There are so many what-ifs in our relationship. What if he doesn't think I'm worth leaving behind the comfort and security of his family's money and status for? What if his father or Liliana convinces him to change his mind and follow through with the marriage? What if he really isn't in love with me and it's lust that will eventually fade away?

These thoughts are plaguing the relationship I so desperately want. My heart wants Conrad, but my head is holding me back. I just need to figure out which organ to listen to.

I leave my mom's house with more than the dress fabric I came here for. She has given me her insight and is clearly on Team Conrad, even though she assured me that she supports whatever decision I make.

With a ramble of thoughts rolling through my mind, I drive the over two hours back to Braxton. I have five days to create the outfit for the banquet on Saturday, on top of working and classes. Maybe with a busy week, I will be too distracted to think about all that is going on with my life. Or maybe, with the anticipation of Saturday, it will make me get lost in my thoughts even more.

CHAPTER THIRTY-ONE

CONRAD

"This goddamn monkey suit is bullshit," Levi grumbles from the couch as he adjusts his tie once again. The guy lives in jeans and old shirts. Anytime we have to dress nice for soccer events, all he does is complain as if he doesn't know this is part of the deal.

"Stop your bitching. You look very handsome." Maddox pinches Levi's hairy cheek and his hand gets slapped for doing so.

"Of course I look handsome, but that doesn't mean I'm not tired of having to dress up for these stupid events."

Camden comes downstairs, dressed in a pair of black slacks and a dark-green button-down shirt with a thin, black tie. "Just be grateful that it isn't a formal event and we don't have to wear tuxes. I'd be faking an illness if that were the case."

"Ugh, don't even say that. I feel like if Coach gets wind of that idea, he would do it just to fuck with us," Levi grumbles.

"Are you ladies ready? The limo is waiting on us." Maddox insisted on getting us a limo for the banquet tonight rather than taking a couple cars. Part of the reason is that this is the first event where we are all twenty-one, and rather than having designated drivers, we get to let loose in the back of a limo.

My roommates, Jules, and I pile into the limo and head toward the girls' apartment. Emree insisted they needed to get ready at her place because sharing a shower with four guys is not okay, and the last time Blaire used Maddox's private bathroom, she walked out to an eyeful of a naked Maddox's ass sleeping on his bed. While he won the owner's bedroom when we moved in, I'll admit that it was the best decision because Mr. Free Spirit likes to be in the nude as much as possible. If we had to share a bathroom with him, there would be a naked Maddox in the hallway frequently.

Maddox pops a champagne bottle and begins filling glasses and passes them out to everyone. "To a kick-ass season," he cheers. "And to another championship under our belt."

Our team killed it last season, even after losing our upperclassman starters when they graduated. Camden turned out to be a great captain, always motivating the team and being there for anyone who needed some extra practice on the side. Our senior year is going to be even better. The team is more in sync than it has ever been.

The limo driver pulls up to the front of Emree and Blaire's apartment, and Camden and I exit and head up to their floor on the elevator. After knocking, we wait for the door to open.

"Just a minute!" someone, I think Blaire, yells from the other side of the door. Camden smiles at me and rolls his eyes.

About three minutes later, the door opens, and it takes every bit of effort not to fall over at the woman before me. My eyes slowly drag down Emree's length. Her long blonde hair is expertly curled and there are a couple new blonde highlights framing her face. Her makeup is more visible than I have ever seen before. Her eyelashes are long and thick, and the way they frame her blue eyes makes them look larger than usual. She has a slightly smoky eye—Emree taught me that term—that makes her look ever so sexy. The best part about her makeup is the cherry-red, plump lips that are begging for my mouth to be on them.

Raking my eyes down her body, I take in the turquoise silk dress that showcases every bit of Emree's grabbable curves. The straps holding it up are so thin they're barely there. The top of the dress is bunched up fabric and dips low enough to give you a good view of her luscious cleavage but still modest. The hem is my favorite part. While Emree is on the shorter side, she has legs that look long on her small frame. They are tan, and her thighs are nice and thick, and the bottom is clinging to the middle of them. She has paired the outfit with a pair of strappy silver heels that add about four inches to her height.

"Fuck, baby, you are killing me." Closing my eyes, I drop my head back and try to throw out all the thoughts about how I want to fuck her with those heels on or the vision I have of pinning her to a wall and lifting that dress, hoisting her up by the thighs and plowing into her. She doesn't need my dirty mind right now. She deserves a gentleman who is going to win her heart back.

She looks down at her dress and smooths a hand over the front. "You like?"

Reaching for her, because I can't go another second without touching her, I pull Emree so that she is plastered against my front. "I fucking love," I mumble against her throat as I inhale her vanilla scent and plant a kiss below her ear.

She giggles, probably from the feeling of the beard I have been growing out. Pulling back, Emree takes in my appearance. She flattens her hand against my black tie. "You clean up pretty well, Dugray."

I kept it traditional with a white button-down shirt, black tie, and black slacks.

Blaire and Camden come up to us, and I would be lying if I didn't say I completely forgot they were here. Blaire, who isn't one to enjoy bright colors like Emree does, is wearing a tight black dress that hits above her knees and has some crisscross design on the bust. Her long, dark hair is pulled up, with a few pieces framing her face.

"You done groping my friend so we can leave?" Blaire's tone is light and paired with a smile as she looks between the two of us.

"I don't know about him, but I'm ready to ride in a limo for the first time." Emree jumps with excitement and starts bouncing down the hallway to the elevator, giving me a perfect view of the back of the dress.

I start charging after her. "Em, what the hell? There's no back." I'm definitely going to struggle all night.

THE ALUMNI really went all out this year. They moved the banquet from its usual spot at a high-end Italian restaurant downtown. The location change came last week when Coach told us there was a large last-minute donation that afforded the additional spending.

While the event is at my family's hotel, I try not to think about it. It's not like the entire staff here knows who I am or that my father is going to walk through the door, ready to kick his disowned son out. Coach knows I'm a Dugray and the son of the billionaire family, but no one else associated with the team does, except my roommates now. I have been able to keep my family's identity under wraps since starting school here. It helps that the majority of college kids don't give a shit about rich people or corporate America.

The banquet hall where our event is being held is large and littered with well-dressed people. There is a scattering of tables that are clearly designated by team, with specific sports equipment in the center. By the stage, there are five large tables with soccer balls as the centerpiece and tableware. The decorations filling the room are a variety of silver and gold, making the room look as if we're attending an upscale wedding and not a college banquet.

"Looks like this table is empty. Let's snag it," Jules states, dragging Mateo that way. We follow, knowing finding a table that can fit the eight of us might be a struggle.

We all take a seat while a waiter comes up to our table to take drink orders. He moves to the next table to collect their orders before disappearing behind a curtain to what I assume is the kitchen. Looking around, I take in the scene around me. Everyone is dressed in their best, and seeing our coaches without their ball caps and athletic shorts will always be surprising to me. Especially Coach Walters, who looks more uncomfortable than Levi does in his slacks, matching jacket, and button-down shirt. He's opted out of a tie, though.

Emree wraps her arm around mine and leans in close. "Do you want to dance?"

On the dance floor in front of the stage, I see a few people moving to the music, but it is nowhere near filled. "Sure, baby." Standing, I grab her hand and lead her as we weave between the tables.

Wrapping my arms around her waist, I marvel at the feel of her warm skin against my hands. Emree's dress is completely backless, with a few thin straps crossing at the back to keep it secured against her body.

With her body against mine and her arms wrapped around my neck, we sway to the music at a lazy pace. Having Emree here as my date, knowing that if I hadn't gotten my head out of my ass and stood up to my father, it would have been Liliana, makes me smile. She is by far the most beautiful woman in the room and having her by my side feels right.

Liliana wasn't happy when I told her the arrangement with my father was off, but after a mini blowup in her hotel room, she packed her things and promptly left and went back to Boston. A woman like her will have no trouble finding a rich man like she has wanted and I wish her nothing but success.

"How do you feel being here?" she asks me, her eyebrows pinched together in worry. She doesn't have to ask specifics, but I know she means being here at my father's hotel.

"I feel okay. Weird because the last time I was here was to meet Liliana, and that feels like a lifetime ago."

Her lips point down at the mention of the woman who was meant to be my future wife.

"Hey, I'm sorry. She shouldn't be brought up, but I can assure you she is a blip in my life. You consume my world, baby, and she doesn't hold a flame to you."

Her eyes become glossy. "Don't go saying sweet things like that, Conrad. You're trying to steal my heart or something."

Smiling, I kiss her on the lips. "Baby, call me a thief because I'm coming after everything that involves you, including that heart," I say against her mouth.

She sobers. "Just promise not to break it again."

"I promise, baby. I've lost you before and it is not something I ever want to go through again. You're meant to be in my life, Em, and I feel that in my heart."

Emree studies me for a moment, her lips tight and brows angled down. She runs her fingers through my hair and smiles. "Then you have it, Conrad."

Cupping her cheek, I bring her mouth to mine in a hard kiss and smile against her. "I promise you won't regret giving it to me." Pulling back, I look Emree in the eyes. "I love you, baby. More than you know."

With sparkling blue eyes and a smile that can make any man

fall to their knees, Emree looks back at me. "I love you. So much."

We sway to the music, getting so lost in each other that I almost forget where we are and my only thought is getting my gorgeous girl home. Everything feels right now. I'm out from under my father's thumb, the school year is coming to a close with a championship under our belts, and I got the girl of my dreams. Even though all is not right with my family, it doesn't feel like a huge loss like it would to most people with a normal family relationship, but the only person I happily keep in regular contact with is my little sister, Alice. She has a good head on her shoulders and doesn't fall into my father's manipulation like her twin, Archer.

The lights dim and a spotlight shines on the stage. "If everyone could take their seats, we are going to start the celebrations and recognitions," our school dean speaks into a mic. Hand in hand, Emree and I head back to our table.

As the dean goes through the different teams' praises, making sure not to point out how terrible our football team is, food is served, and we chow down while a few different administrators and coaches go up to speak. They play a slideshow of various snapshots from games and practices.

After all the other teams' coaches have spoken and passed out various awards to their players, Coach Walters passes the girls' soccer coach on the stage and grabs the mic.

"Listen, I'm not good at this fancy stuff, but it's part of the requirement for being the coach, so I guess I need to do it," he grumbles, and the team laughs. "First off, I would like to say a huge congratulations to the girls' soccer team. You all have blown me away with your determination and drive this season, and even though you came in second, know that you all are great players, and I can feel it in my gut that next season is yours for the taking." The girls' coach is wiping her eyes from her table. "And Coach Eastman, you're one hell of a leader, and the way you lead your team is admirable."

As if we are all thinking the same thing, each of us on the guys' team stands and claps for not only our coeds but Coach Eastman. She and all her players are smiling as we show our admiration.

Once everyone settles down, Coach continues. "Boys, you all continue to prove everyone wrong. Not only are we one of the smaller schools and that means funding is nowhere near what these larger universities have, but this season should have been one of our worst, considering we lost the majority of our starters who graduated last year."

Coach looks over at Camden, who is leaning against the table, hanging on to every word. "Camden, when you came to this school, you were a punk-ass kid who didn't respect authority and thought showing up late to practice and mouthing off would be okay, and boy, were you in for a rude awakening." We're all laughing, remembering freshman Camden. "The man before me is not at all like that kid. You have shifted into the team captain role flawlessly and taken our new players under your wing. You're a born leader, young man."

Admiration and appreciation light up on Camden's face as he listens to our coach. Growing up without a father, I know Camden struggled to take orders from male authority. It took a while for him to warm up to his high school coach years ago and they eventually became close. Coming to a new team, Camden was reluctant to accept being told what to do, but Coach Walters was straightforward with Camden about how he needed to get his act together, and he did.

Coach continues to thank his assistant coaches and show his appreciation for the rest of his players. He assigns awards that all the players have voted on, from the best penalty kicks and goals of the season to who had the most embarrassing moments. It's all in good fun, and when Mateo—our resident hothead—goes up for his most red cards award, he pretends to be mad, but we all know he secretly loves going off on the refs during a game.

Once Coach is finished singing our praises and handing out awards, the dean takes the stage again. "I'm sure many of you noticed the change in venue, and we were grateful enough to have a last-minute donor want to make sure this banquet was the best we have ever had." He smiles wide, and I swear if it were possible, there would be money signs in his eyes. "Not only did he want to make tonight great for us, but he was also generous enough to donate more than enough money to the sports programs so that we are able to afford all new equipment and uniforms for next season."

Cheers erupt all around us, booming from wall to wall in the room.

"I would like to say a special thank you to our generous donor. Please welcome him up here." The dean claps and looks off to the side of the stage as a man climbs the stairs. "Mr. Howard Dugray."

My veins turn to ice as I watch my father walk across the stage, his ever-present fake smile on his face as he approaches the dean. Howard Dugray is dressed like he always is, in a slim-fit suit. This one is all black, making him come off as more intimidating than he really is. I'm sure that is for my benefit. His dark suit matches the presence he looms over me, like a rainy cloud on an otherwise beautiful day.

And as that rainy cloud, he is like a torrential downpour, here to drown my happiness.

My father takes the mic the dean offers him, his phony smile growing as he is now in the spotlight. "Thank you, Dean Patel. I am honored to be able to contribute to such a wonderful school and help these young people in their coming season."

My skin prickles with eyes on me, most likely my friends' and Coach's. Those are the only ones who know what having this man here means.

And Emree.

She grips my hand, which is balled in a fist on my thigh. Her simple touch cools down my overheated skin at the sight of the man who wanted to ruin my life. Ruin any chances with the love of my life. The mere sight of him makes my blood boil. Never has he shown up for a single school event since I started preschool. Not one award, not when I went to the finals in a spelling bee in sixth grade, and not a single soccer game since I started playing at seven years old.

He never cared, so why is he here now?

"As many of you can probably connect, I am the father of your very own Conrad Dugray," he says into the mic as he waves a hand in my direction, looking like the picture of a proud father. A lie. "He has been a student at Braxton for the last three years. Me and his beautiful mother, who is here with me tonight, could not be happier with all he has achieved here, alongside his team. With next year being his last one before he joins me in the real world, I wanted to make it the best. Anything these players need will be readily available. You will have nothing but the best equipment and resources to bring home more championships."

Grinding my molars together, I try not to let the anger inside me show on my face. I should have known it would not be as easy as I thought to walk away from the Dugray family. My father is going to use his power to control me once again. The only difference is I don't need anything he has to offer. Even if he takes away my car or tries to revoke the payments to the school until I graduate, I have more than enough from my inheritance from my grandfather.

THE HURT OF LETTING GO

He can't control me. Not anymore.

After saying a few parting words, my father exits the stage to sit at a table off to the side of the room filled with administrators and my mom. I'm wondering if he has been here the whole time or snuck in when the lights dimmed since I never noticed him before. Mom is dressed to the nines and playing the doting trophy wife as she laughs and smiles at the people surrounding them.

Light chatter fills the room as it becomes bright again. Looking away from my father's table, I scan my own and see several sets of eyes on me.

"Dude, why didn't you ever tell us your dad is, like, a billionaire or something?" one of the freshmen who joined our table asks with excitement in his tone.

Camden blows out an annoyed breath. "Jonny? Why don't you go join that table over there? It's filled with girls. Go get lucky, kid."

Jonny looks to where he is pointing and sure enough, one of the other men's soccer tables has a group of volleyball girls surrounding it. He's out of his seat and over there in a matter of seconds.

Now that it is just our core group, once again, concerning eyes are back on me. "How're you feeling, man?" Maddox asks. Gone is his joking and light tone, replaced with worry and a slight edge to how he asks me.

Out of all of my friends, Maddox understands the most about my family. He spent more time with his nanny than either of his parents because they would rather travel than be around their kids. It's not that they don't care for their children, it's more that they enjoy the life of acting like they don't have any.

Taking a calming breath, I release it slowly. "He's back with his controlling ways, but he's not going to get to me."

Just then, a hand clamps down on my shoulder. Hard. "Well, if it isn't my *son*. How are we doing, Conrad?"

Without looking back at him, I answer, "Been a whole lot better since getting the fuck away from you."

The hand on me tightens, and I try not to flinch at the slight pain. "Is that any way to speak to your father?"

Standing, I come face-to-face with him. "Wouldn't know. Didn't really have one of those growing up."

Looking around, I spot my mother at the drink station with the dean and a few other people who I assume are alumni. She's his pawn, playing her part to put on a good show, and I'm sure Mom was bribed to come here. It wouldn't be the first time my father promised her a new piece of jewelry or upgraded her car in exchange for playing the doting wife.

My father masks it well, but I see the anger flash through his eyes. He would love nothing more than to go off on me right now like he usually would, but in a room full of people, he needs to be on his best behavior.

Howard looks past my shoulder at something, or someone, behind me. "Well, is this the whore you gave up your future for? And what is in your ears? You look like you're ready to join a gang. Is this really the image you want to display to people?"

A gasp comes from the other side of the table, and I look over to see Blaire's hand covering her mouth, eyes wide with shock. Looking back at my father, I square my shoulders. He may have a looming presence, but I have height and size over him, making me more intimidating in a physical sense.

"Keep her out of your mouth and show some respect to a woman."

He offers up a dark chuckle and looks back at Emree. "I know a whore when I see one, son, and she is a whore. Her body was made for fucking. At least you chose well for yourself, but to give up your future for a good fuck toy? I told you once you marry Liliana, you can have whatever piece you want on the side." His eyes travel up and down Emree's body, and she shrinks at the obvious gawking. "Wouldn't let this one go after the marriage. All those curves make for something good to hold on to."

"Get the fuck out of here," I say through clenched teeth. "I'm done with you, with your shitty obligations and your lack of care for your own family. Just get out of my fucking life."

The side of his mouth rises in a patronizing smirk. "You really thought it would be that easy? Even if you came crawling back, no way would I let you have my company. But I do plan on making your life a miserable hell." Leaning in, he whispers in my ear, "Disobey me and find out how shitty I can make your life, Conrad." He turns and strides across the hall toward the exit. My mother must see him exit because she says something to the group she has been talking to and follows him out. Not saying a word to her own son.

The sounds in the room fade around me as I turn and cup my hands around Emree's face. She looks as if she is in shock, not looking me in the eyes. "Baby, please look at me." She doesn't. "Give me those eyes, Emree. I need to know you're okay."

After stroking her cheek a few times, she finally lifts those beautiful blue eyes to meet mine.

"Hey, baby," I say softly. "I love you. I love you so much, Emree, and I am so sorry he said all of that. None of it was true, okay?"

Her eyes begin to fill with tears, but they don't fall.

"He's horrible," she whispers as she tries to blink away the moisture collecting in her eyes.

Smiling, I continue stroking her cheek as my other hand moves to her nape, pulling her toward me so I can place a chaste kiss on her lips. "I know, baby. But something really important I need you to understand is that nothing he says is true. He is a cruel man who is angry someone has gone against him, and he is trying to take that out on you because he knows it will hurt me."

She musters up a weak smile. "I know. And I love you too."

While I believe her words, part of me is worried about my father's promise to ruin my life and it tearing the two of us apart.

CHAPTER THIRTY-TWO

EMREE

Not sure I have ever been at a loss for words like I am right now. The banquet has ended, and as we pile back into the limo, it feels different than when we first got in here earlier in the evening. Now everyone is somber after the encounter with Mr. Dugray. Conrad has been quiet along with everyone else, but he has not stopped touching me in some way. With a hand on my hip or his fingers twined with mine, we have remained connected since leaving the hall.

The words his father said to Conrad and the things he said about me were cruel, and I have never met a person as horrible as that man. Conrad had told me a little bit about his father, but nothing could have prepared me for the man himself.

As the limo driver speeds through downtown, an awkward silence fills the car.

"Well, enough of this," Maddox announces as he reaches for a chilled bottle of champagne. "Conrad's dad is a dick. He said some shitty stuff that is in no way true, and we're moving past it." He fills up the glasses we used on the drive over and begins passing them out.

With Maddox breaking the silence, everyone relaxes and

falls into casual conversation. During the drive, Conrad's hand doesn't leave my thigh the entire time, and when I cover it with my own, he smiles over at me. I want him to know that no matter what, there is an us. His father can throw every hurtful word at me and while they will sting, they will not make me love this man at my side any less.

The divider separating the driver from us lowers and the music drops a few notches. "Mr. Stone, are we taking the girls back to the apartment or heading to your residence?" he asks while looking through the rearview mirror.

Maddox looks at Blaire and me as Conrad's hand on my thigh tightens. He needs me tonight, and I don't feel like being away from him after what happened with his father.

Blaire has a shy smile on her face and red cheeks as Camden whispers in her ear. "Um, Em, I planned on staying with Camden tonight. Are you going back to the apartment or…" She leaves the question hanging in the air.

Conrad's thumb begins rubbing circles into my thigh.

"Thinking I'll stay at the guys' place as well."

Without looking at me, I see the side of his mouth tip up.

He goes back to stroking my thigh as everyone chatters and enjoys the minibar provided by the limo service. I stop after my second glass, wanting to have a clear head. Tonight is the first time I will be sleeping over since our breakup, and it feels like our first time all over again.

While I wasn't a virgin when I met Conrad, I had such a crush on him for years that the buildup to us getting together at a party meant more to me than he could ever know. The two guys before him don't hold a candle to Conrad Dugray. When I'm intimate with him, it feels as if I have known this man my entire life. I trust him completely, with my heart and body. That is probably why it was harder than anything when he ended us because I have never given that much of myself to another person.

He says he won't hurt me again, and I need to believe him when he says he loves me and won't let me go. If I keep my heart closed off to Conrad, it will only hurt me in the end. He deserves a second chance, especially with how he has treated me with nothing but care since coming back.

The limo comes to a halt, breaking me from my thoughts and causing the flutter of nerves in my stomach to flourish, knowing we are at his house and what is to come. Conrad would never pressure me into having sex if I didn't want to or wasn't ready, but I think I am. I love him and miss being with him in the most physically intimate way there is.

Our friends stumble, thanks to the copious amount of alcohol Maddox handed out, as they exit the vehicle. Everyone is laughing and having fun while Conrad and I remain quiet as we follow our friends into the house. His arm is wrapped around my waist, and the heat from his hand is burning through my thin dress.

Once inside, Maddox strolls into the kitchen while everyone else lounges on the couches. "Can you believe the shit they fed us at this thing? We're athletes. I don't need a fancy-ass dry and flavorless chicken and veggies meal. We need substance," Maddox yells from the kitchen.

Conrad and I remain joined but stand behind the couches rather than joining everyone else. I think we both have the same idea in our minds but don't want to be rude and leave our friends.

"Do you plan on making yourself something better? Because I still have nightmares from the pasta dish you almost killed me with." Blaire laughs from her spot on Camden's lap. She's sitting across him as he lazily strokes her thigh.

Maddox comes back into the living room with a sandwich and a water bottle. "Of course not, and you did not almost die. It wasn't that spicy." He plops down onto the couch beside Levi.

Laughter fills the room at Maddox's denial of his terrible cooking.

"Dude, pretty sure you gave me a stomach ulcer from that meal. Who puts that many jalapeños and red pepper flakes in a pasta dish anyway?" Mateo asks.

"Someone with a sophisticated palate," Maddox answers before ripping off a large bite of his sandwich.

Conrad's hand on my waist tightens, and I know he's about to give our friends an excuse about why we're going upstairs, but before he can, Maddox speaks with a mouthful of food. "You two going to stand there all night or go upstairs and screw? We can all smell the sexual desires going on there."

My face heats up as the guys laugh. "Ew, I don't ever want to hear the words *sexual desires* come out of your mouth again." Jules's face is of pure disgust.

"Adults have sex, Julesy. Just because you're celibate doesn't mean we all are."

She rolls her eyes and goes back to watching some alligator-catching show they put on TV. Conrad looks down at me and smiles. He kisses my forehead before addressing our friends. "Good night, everyone."

"Good night, you horndogs," Maddox tells us, his voice reflecting an evident smile on his face.

Conrad links our hands together and has me following him up the stairs. As we walk down the hallways toward his room, the sounds of the TV fade away.

All the guys' rooms are on the second floor. Maddox has the owner's suite at the end of the hallway to the left. Coming up the stairs, taking a right, Conrad's room is the first door on the left. On the right between his and Camden's rooms is the bathroom they share, and down at the end on the right is Levi's room. While Maddox was lucky enough to get his own private bathroom, Conrad, Levi, Mateo, and Camden share the one full bathroom and there is a half bath downstairs.

When I had stayed over before, it was unsettling sharing a bathroom with four guys, especially when they have a tendency to not always shut the door when they use the toilet. There were too many encounters with them in the early morning, and Mateo has no shame if you catch him in nothing but a pair of boxers peeing over the toilet.

Conrad turns the knob on his bedroom door and holds it open for me. I enter, inhaling the familiar scent of his leather and sandalwood cologne. The door clicks and when I turn, Conrad is locking it. He twists the doorknob, making sure that the door is truly locked.

I raise my eyebrow at him in question.

He shakes his head. "Don't ask, but I will say I have invasive roommates."

The air in the room changes as we stare at each other. Now that we're together, I don't know what I was nervous about earlier. This is Conrad. The man who has cherished me, admiring my body and showing me he would love me over anything else, even his family. There is no reason to feel anything but at home with him.

Conrad's eyes darken as he takes me in from head to toe. I'm still in my heels, and I would have shucked them off the moment we got in here, but the way he is looking at them makes the pain worth it.

"Come here, baby," he tells me, his voice low as if he is struggling to control himself.

Without a second thought, I take a few steps and close the distance between us. The sound of my heels clicking against his hardwood floor is the only noise in the otherwise quiet room. Conrad watches my every movement with little expression on his face, but I can see the hunger in his eyes.

When I'm within arm's reach, Conrad grips the nape of my neck and jerks me forward. "Fuck, I've missed you," he whispers into my shoulder as he drops a kiss to the exposed skin there. "You've been killing me in this dress tonight. You were by far the most stunning woman in that hall. Not sure how anyone got anything done when you were there, distracting them with all these curves and, fuck, your legs in these heels." His hands skim down my body, and he gives my ass a hard squeeze before coming back up to cup my face.

Smiling, I look into his eyes, which are a storm of desire. "Thank you, but I'm sure you're overexaggerating."

He doesn't laugh along with me, but a slight frown graces his face. "You just don't get it, do you?"

"Get what?"

He strokes my cheek with the pad of his thumb. "How unbelievably beautiful you are."

While I'm not usually uncomfortable with compliments and would laugh at his words, Conrad says them with such purpose and sincerity that I don't have a choice but to believe him. That, mixed with the need for me in his eyes, has my stomach fluttering, knowing this man loves me.

Even in my heels, I barely come up to Conrad's shoulders. Pushing up on my tiptoes, I press my lips to his in a soft kiss. He grips my hips, pulling my body against his, and deepens the kiss. Our lips glide against each other's slowly as I run my nails through the hair at the back of his head.

A rumbling comes from Conrad's chest, and he grips the bottom of my dress. "As much as I want to rip this off, I'm going to be gentle with your dress since you made it," he says against my mouth.

At an agonizing pace, he lifts my dress while continuing our kiss, his tongue exploring mine. He breaks apart from my lips to slip the material over my head and sucks in a breath when he leans back to take me in.

"Shit, you've been naked under this thing all night?" His voice is thick as he takes in my bare body.

Shrugging my shoulders, I look at my dress clutched in his hand. "It's kind of thin and no one wants underwear lines."

Burying his face in my neck, Conrad inhales. "It's a good thing I didn't know that before now, or we would have never made it out tonight."

His hands begin roaming my naked form, and I moan at the feeling of his rough hands on my smooth skin. Where Conrad is polished and perfect all over, his hands have always been a contrast to everything else. They are heavily calloused from working out and lifting weights. He says he likes having calluses because it shows that he's working hard while he is in the gym as if his body couldn't tell him that.

A squeak escapes me as he grabs the backs of my legs, lifting me up. I automatically wrap my legs around his waist and hold on to his shoulders as he walks us to his bed. Instead of laying me down, Conrad sits on the end and holds me in his lap as he unbuckles my heels and drops them to the floor.

Pulling back from the spot on my neck he was kissing and sucking, he looks me in the eyes. "I love you, you know."

Lifting my hand, I push the hair back from his face. He hasn't gotten a haircut in a while, and the strands are longer than I have ever seen. "Yeah, I know that, Conrad."

His hands run up and down my back in a soothing motion rather than a sexual one, and considering I'm completely naked on his lap, I'm kind of surprised. "I never want to hurt you like I did. You're too important to me."

Once again, his words make my chest swell. Resting my forehead against his, I bring myself closer until we are chest to chest. "I love you. Now make love to me."

He doesn't hesitate as he lifts me up with ease and lays me on his unmade bed. The sheets are cold against my bare back, and my body shivers without the heat from Conrad as he stands above me, unbuttoning his shirt.

Watching him slowly release each button is torture, and the

moment he has the last one undone and shucks off his dress shirt, I sit up and wrap my hand around his neck, pulling him down to me. He holds himself above my body as we get lost in a sloppy kiss. One of his hands is running up and down my skin, paying extra attention to my full breast and the curve of my hip. That hand moves lower until he's cupping between my legs. I spread them, allowing him better access.

The moment his long finger enters me, my head falls back, and I let out a moan. "I was really trying to go slow tonight, but the sounds coming out of you and feeling how ready you are for me are making it hard," Conrad tells me as he kisses and sucks at my chest.

Gripping the back of his hair, I bring his head up to look me in the eyes. "Slow isn't what I need tonight. I've missed you too much for that."

He smirks as he removes his hand, and I suddenly miss the feeling of him being there. "Let me give my girl what she wants then."

Conrad kisses me long and hard. His tongue glides with mine as I clutch him to me, needing to feel his body against mine. One hand snakes between us, and I undo his belt and the button of his slacks in record time. Conrad moans against my mouth as my hand slides into the front of his pants, and I grip his length, giving him a long stroke.

"Fuck, I need you," he groans as he shucks his pants and underwear off and reaches into the nightstand. His naked body comes back over me, and he rips the condom open with his teeth as he stares down at me.

A thought that has never entered my mind overfills it, and I wrap my hand around the condom in his hand. "I'm clean and you know I have the shot. Are you...were you using protection while we weren't together?"

His eyebrows pinch together. "You think I was fucking around while we were apart?"

For an entire month, we weren't together, and technically, he was forming a relationship with another woman who was meant to be his fiancée. "I would understand if you were. You and Liliana were going to be engaged."

Conrad holds his body up so that he isn't touching every part of mine. "First off, we don't talk about other people while in bed together. Let's make that a rule. Second, there is no one besides you. Even the thought of fucking someone else repulses me, so no, I was not with anyone while we were apart."

Before I can say another word, Conrad plasters his body to mine and captures my mouth in a bruising kiss. With the condom forgotten, Conrad grips himself, positioned at my entrance. In one deep thrust, he enters me and I suck in a breath, taken aback by the invasion.

At a loss for words, I moan as he pulls out and pushes back into me. Never having had sex without a condom, the feeling is new and more intense than ever before. And by the way Conrad is struggling above me, I think he is feeling it too.

"Oh god." My body sets off, and I grip his shoulders as I ride it out. Shaking, I barely register Conrad moving above me.

Feeling as if I'm on cloud nine, I smile as Conrad wraps his arm around my waist and speeds up as he seeks out his own release. Low grunts come out of him with every thrust, and I hold on to his back as my body begins sliding up the bed with his movements. With one last deep thrust, Conrad goes still, and I wrap my arms and legs tight around him, enjoying the feeling of him being this close for just a moment longer.

Conrad collapses on top of me, out of breath and slick with sweat. Rubbing my hands through his hair, I take in this moment. Never have I felt more connected to a person before, and experiencing this with the man I love and who loves me back makes it that much more intense.

"I love you," he whispers in my ear. Pulling back, he looks me in the eyes. "Never felt anything like that before. Thank you, baby." He kisses my cheek and slips out of me. The loss of him makes my body cold, and I already miss him.

Sitting up, I catch Conrad pulling on a pair of boxer briefs and start to worry. He has never treated me as a "hit it and quit it" hookup, but why would he be getting dressed?

"Be right back," he kisses my forehead and slips out of the room.

Feeling awkward, I pull the sheets up and cover my body. In under a minute, he comes back into the room with an ice water. My heart swells as he comes to the side of the bed I'm on and hands it to me.

Without another word, he takes his clothes off and climbs back into bed with me, providing me once again with his body heat. With my back to his chest and my head tucked under his chin, I fall into the most peaceful sleep I have ever had and dream of a future with this man I love who makes me feel cherished and safe.

CHAPTER THIRTY-THREE

CONRAD

While soccer season isn't here yet, Coach Walters doesn't let us slack off during spring. This Saturday, we're having a scrimmage match against one of the colleges close by. Their field isn't nearly as nice as ours since we use our school's football stadium, but we make do.

The stands are littered with family and friends. Those are the only ones allowed at off-season games. Emree, Blaire, Jules, and her roommate Piper are out there somewhere. Knowing Em and Jules, they're loading up on snacks from the concession. Every game, those two can be found with their laps filled with nachos, hot dogs, and popcorn. I swear, sometimes I don't even think they're here for us and enjoy the food more.

As we're stretching and a few players are kicking some soccer balls around on the field, I search the crowd for my beautiful blonde girlfriend in the bright-pink jersey with my name and number on the back. While our school colors are blue and gold, Emree has decided to do a twist on our jerseys and make them more her style, which means adding pink. It makes finding her in a sea of blue and gold easier, so I'm not one to complain.

Spotting her in the second row of bleachers, I smile as she takes a large bite of a burger, getting ketchup and mustard all over her face. She quickly wipes at her cheeks and waves at me when she notices I'm looking at her. I can't stop the smile that stretches across my face and wave back.

"Dude, you lose your balls or something? You're smiling like a little girl." Mateo laughs from where he and Maddox are kicking the ball back and forth to my right.

Maddox points a finger at Mateo after he sobers up. "We lost another one. You better watch yourself, McKay. Don't need another one of us pussy-whipped."

His face drops in surprise. "Me? Why don't you talk to Levi over there, who's making goo-goo eyes at Piper?"

Levi, who is warming up by catching balls Camden kicks at him, stops after jumping up in the air and catching a kick about two feet above him. "Fuck you, man. I'm focused on the game."

Maddox smirks. "But you do like our little freshman."

Our goalie goes back to warming up and ignores Maddox but grumbles under his breath in the process. As I stretch out my hamstrings, the referee blows the whistle to begin the game.

One of the best things about the roommates I have is that we are all starters and some of the most talented on the team. Camden and Maddox are both forwards and work perfectly together. I have never seen two teammates in such sync as they make their way through the other team's defenders and get the ball right into the net. Mateo and I are on the defense, and with his quick feet and my ruthlessness, we do well at stopping anyone from getting past us to our goalie. Levi is a monster in the goal. Being as tall and large as he is, the guy takes up most of the goal without even moving.

We get into our positions after the coin flip, and as we wait for the official whistle to start, I tune out everything around us. Something you have to learn from playing sports is that all of your focus goes to what is happening on the field. None of the noise of screaming fans and ringing cowbells matters. My only focus is what goes on while I am on this turf.

Maddox captures the ball and begins dribbling it toward the other team's goal, dodging their defenders on the way. When Maddox starts to get swarmed, he does a fake pass to our teammate, Rodrick, and when the other team is distracted, he makes a real pass to Camden, who kicks it straight into the goal.

We fall into a rhythm and dominate on the field. The other team gets one goal past Levi, but he deflects several more. Before halftime, we are leading three to one, and I'm feeling confident with how well this team is working together, seeing as how we aren't losing anyone on the field this school year to graduating.

The halftime whistle blows, and we all jog off the field, grabbing cups filled with water. Coach gathers us in a circle and starts his midgame pep talk. It's not as intense since we are winning and this is not a game that matters, but he gets amped up for the second half when some players look exhausted.

Coach Walters makes the decision to pull Maddox and Mateo and throw in some sophomores so they can get some game time. Mateo, our designated hothead, looks pissed, but Maddox pulls him to the bench before Coach can see.

We head back on the field and continue our ruthless defeat. The opposing team isn't able to get another ball past Levi, while Camden, along with the sophomore, gets an additional goal and we take the win four to one. As the final whistle blows, we all run together and cheer, celebrating how well we work together and how this one day is setting into motion how the next season is going to go.

After our celebration, both teams line up to tell each other "Good game" and slap hands. Coach Walters maintains his happiness for our win as he talks to the other team's coach. He always told us that we can celebrate every win to an extent but to remain humble because we can be knocked down several pegs at any moment.

As we head back into the locker room, my eyes are drawn to Emree. She is standing on her chair and holding a sign that says *Conrad is the #1 player*. If she wasn't so adorable, it would be embarrassing, but this is all part of her bubbly personality.

Since we are guests, the locker room assigned to us is technically the girls', and I can't say I'm complaining about it. The smell here is drastically better than the sour and musky smell of the mens'.

Once everyone is inside and sitting, Coach addresses the team. "You boys continue to make me proud. Even though this game did not count on paper, it mattered. You put your all into it and that's what counts the most."

Camden stands. "Never did I think being a team captain would be something I would want to do or even be good at. Not sure why all you idiots voted for me, but here we are." We all laugh because before the season started and Camden got voted as team captain, he thought it was a joke. "Being the captain of a team like the one we have makes it easy. You are all great players, and it has been an honor to be your captain, and I hope you will want me to continue this position next season."

There is no doubt in my mind that he will be chosen again. If this year has shown us anything, it's that Camden Collins is a born leader and a great one at that. He doesn't belittle anyone and is great at encouraging us when we need it. Our team last season was great, but losing many of our seniors put the team in a funk, and he was a big part of getting us out of it.

"That's enough with the feelings. Get changed and let's get out of their locker room," Coach announces before walking off. He's never been one for long, drawn-out pep talks and is more of a straight-to-the-point kind of guy.

The guys start undressing and heading to the showers. I

head over to try and get in first so I can get out of here and maybe take Emree out tonight.

After washing off, I head over to where I left my stuff. Levi and Maddox are there, still in their uniforms. Maddox strips down to nothing and rests his hands on his hips. "Ah, nothing better than airing out some sweaty junk."

"My man, I know the feeling is great, but can you not get your dick so close to my face?" Mateo states from where he is sitting on the bench, with a clear view of Maddox's package.

Maddox ignores his request. "Take in all that is a well-gifted body. Not sure what I did to be given this wonderful cock, but I'm not complaining and neither are the ladies."

Camden comes in with a towel around his waist and his hair wet from a shower. "Cover yourself and get in the shower. We already see your dick enough at the house. I don't want you flaunting your stuff here as well."

Maddox is notorious for being nude around the house. He has gotten better about it with Blaire and Emree being around, but his room is still a zone we all avoid. Each of us has made the mistake of trying to sneak into his room to use the shower, coming across a naked Maddox in bed.

Maddox struts through the locker room with his towel slung over his shoulder, every bit of him still on display. Levi rolls his eyes and heads toward the showers. We're practically immune to Maddox's antics but try to keep him under control as much as possible.

As I start putting my clothes on, a fully dressed Camden takes a seat on the bench beside me. "Wanted to check in on you. How are you doing after the shit that went down with your dad at the banquet?" Camden keeps his voice low. The only ones who know about my family struggles are my roommates and Coach Walters.

Talking about my feelings has never been something I was accustomed to. Growing up in a cold family, we never discussed anything other than trivial topics and achievements in our lives, and even those conversations were rare. Camden grew up with a single mom and younger sister, so he has been more in touch with his feelings than probably any of us. I think that makes him the ideal team captain because he is sympathetic and understanding of what someone is going through.

Shrugging on a pair of jeans, I think about my response to him as I pull on a white T-shirt. "Not much to really think about. He gave me an ultimatum and didn't like my decision."

"You think he'll do anything about it like he says?"

This has been on my mind since last weekend. While I don't need my dad or his help or money, thanks to my inheritance, he is a powerful, manipulative man. Not sure what he would have planned, but now I feel as if I should be on alert for any kind of moves he wants to make to mess with my life.

"He could be all talk and no bite, but I've never been on the receiving end of his wrath, so who's to tell?"

Camden watches me as I slip on my sneakers. "You think he'd come after Em?"

My body freezes. Messing with my life is one thing, but if he comes near Emree, I'm done, and I won't be holding back going toe to toe with him.

"He would be making the biggest mistake of his life," I tell Camden as I sling my bag over my shoulder. "I'm heading out. Going to take Em to dinner. See you guys back at the house."

As I walk through the locker room, all the guys are joking and laughing with each other. While this team is like a family to me and enjoying a victory with them is something I have always partaken in, being with my girl is more desirable at the moment. Some may call me whipped, but at least I know Camden understands it because I have no doubt he is going to be ditching the guys and grabbing Blaire.

Stepping outside the locker room, I'm hit with the heat of Florida's April sun. Summer is approaching and so is the end of the semester. We only have one more year at Braxton U before all of us are thrown out into the real world. With my new life changes, I'm not sure what will happen after graduation, but during the summer, I'll take time to reach out to a few of my dad's business associates because while I may be removed from the Dugray family, the name alone leaves some doors open for me. I've met and made connections with these men and women since my freshman year of high school when I started shadowing my dad in the office during summers. While many of them are assholes like my father, I actually grew fond of a few who slid me their business cards when my dad wasn't looking.

Searching the parking lot, I look for Blaire's red sedan. She and Emree drove together, and it worked out well because Camden and I took my car and now he can go with his girl and I can take mine.

The front of the lot is filled with players' cars since we had to be here early, so I start walking to the back while looking around. Once I'm almost near the end, I see the two of them sitting on Blaire's hood with a bucket of popcorn between them. The moment Emree sees me, her face lights up and her mouth tips into a smile.

When I reach the car, I drop my bag on the floor and grab Em's ankle, pulling her to the end of the hood so she is settled between my legs. "Enjoy the game, baby?" I ask against her mouth.

Wrapping her arms around my neck, she grins and I feel the movement against my lips. "I always enjoy watching you play, especially in those tight shorts that show off your bubble butt."

Leaning back, I arch a brow at her. "Bubble butt?"

Em looks at Blaire and the two giggle like schoolgirls. "We had a little fun with Jules and Piper and ranked which players on your team have the best ass." Her grip on my neck tightens as she brings my head closer. "You and that nice butt were in the top five."

She brushes her lips against mine, but I pull away before she can lay a real kiss on me. "Top five? What the fuck, Em?"

"It was close, but Levi's tush is just perfectly round and voluptuous. Plus, he likes to flaunt it while in the goal. Pushing his butt out while squatting and all that. He really wasn't playing fair."

"It's true, Con. Your boy really flaunts it while he's waiting for someone to try and score," Blaire chimes in.

Looking between the two, I wonder if the girls were even watching the game at all. "I'm feeling a bit objectified right now, and I didn't even end up winning. That's some bullshit."

Emree rubs her hand through my hair on the side of my head in a soothing motion. "Aw, don't be hurt. You still have a fantastic ass, babe."

"My ego is crushed. I may need you to make up for it." Smiling, I decide to milk this because Emree has a loving heart and if she thinks this hurts me, she will try to make it up to me.

Blaire cuts in before my girl can say anything. "Oh no, don't let him play you, Emmy. His ego is perfectly fine."

My head snaps in her direction and my eyes narrow at the brunette still sitting on the hood. "Don't you have a boyfriend to go find?"

As if he knows we are talking about him, Camden walks up to us. "Why are you giving my girlfriend a death glare?"

"Because she and the others voted Levi for best ass on the team."

Camden stops in his tracks just a few steps away from us. "What the hell, Gray Eyes?"

Blaire, the sweetest of our friend group, lays a good punch to my arm as she slides down the hood of her car. "Way to upset him. He didn't even make the top five and now this will crush his heart."

Camden is now getting the "best ass award" discussion that

THE HURT OF LETTING GO

I got, but he doesn't get the cushion of knowing he is the runner-up. That has to be a hard blow for him.

Emree jumps off the hood with her popcorn in hand. "Way to start issues in paradise," she says, peering at our friends as Camden rolls his eyes.

Choosing to ignore the couple's spat, I grab my girl's hand and pull her forward. "Want to go on a date with me?"

Her eyes light up as she smiles at me. "I hope you don't plan on a big dinner or something because we kind of ate through the concession stand."

A laugh rumbles through me. "I swear you ladies only come to our games for the food, and watching us play is just a bonus."

"Don't be silly." She slaps my chest. "The nice butts are the bonus. Watching you play is an obligation," she jokes.

Rolling my eyes, I sling my arm over her shoulders as she laughs. We say goodbye to our friends as they make out in the parking lot, clearly past the loss of the "best ass award," and head to my car.

Nothing is better than this feeling right here. Our team is going to be killing it next year, and I have the most amazing woman by my side. A woman I know would be there for me no matter what and whom I love more than anything.

CHAPTER THIRTY-FOUR

EMREE

Tuesdays are sluggish nights at Whiskey Joe's and not working with my best friend makes it even worse. Garrett had a new hire flake this week, so he needed us to pick up the slack. Luckily, I got off easily and didn't end up getting a double shift on the weekend because those are torture.

The bar is pretty empty, for it being just a little past six, but a few of our regulars are at the bar, and there is a group of college kids hanging out on the patio and ordering drinks and appetizers. They're keeping me busy, at least.

A chime from the front door rings through the deserted area, and I'm grateful there is going to be another body in here to serve. Slow shifts make the time go by much slower than it really is, so I'm happy to wait on more tables.

Turning to greet the new customer, all the air leaves my lungs as my eyes lock with Howard Dugray's. Conrad's father looks out of place in this college bar wearing his fitted gray suit and black tie. His hair is perfectly slicked back, and he is sporting a clean face with not even a five-o'clock shadow.

Mr. Dugray's mouth slides up on one side when he sees me

standing there, and the look is somewhere between menacing and leery. He's standing about ten feet from me, but I can feel his presence as if he were right beside me.

With just a few long strides, Mr. Dugray is standing in front of me, looking down with that same crooked smirk. "Well, if it isn't my son's little whore."

Squaring my shoulders, I make myself look as tall as possible. "Good evening, sir. May I get you a table, or will you be sitting at the bar?"

His eyebrow rises at me, blatantly ignoring his disrespectful statement. "A table. In your section, of course."

Grabbing a menu and silverware from the hostess's post, I lead him to a table in the back—away from the bar, because the last thing I want is for anyone to hear his rude comments directed at me.

Setting the items down at one of the spots at the four-person table, I step back to allow Conrad's father to sit.

"This place is exactly somewhere I imagined someone like you working. A scholarship kid from a single, young mother in a town not worth remembering the name of. No surprise here."

My blood runs cold at his mentioning my personal life and where I come from. "How do you know those things about me?"

Howard leans back in the seat and unbuttons his suit jacket. "When my son tells me he is ruining his life and abandoning the plans I set for him before birth for a woman, you think I wouldn't find out who that woman is?"

"Maybe he made those decisions because he was tired of living *his* life the way *you* wanted him to."

Nostrils flaring, Howard leans forward with one long finger pressed onto the tabletop. "Not sure I like the service at this place. Bring me a scotch neat and maybe I will reconsider that tip."

Plastering on my most perfect fake smile, I lean down so that we're at eye level. "You can shove your tip up your ass, *sir*." Standing, I look toward the bar to make sure my coworker or Garrett doesn't think anything is off. "I'll go ahead and grab that drink for you." Without another word, I turn and head toward the bar.

Once I have the drink from Garrett, who eyes Howard, I turn and head back in that direction. He is leaning back in the chair again and one of his legs is resting on the opposite knee as he scrolls through his phone.

"Here you are," I announce cheerfully as I set the drink down.

"Sit," Howard demands without looking up from the phone.

Cocking my hip out, I rest my hand there and narrow my eyes at him. "Excuse me?"

With a sigh, he looks up from his phone. "Sit. I'd like a word with you, and based on the fact that I'm your only table, you have the time."

He's not wrong. I've already checked on the group on the patio, and they got fresh refills and had finished their apps.

Reluctantly, I take the seat across from him. Howard swirls the amber liquid in the glass and takes a sip. "Clearly you don't have top-shelf liquor here."

"Did you come here to insult my place of work, or is there a purpose for your visit?"

"Obviously I would never willingly choose to spend my time in a place like this." He sneers as he looks around one of my favorite places to be. Whiskey Joe's may not be the fanciest establishment, but we have a great team and loyal customers who love coming here on the regular.

"Then why did you grace us with your presence?"

That smirk appears on his face again, and my stomach clenches, knowing the reason he is here could not be good. "I'm assuming my son thinks he doesn't need me and that's why he has decided to be *independent*."

Raising a brow, I try not to give my answer away. "Not sure what you mean by that, but your son wants a life of his own and not one that you are forcing on him."

"It's cute how you defend him." Howard leans forward and rests his forearms on the table. "I'll cut to the chase because I want to get out of here."

"That makes two of us."

His nostrils flare at my snarky comeback, and I get the feeling people in Howard Dugray's life don't talk back to him much, if at all. "Conrad thinks he is safe with that trust fund of his from my father and while I don't have direct access to it, I have excellent lawyers that are confident I can win power of attorney over it, and that means I will manage every bit of what is in there."

The confident smile and tone of voice worry me. I know nothing about wills or what a lawyer can and cannot do. He has the upper hand in this conversation, and I wish I paid more attention in the law class I took my senior year of high school, although I don't think this would be a priority topic.

"What are you trying to say?"

"I'm saying that my son is too stubborn to listen to me and thinks I won't make any moves, but you seem like you truly love him. So I will give you two options: stay with my son and I take everything from him, including any job opportunities he was being hopeful for after graduation, or end your relationship and he won't have any reason not to fulfill the plans we had until you came along."

Everything around me fades away as his words sink in. Howard Dugray is a powerful man and, from what I have seen, a ruthless one at that. The fact that he is willing to ruin his own son's life shows he has no empathy and a cold, dead heart.

"Why can't you just let him be?" I whisper.

Howard lets out a sinister laugh that gains the attention of other patrons. "My son went against me, and that's unacceptable in my world. There are consequences for your actions, and these are his. You should be grateful I'm leaving the decision up to you instead of doing as I please. I would say I'm being fairly generous."

This man is pure evil. I will never understand people like him. Parents like him. My mom did everything to make my life better and motivated me to follow my dreams and what I love. For Conrad's dad to want this much control over his son's life, even at the expense of his happiness, is pathetic as a father.

Throwing back the last of his drink, Mr. Dugray stands and straightens his suit jacket. "You have until the weekend to make your decision. But know this, Miss Anders, there really is only one right option. Let's hope you're smart enough to know which it is." After tossing a twenty-dollar bill on the table, he heads toward the double doors he entered through not too long ago, and even though it is a warm spring night, goose bumps form on my bare arms as a shiver runs up my body.

"You okay?" Garrett asks from in front of me, and I realize I've been sitting at this table for much longer than I should have been.

Hopping up, I plaster on a cheerful smile. "For sure, boss. Sorry about that."

"You're fine, Em. I'm more worried about whatever the suit said to you to make your face drop like it did."

A boss like Garrett is what most people wish for. He truly cares about his employees and even though he isn't one to be comfortable with heart-to-hearts, there are moments you can see the softer side of him.

"Just a jackass who came into my life recently."

Garrett's eyes soften as he studies my face. "If he comes back in here, he's not welcome. This is a jackass-free zone, aside from that Maddox guy you seem to like."

A laugh sneaks out of me. Garrett has never been a fan of Maddox's after a drunken striptease on one of the tables that ended in Camden and Levi having to haul a half-naked and feisty Maddox out of the bar. Garrett still glares at Maddox anytime he comes in, even though this happened over a year ago.

Garrett goes back to doing his manager duties while I check in with my group on the patio and take away empty plates and cups. They're finishing off the rest of the bucket of beer and closing out their tab, which means I've lost my only table, and the night will be even slower. Hopefully, we get some more people in tonight so I can zone out and forget about the conversation I had with Conrad's father for just a few hours.

THE REST of my shift picks up some as the night goes on, and I get a few tables of customers. Waiting on patrons helps to distract me from the mess of an ultimatum Howard Dugray gave me tonight. This man has ruined my relationship once before and here he is again, set out to completely destroy it.

Conrad texted me tonight, asking if I would come stay at the house, but with everything that went on with his dad, I don't want to be around him when my mind is somewhere else. He would be able to tell something is wrong, and I have so much to think about.

On the drive to my apartment, my mind gets lost in the two decisions I have. Staying with Conrad not only takes away the safety he has of his inheritance, but those job connections he planned to use over the summer are in jeopardy now. Losing those opportunities would crush him and without the job security he'd have if he followed through with his father's demands, this leaves Conrad's future up in the air.

Part of me thinks I shouldn't even be considering Mr. Dugray's option of breaking it off with Conrad because that would be like tearing my heart apart again, and knowing that I would hurt him in the process puts weight in my stomach. He has laid his heart out to me and chosen our relationship over his family.

What I want more than anything is for Conrad to have a happy life, whether that is with me or not. Though it would hurt me more than anything, letting him go to succeed in the life that was meant for him may be the better option.

The drive to my apartment is a blur, and when I open the door, the sound of the TV playing in the living room greets me. Blaire had the night off and needed the time to study for her upcoming exams. After dumping my bag and shoes by the front door, I make my way into the apartment. The place is dark except for the soft glow from the TV. Blaire is curled up on the couch with a throw blanket tucked around her body.

She looks up at me when I plop down on the opposite couch. "Based on the look on your face, I'm going to assume it was either a slow shift or you dealt with some real jerks tonight."

My mind goes straight to Howard Dugray, who could be categorized as the biggest jackass of all time. "A little bit of both," I whisper to my best friend.

Blaire eyes me warily as she sits up. "Everything okay?"

While I did debate internally if I should tell Blaire about what happened with Conrad's father, I ultimately came to the conclusion that I needed to talk to someone about this. Holding it in would tear me apart more than it already is.

"Conrad's father showed up at the bar and basically threatened Conrad's future unless I end our relationship."

Her mouth pops open. "What do you mean?"

For the next twenty minutes, I tell Blaire about my entire conversation with Conrad's father, and her facial expressions shift from shock to anger to sadness because she knows no matter what decision I make, Conrad will be hurt as a result.

"What are you going to do?" she asks me after we sit in silence for a minute.

Taking a deep breath, I look down at my hands that have been toying with the blanket covering my lap. "I have no idea."

CHAPTER THIRTY-FIVE

CONRAD

"Why did you never tell us this shit hurt so bad?" I grumble to Levi when I come out to the front of the tattoo shop.

The bastard laughs. "Never took you for a wimp."

"Call me a wimp all you want, but my arm is on fire from that shit."

When Levi brought us to the tattoo shop where he gets work done, never did I think getting a tattoo would be something I wanted, but here we are. There was a drawing in Levi's artist's book that I was interested in. He had some time available today because of a cancelation, and I did something I thought I would never do and permanently marked my skin.

The freedom to do what I want feels great; the stinging from the needles does not.

Once I pay and am told how to care for the tattoo for the next couple of weeks, Levi and I head out to meet our friends at the house before we go to Whiskey Joe's for some drinks and games on the patio. With how busy Blaire and Emree have been with work, it has been hard to get everyone together, and Garrett was cool enough to schedule the two off this Friday.

Pulling into the driveway, I notice that a couple of the guys' cars are already gone, but Emree's is sitting in my driveway. Since our plan was for her and Blaire to meet us at the bar, I'm confused why her car is here and some of my roommates are gone.

"Hey, man, why don't I meet you there? I think my girl is inside, and I'm going to see what's up," I tell Levi when he pulls up to the curb in front of our house.

He nods in response, and I hop out of his car and head up the driveway. The sound of tires rolling against asphalt drifts away as Levi's car disappears down the road. The front door is unlocked, and inside is Emree sitting on the couch with her hands in her lap.

While she is just as beautiful as she always is, her face is tense with what I can only assume is worry. "Hey, baby. What are you doing here?"

The door slams behind me as I walk toward Em. She gives me a sad smile but doesn't stand to greet me. "Hi. What happened to your arm?"

The tattoo was going to be a surprise because part of me assumed she would try to talk me out of it if she thought I was being impulsive. "Don't be mad I didn't tell you, but I got a tattoo."

Her eyes widen. "What?" She is out of her seat and beside me in an instant, lifting my sleeve. "Why? What did you get? You realize this is permanent, Conrad?"

A chuckle comes out of me. "Yeah, baby. I know it's real."

She's looking at the blob of ink through the protective wrap I have to wear for a few days. "I can't believe you got a tattoo. Why the sudden, spur-of-the-moment decision? And what even is it?"

"Just another thing I would have never been able to do under my father's dictatorship. I feel like I should be making a 'Conrad is finally free' bucket list. You know I've never let myself get blackout drunk before in case I do something stupid and someone catches it on video? He laid into me how important my image was all my life, and I've tried so fucking hard to maintain that, but I'm tired." I look down at the blob and smile. "And it's a skull. I thought it was cool."

Emree's face falls at the mention of my father, and her hand drops from my arm. "I actually need to talk to you about something. But we will revisit the conversation that you got a skull tattooed on you."

Narrowing my eyes, I raise a brow. "What are you talking about?"

"Let's sit," she states as she pulls away and returns to the single-seater sofa she had been sitting on. I take up the other couch and sit on the edge, nervous about whatever she has to tell me. "Your dad showed up at the bar on Tuesday night and basically threatened me. Told me to break up with you, or he would find any way he can to take the trust fund set up by your grandfather."

Of all the things my mind was conjuring up that could have come out of her mouth, my father blackmailing Emree was not one of them. While I should not be surprised he would try something like this, knowing that my father threatened Em to try and hurt me boils my blood.

Standing, I run my hands through my hair and tug on the strands. "This *fucking* man just won't stop." I'm pacing the area between the coffee table and the television. Stopping, I turn to face Em. "What did he say he'd do to try and get the trust fund? He can't do that."

She offers a sad smile. "He didn't go into much detail but basically said he has the best lawyers in the country and would do everything to bring you down." Emree bites her lip and looks unsure of herself. "There's more than that, though."

"Just lay it all out." Once she tells me everything, I can take it all in and figure out a plan to get this man the fuck out of my life.

"He mentioned he would also do everything to ruin any business relationships you try to form with acquaintances he's introduced you to over the years."

"Fuck!" I kick the side of the sofa, wishing it were my father's face. "He's playing dirty and has the upper hand. He'll do anything to ruin my life and this is bullshit."

Emree remains quiet as I let out my frustration. After I have cooled down some, Emree breaks the long stretch of silence. "There may be something we could do."

My ears twitch with interest, and I take a seat. "I'm listening."

"Blaire said that her mom knows a popular and well-known lawyer in Texas. It turns out that her friend is connected to the largest estate planning lawyer where you're from, which I guess is the type you would need. I told Blaire's mom's friend what was happening and the threats your father made, and she relayed the information to one of the partners in Boston. The moment he heard your name, he said he would take you as a client at any time you needed him."

My mind is spinning with all the information Emree has given me. Not only did she not cower to my father's demands, but my girl went out and sought out someone who could help us.

"Why would he help me?" Usually when someone hears the name Dugray, they bend over backward to do anything for my father. The fact that this lawyer is willing to help me and not Howard seems suspicious.

Emree chews on her bottom lip. "Well, this part is kind of hard to tell you, but it's the reason he's so willing to help you and not your father. The lawyer, Mr. Groves, has history with your father and, um, well…his wife."

Groaning, I lean back against the couch and close my eyes. "My father had an affair with his wife, didn't he?"

"Yes," she whispers. "Mr. Groves was actually all too happy to be on your side against your father. He even said he would take your case pro bono."

I can't help but laugh. "Well, I guess using his enemies against him could work in our favor."

Emree studies me from her seat. "What are you going to do?"

That's a loaded question if I've ever been asked one. I'm still fuming that my father even approached Emree and that she had to endure threats from him. I make a mental note to talk to Garrett about adding him to their ban list at the bar, which usually consists of patrons who have gotten too out of hand. I want to know that away from me, Em is safe from my father.

Wiping my hands on my jeans, I stand and try to push away the thoughts of all the drama going on in my life. "I'm going to come kiss my girlfriend, and we're going to go meet our friends for a fun night at the bar. We'll deal with all the other shit after tonight."

Without another word, I grab Emree's hand and pull her up and into me. She gasps in surprise as I press my lips to hers and enjoy her softness in my arms. She relaxes, and I use that to my advantage and run my tongue across her lips. She wraps her arms around my neck and opens, allowing me to deepen the kiss. She moans the moment my tongue mingles with hers.

Pulling back, I rest my forehead against Emree's. Our ragged breaths are the only sound in the room. "As much as I want to continue this and take you upstairs, we have a few people waiting for us, and I'd love nothing more than to enjoy tonight with our friends and forget about everything with my dad."

She smiles and runs her nails against my scalp. "Trust me,

forgetting about your father is at the top of my to-do list, but I'm worried. How are we going to handle this?"

"Together," I tell her as I tuck a piece of hair behind her ear. "We'll figure it out, and when we go against the big, bad dickhead, we'll win. But the most important thing is that we're together doing it."

"I love you," she whispers with a smile on her face.

"I will always love you, baby."

We may have a hell of a fight coming up, but the most important part is that I have my girl—the love of my life—by my side. Knowing that she came to me with the ultimatum my father gave her shows me that she is in this for the long haul. Emree is willing to stand beside me in any fight, and that makes me love this beautiful woman even more.

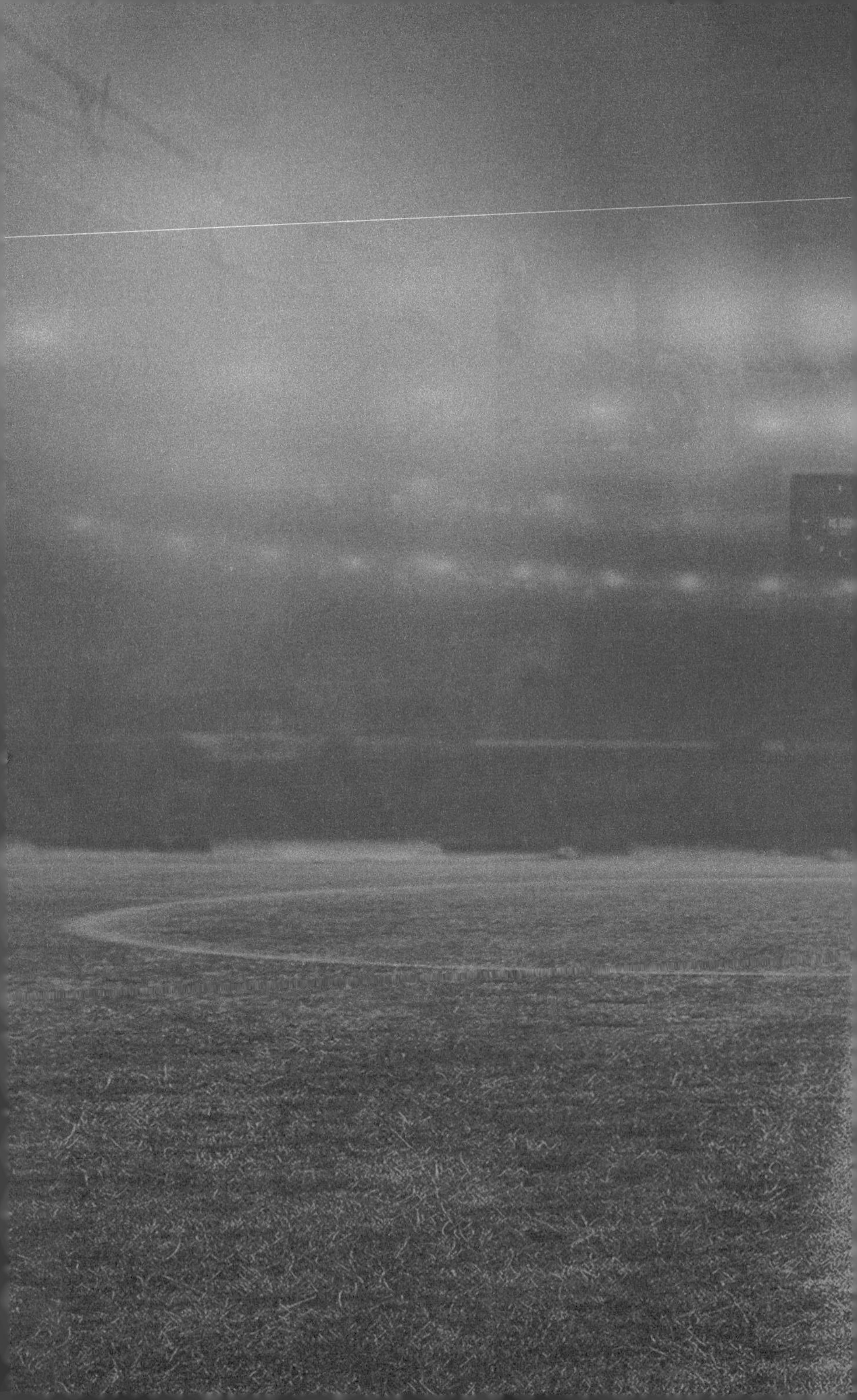

CHAPTER THIRTY-SIX

EMREE

There have only been two times in my life that I have left Florida. One was for a summer school trip to the caves in Georgia. The second was our spring break a couple months ago to Maddox's family's vacation home in South Carolina. Neither of these involved me getting on a plane and flying thousands of feet in the air.

Being so high in the sky has my nerves rattling. My ears have been popping and feel clogged, yet Conrad is sitting beside me as comfortably as ever. He distracted me in the airport before our flight by telling me about all the places he had traveled to. The farthest distance he has ever gone to was Bali for a summer trip between high school and college. I couldn't even imagine being in this recycled air tank for that long. The seats are uncomfortable and there is a baby crying in the back that sounds like how I feel.

Conrad and I are flying to Boston, Massachusetts, to meet with Mr. Groves. After a week of back-and-forth conversations between the two, Mr. Groves came up with a strategy to set up a meeting with Howard Dugray at his office. The details are somewhat gray to me since a lot of what Mr. Groves said was in lawyer terms, but Conrad seems to know what he needs to do and that makes me less worried.

"Everyone, please fasten your seat belts and put your seats back in the upright position as we prepare for landing," the flight attendant announces over the speaker. I close my eyes and take deep breaths as I prepare for my first flight touchdown.

The landing is rocky, and I'm pretty sure I cracked a molar clenching my teeth so hard. Conrad is right beside me, holding my hand through it all. Once we are on the ground, I feel more relaxed.

"You did great, baby," Conrad whispers in my ear as everyone on the plane stands to be the first one out. I smile as he kisses my cheek.

We take a cab to our hotel in the center of the city and check in for the night. The meeting with Mr. Groves is at eight in the morning. We had to take a later flight since we both had classes. Conrad has seemed surprisingly calm about this entire setup, but I'm wondering if he is hiding his emotions for my sake. He tells me that there is no heartbreak with the dynamic between him and his family now, but I can see something in his eyes at times when he doesn't think someone is watching.

Since it's late, we decide to have dinner at the hotel instead of exploring Boston. Alice, Conrad's little sister, lives with their parents while attending her first year at Boston College. Tonight she has a study group session but said she is able to skip it this week to meet us for dinner.

We're currently seated at a booth in the upscale hotel restaurant, and the hostess makes her way toward us with a beautiful young woman. She's dressed in a perfectly fitted pair of flared corduroy pants, a black fitted long-sleeved shirt, and black loafers. Her blonde hair is flowing around her in large curls. Conrad's face lights up with a genuine smile when he sees her.

He gets out of the booth, and the girl, who I assume is Alice, dives into his open arms. Conrad runs his hand down her long, blonde hair as she clutches him as close as possible. Even though I have seen the worst of Conrad's family, I can't help but wonder how these two came out as loving as they did.

Pulling apart, Alice wipes under her eyes and smiles up at her brother. "I'm so happy for you that you were able to stand up to him."

Conrad grips his sister's shoulders. "You can too, Alice. I've told you I'll help with anything."

"I know," she tells him with a soft smile. Turning in my direction, her smile widens. "You must be Emree."

Nodding, I stand to join them and give her a warm hug. "It's great to finally meet you. Conrad has told me so much about you and the fun you both had growing up."

We all take a seat in the booth. Conrad and I go back to where we were sitting, and Alice is across from us. The waitress comes over with the drinks we asked for when we first got here, and Alice orders water.

Conrad asks her about the final semester of her first year of college and if she has enjoyed this experience. Alice's hands are moving all over the place and her face is expressive as she tells him all about what she has learned and the friends she's made.

According to what Conrad has told me, Alice was more sheltered than he was. She was never allowed to date, and her father monitored who her friends were. They usually had to be daughters of men Howard knew. Luckily, Conrad was there to help sneak her out to parties or sports games when their dad was out of town. Without him, I feel as though a deep depression would have taken over Alice. Losing him when he went off to college had to have been hard on her.

Our waitress comes by once again, and we order our dinner. This time she leaves a basket of warm bread on the table that I am more than happy to indulge in.

"Tell me about yourself, Emree. I've only gotten little bits and pieces from Conny and want to get to know more about the girl who has my brother taking control of his own life."

Swallowing the bite of bread in my mouth, I wipe my face to make sure no crumbs are left behind. "Well, I don't think there is much to tell. You probably know about how Conrad and I met, so I won't bore you with that. I'm from a small town in Florida and was raised by a single mom. I'm going to school for fashion management and design. I would love nothing more than to one day have my own fashion line."

"Her designs are sick too. You should have her come up with some outfits for you, Alice. You'd like her style."

Alice's face lights up. "I would love that. Based on your outfit alone, I have a feeling you'd be able to put together something perfect."

We spend the rest of the evening in relaxed conversation with Alice while enjoying a five-star meal. Neither of them brings up the reason why we're in Boston or any of their family members. It's natural too. As if not talking about their parents and brother is normal. I have tried to understand the Dugray family, but it is useless. I'm happy Conrad and Alice have each other, but Howard, Annie, and Archer will never make sense to me.

For hours, we sit together, and I enjoy getting to know Alice. She's quiet but has a great personality, and I can see us being friends. She would get along great with the rest of the girls in our friend group too.

With our meeting early in the morning, Conrad and I reluctantly say goodbye to Alice. It's a sad parting because he knows she is going back to the house he hates, but we promise to have more visits here or have her fly out to us. I can tell by the way he clings to her that Conrad misses his sister.

THE HURT OF LETTING GO

THE CONFERENCE ROOM we are in is bright, with floor-to-ceiling windows that overlook downtown Boston. There is a long table that is almost the length of the room and there are well over a dozen chairs surrounding it. Conrad and I are occupying two of those chairs while Mr. Groves's assistant passes out water bottles. Mr. Groves himself has been rambling on with Conrad about what to say and how today will go.

Mr. Groves ends the conversation and walks over to the small counter against the wall stocked with fruit, snacks, and a mini-fridge, where his assistant is now organizing items.

Leaning over, I kiss Conrad's shoulder. "You doing okay?"

His hand on my thigh tightens as he smiles over at me. "Doing a lot better than I thought I would. More concerned with how I'm not going to rip my father's head off for threatening you."

My heart swells. He keeps worrying about me more than himself, and I try to reassure him that I handled myself well and will be okay.

"Focus on keeping a serious face against your father during this meeting. He thinks he is so sure of himself that he can somehow get control over your trust, but he is in over his head and needs to be taken down a few notches."

Conrad chuckles, but it is cut off by a knock on the door. The woman who works at the front desk of the large office enters, and following her is Howard Dugray and another woman with blonde hair in a fitted black dress carrying a folder in her arms. Conrad's father is dressed much like he was when he came to Whiskey Joe's, except this time it is a dark blue, almost black suit with a white shirt underneath.

"Well, if it isn't my son and his lovely little girlfriend,"

Howard says in a mocking tone as he takes the seat across from Conrad. The woman with him occupies the seat crossways from me.

"Morning, Howard. Leslie." Mr. Groves takes his seat at the end of the conference table as he greets the two new guests.

Conrad's father gives Mr. Groves his attention and a devious smile grows on his face. "Anthony. How's the wife?"

Mr. Groves doesn't let the double entendre affect him. "She's wonderful," he tells Howard with a smile. "How about we get started with why we set this meeting up?"

"Proceed." Howard waves a hand at Mr. Groves.

"It appears you have made some threats to Miss Anders here about your son's inheritance from his grandfather. After reviewing the paperwork from your father's estate lawyer, I'm going to assume you weren't able to get ahold of that to look at it yourself?" Mr. Groves's tone is serious and stern.

Howard does a good job of keeping a poker face, but I see a small slip in the way his eyebrow twitches. "No, I haven't had the chance to yet."

"Well, you probably won't get that chance. I'll give you an idea of what it states. Your father has left a generous amount of thirty million dollars to your son and only your son. The conditions of the inheritance are that Conrad must complete high school, graduate from college with the minimum of a bachelor's degree, marry, have his first child, and retire. Those are all the milestones he must reach to obtain the money that was left. After each achievement, he will get a certain amount."

My breath catches at the amount of money. Conrad never told me the amount, and I didn't want to know, but hearing how much his grandfather left behind leaves me speechless.

Mr. Groves continues. "One of the other conditions in the will is that not a single one of his sons, including you, is to touch a cent of Conrad's or any of the other grandchildren's money. It seems dear old Dad didn't leave anything to you all besides his businesses, which I'm sure he would have left to Conrad if he were old enough."

Howard's jaw is clenched, and his face turns several shades of red. "I don't fucking believe you."

"Oh, trust him. You're not allowed access, but if you really want to, I can show you the part of the will where it says you aren't allowed near my inheritance," Conrad says with a smile.

His father glares at him, and Conrad doesn't even flinch. He only smiles. The two maintain eye contact in a stare-off until Howard is the one to break the awkward silence. "You little shit. Do you really think you can win this fight?"

"Actually, he has a much better chance than you would think. Not only was your father's will extremely detailed, but couple that with the fact that the best estate lawyers on the East Coast won't touch your case after I spoke with them, it bodes well for your son." Every word comes out smoothly as Mr. Groves sits reclined in his chair.

Howard's chair rolls against the carpet as he quickly stands. "Don't think this is over, Conrad. You made a mistake going against me, boy. I don't give a shit what your little lawyer here says."

Conrad leans forward and rests his hands on the table. "Do your damage, but you're done threatening and trying to hurt us. Come near Emree again, and we'll file a restraining order. Find whatever lawyer you think will help you, and we'll come right back here. You're out of moves, *Dad*. Time to give up."

With flared nostrils and a tight jaw, Howard Dugray turns and jerks the door open, storming out of the conference room. His assistant, Leslie, gives us a small smile before grabbing her folder and following her boss with her head down.

"That went much better than I thought," Mr. Groves cheerfully states.

Conrad grabs my hand under the table and gives it a squeeze. "Thank you again for doing all this. Not sure I would have known how to handle a situation like this without your help."

The well-dressed lawyer waves a hand. "Don't mention it. Anything to knock Howard down a few notches. You held your own well, kid. I may not be able to help with your dad running your name through the mud, but if you're looking to get into the business end of law, let me know." He stands and comes over to shake our hands. "It was nice meeting you both. Hopefully, we won't have to do this again."

With a smile, Mr. Groves and his assistant exit the conference room, leaving the door cracked open on their way out.

Grabbing Conrad's hand, I bring it to my lips and place a kiss on his knuckles. "How do you feel?"

He removes his hand from my grip and cups my jaw. "Free."

CHAPTER THIRTY-SEVEN

CONRAD

"Fuck. Right there."

"Oh god, deeper."

"A little to the left. Yes, that's the spot. Keep hitting that spot."

"If I didn't know any better, I'd say what's going on in this room is a bad porno," Coach Walter announces as he enters the locker room.

"Watch a lot of porn, Coach?" Maddox asks with a laugh.

Coach cuts to him with a look that has even me nervous. "Shut the hell up, Stone, or you're missing your massage turn."

The locker room is currently filled with students in the sports therapy program who are looking for more hands-on experience needed for their degree. They have worked with all the sports players, but not near enough, in my opinion.

Maddox turns without a word and goes back to sitting on the bench and waiting his turn.

"Coach, I think we should have a full-time masseuse on staff," Camden states from where he is getting his back rubbed on one of the three tables placed in the locker room.

Coach leans against his office door that is off to the side of the locker room exit. "I'll make sure to add that to the budget request for next year. I'm sure the dean will be ecstatic to add a personal masseuse for you all."

"That would be great," one of the freshmen cheers from the back of the line.

Coach shakes his head and ducks into his office, clearly disappointed his player missed the obvious sarcasm.

"You all ready for final exams next week?" I ask Levi, who is waiting in line beside me.

He shrugs his shoulders. "I only have one left, so not sweating it so much. English is my best subject."

"Seeing as how you're an *English* major, I would like to think so," Maddox comments. "If it wasn't your best subject, I would reconsider your future."

Another player leaves the table, and Levi stands to take his turn. The woman, who is putting lotion on her hands, turns and her eyes widen as she takes in all that is Levi and his several tattoos. This is the usual reaction he gets from women, but the guy is completely clueless about the effect he has on the opposite sex.

"Um, Conny. Have you seen the news lately?" Maddox asks as he looks at something on his phone.

"You know I don't watch that shit," I tell him.

Maddox looks up and stretches his arm toward me with his phone in his hand. "You may want to see this."

My eyes scan the article open on his phone, and my jaw drops.

BILLIONAIRE BUSINESSMAN, HOWARD DUGRAY, ARRESTED FOR EMBEZZLING CHARITY FUNDS

BY ELIAS JAMES

I go on to read more of the article. The number of years my father has been stealing money from his own charity for heart disease, which my grandfather died of. How my father's assistant has been collecting enough evidence against him and how she is also filing sexual harassment charges against him. There is a photo of my father in one of his well-fitted suits with his hands cuffed behind his back while being escorted out of his Boston office. Reading through something that is tearing apart my father would usually bring most sons sadness, but I can't help but smile, knowing that he got what he deserves.

Karma is a bitch, and my father has now met his fate. Piss-poor actions always come around, and he has had this coming for a while now.

Locking the phone, I hand it back to Maddox. "Couldn't have happened to a more deserving person."

He gives me a smile and a knowing nod. Maddox may have a better relationship with his parents than I do, but he still gets it. Family doesn't always mean blood, and I feel more love and care from my good friends and Emree than I ever had from my parents.

My phone dings from inside my pocket. Pulling it out, I read the text from my sister.

> **ALICE**
> Mom won't stop crying and Archer is on a rampage. All the kids at school are talking about it. I left the dorm and am staying with Mom, but it's bad, Conny.

> **ME**
> I'm sorry. You can come here if you need to escape it all. You're always more than welcome. I love you, little sis.

Although my family and I have no relationship anymore, Alice is not someone I could go without having in my life. My sister is a sweet and kindhearted person who is more out of place in the Dugray family than I am. Even though we live almost two thousand miles away from each other, I have tried my best to keep in touch with her, especially after what happened with my father.

After all the players get their massages, Coach dismisses us and tells everyone to take the next few days off to focus on final exams. Levi smiles, knowing he basically has a few free days other than his one exam and work.

The guys want to have a BBQ tonight to celebrate the end of the semester, so Mateo and I stop at the grocery store to get some food to grill and different snacks and drinks. Most of us haven't been too big on the larger parties we used to have, so these smaller get-togethers are more common.

When we get back to the house, there are already a couple of extra cars parked on the side of the road. Two I recognize as Jules's and Blaire's, but there is also an older sedan I've never seen before.

"You know who that other car belongs to?" I ask Mateo as we unload the trunk.

He shakes his head as he looks away from the stranger's vehicle. "No clue. Let's hope Maddox didn't go rogue and invite more people over than we talked about."

Knowing our roommate, I can see him bypassing our agreement and turning this get-together into a full-blown rager.

With our arms full of grocery bags, Mateo and I make our way into the house. The smell of homemade tomato sauce fills my senses, and there is music playing softly in the background. Rounding our way into the kitchen, I take in Emree at the stove, stirring something in the pot with a wooden spoon in her hand.

"Now you want to make sure if the heat is high that you're constantly stirring the sauce so that it doesn't burn on the bottom. If you lower the heat, it's fine to leave and just stir occasionally." Blaire is beside my girl, explaining the art of sauce making, and I can't help but laugh because something so simple should be common knowledge, but Emree is simple when it comes to the kitchen. As in, she is all about foods that need to be reheated via a microwave or oven. Sautéeing and mixing are not her forte.

"Hey, Mad, why don't you come get a much-needed lesson in the kitchen?" I laugh as I call out to him.

Maddox doesn't look over but yells back, "How about you suck my dick, Dugray?" His focus is on something on the other side of the room, and when I walk over, I see Trazia and Jules talking. Trazia throws her head back as she laughs, and Maddox groans and gets up from his seat.

"You okay, man?" I ask him.

He tosses his empty beer bottle in the trash and opens the cooler to grab another one. "Just fine." He looks around our group of friends and then back at me. "Can you all stop being opposed to bigger parties? I need to get laid, and if you all keep up with these small gatherings, I'm going to fuck Jules eventually."

"Touch my best friend, and you're dead," Mateo answers from the patio. The sliding door is open, and he and Levi are sitting at the table we have back there, and Camden is firing up the grill.

Maddox scoffs and goes to join Camden off to the side of the backyard.

A pair of hands snakes around my waist and settles on my lower stomach. "Welcome home, handsome."

The smile on my face grows easily as I rest my hands over Em's. I like the sound of that. *Home*. Not so much the house I share with the guys, but her. "How was your day, little chef?"

Her laugh shakes me since her front is plastered to my back. Emree unlinks her hands, and I turn to face her. "It was good. My dress was a big hit with my professor. She actually wanted to keep it for her class as an example for next year."

"That's amazing, baby." Framing her face with my palms, I pull her in for a congratulatory kiss. Emree's hands settle on my hips as I taste her for the first time today. With our school schedules and needing to get ready for exams, I haven't seen much of her over the week.

"How about you? How was your day? Have you...um... watched TV at all today?"

She's trying to ask me if I've seen the news about my dad without asking me directly. "I haven't, but Maddox was kind enough to inform me of just another reason why my father is scum."

With sad eyes, Emree cups my chin and runs her thumb over the short stubble there. "While I'm sure you're not surprised, I'm sorry nonetheless. It's hard knowing how shitty your parent is."

One of the connections Emree and I have is that we were fathered by shitty men. Both are horrible in their own way, and luckily Em has never had to even meet hers, but it's a bond we have.

Grabbing her wrist, I turn her arm and place a kiss over her pulse point before resting it against my chest, right where my heart is. "He doesn't matter to me anymore. I can't let broken relationships and people like him bring me down. That isn't my family anymore. You are, Em. I love you more than anything and plan to make a life with you. I've been an idiot in the past, and there is so much I regret, but that won't ever happen again."

Tears well up in her eyes, and I wipe them again. "You're it for me, baby. I want it all. Marriage and babies. I want to watch the sunrise with you in the mornings and make love to you each night. See our kids grow inside this beautiful body of yours and watch them run around our home. We'll grow old together, and I'll enjoy every minute of this life because it will be with you by my side."

A sob escapes her as more tears fall heavily now. "You really know how to woo a girl."

"I have a lot to make up for."

She smiles and runs her hand through my hair. "I think you've done more than enough. You've shown me how important I am to you with your words and actions, and that's more than I could have asked for." She reaches up on her toes to give me a soft kiss.

Before I can tell her that it isn't enough and I'll continue to make it up to her, Blaire calls her back over to the stove to show her how to cut and season chicken breasts.

Looking around at my group of friends, I can't help but smile. This is what family is. Not people who are tied to you by the blood that runs through your veins, but the people who are there for you no matter what. The ones who love and truly care for you, no matter what.

This is my family. And I'll never let them go.

EPILOGUE

CONRAD

A YEAR LATER

Graduation day is finally here, and I couldn't be happier to close this chapter of my life and start the next one.

With how large the graduating class is, it has become a three-day event. Today it is me, Emree, and Camden. Mateo, Jules, and Levi are tomorrow, and Blaire and Maddox are Friday. All of our friends are in the stands, and when I glance out, I can't help but smile. That's my family out there, and I couldn't imagine today being any better.

Emree's, Blaire's, and Camden's moms are out there along with Trazia. Our friends made sure to save them some seats. Everyone is gathered together, taking up an entire row of seats. Trazia is smiling as she and her mom wave at Camden. Jules and Mateo are laughing, and Levi is looking like the grumpy lumberjack that he is while Maddox can't stop staring at Traz.

With my father serving a twenty-five-year sentence in prison—fifteen for good behavior—and my relationship with my mom and brother, Archer, still rocky, none of my family has been able to make it here today. Alice wanted to—and requested we take tons of pictures—but she has her own exams and is finishing her second year of college.

The ceremony begins, and I wait for my girl's name to be called as the dean goes through the long list of *A*s. When he finally does, I stand and cheer as loud as I can for her. She deserves all the support, and based on the screams from the stands, she is getting it.

Emree has worked her ass off this last year, and it paid off in the long run. After a glowing recommendation from her professor, who is the head of the art and design department, Emree was offered a paid internship with a dress designer she admired. She said her portfolio and the designs she has drawn but not created yet blew them away. This is a massive opportunity for her, and I couldn't be more proud.

The best part is that the internship is in DC, where I just so happened to get a job with the Hilton corporation on the marketing team. My connection with Mr. Groves paid off in more ways than I can count, and it turns out one of his clients is the CEO of the Hilton, and after learning about my background, the marketing director reached out.

Emree and I have made plans to move out to Virginia, just outside of DC, so that we are close enough to both our jobs because she didn't want to be too in the city. We already have a house set up to rent and are working on packing up her apartment before we go to stay with her mom for part of the summer.

More names are called, and at the three-hour mark, they make the traditional announcement for graduates to flip their tassels, and everyone erupts in cheers.

The plethora of students are corralled outside, where we wait around to meet our families. Several people are crying as they hug each other, and I can't help but chuckle at how emotional some take graduation. The four years at Braxton were amazing, and I have found not only the love of my life but a lifelong family.

"Con!" someone shouts, and when I turn toward the voice, Emree is running toward me. Her gown is blowing in the wind, revealing the turquoise silk dress she made that I love so much.

Bending my knees, I prepare for her embrace, and without slowing down, she jumps into my arms and wraps those beautiful legs around my waist. "We did it," she mumbles against my lips.

With a smile, I hold her to me with one arm and grip her hair with my other hand, pulling her mouth closer to mine. She eagerly accepts my hungry kiss by framing my face with her hands and molding her lips to mine. We're all teeth and tongue in what I'm sure is not a school-appropriate kiss, but I couldn't care less. This is the start of the rest of our lives together, and I'm ready to celebrate with her in every way.

"This is your official announcement that the moms are on their way over and you're getting some weird looks from just about everyone around you." Maddox breaks through my Emree fog as, for a second, I forget where we are.

Pulling back, I place one final kiss on Emree's puffy lips and set her on the ground. She stumbles a little in her silver heels but steadies herself with the use of my shoulders. Em looks up at me with a knowing smile, and that one look has my pants getting even tighter. Thankfully, the gown helps to cover my excitement.

The rest of our family walks up, and Emree's mom, Margret, comes forward and engulfs her daughter in a tight hug. "I'm so incredibly proud of you, sweetie," she whispers in her daughter's ear. I smile, knowing how much this means to not only Emree but her mom. Margret never went back to finish school, and her dream was for her daughter to have a different experience than she did.

"Well, let's get out of this madness and back to the boys'

house for a celebration," Camden's mom announces. Her arm is wrapped around her son's waist, and he is holding her tight to him. "Maddox's parents were sweet enough to get everything set up during the ceremony."

We decided to have the graduation party today since the next two ceremonies are at night, and we have to be moved out of the house by this weekend.

We all load into a variety of vehicles and head toward the house that started to feel like a home in the last four years. I grew up in the house back in Blackburn and lived there for eighteen years, yet this two-story, six-bedroom structure feels more like home to me than Blackburn ever did.

Hand in hand, Emree and I make our way into the house. The moment we walk through the door, I'm blown away by the setup, knowing the parents went all out to celebrate us. The front door is covered in a sign that says *CONGRATULATIONS* vertically, with the year 2024 floating all around it. There are balloons in our school colors surrounding the top and sides of the door too.

Inside is even more extravagant. There are pictures of all of us throughout our college years. Several are from college games, and I can't help but laugh at the difference between freshman year to now. We all looked like babies, and I can't believe how adult I thought I was back then. I knew nothing as an immature eighteen-year-old and was only living the life I thought I was supposed to. Now, four years later, I'm living for myself and my happiness.

EMREE

With a full belly, I sink back into my chair and smile as I take in everything around me. I'm going to miss this. Our friends are sitting around the patio table we have hung out at so many times over the last year and a half. The sun has gone down, and our parents are long gone, but none of us have been in the mood to leave yet. I think knowing this is the last time we will all be together like this for a while is hitting some of us hard. I know it is for me.

Conrad is lazily rubbing my leg as we laugh about stories over the years. Many of the best ones are centered around Maddox and his lack of filter when it comes to what comes out of his mouth. We've had a lot of great memories together and some sad ones, but my years at Braxton, and especially with this group, will stay with me forever.

Standing, Conrad leans over and kisses my cheek. "While we're all together because I'm not sure when the next time this will happen, there's something I need to do."

Leaning forward, I look at him, silently questioning what is going on. He just smiles and reaches his hand out for my own. I grab it, and Conrad pulls me up so that I'm standing in front of him.

"Emree, the day I met you was the moment my life changed forever. Never did I think this beautiful, fun-loving girl would alter my life for the better. For so long, I was living my life for someone else, and that included not loving you the way you deserve to be loved, but I was finally able to pull my head out of my ass and see that you're meant for me, baby. I have no doubt that we were put on this planet for each other."

He drops to one knee and stuffs his hand into his pocket, retrieving a red velvet box. Opening the lid, he reveals a gold band ring with the most stunning pear-cut diamond shining on top. Conrad grabs one of my hands while holding the box in the other.

Tears are unashamedly flowing down my face as he stares into my eyes with so much love. "While I have messed up our relationship in the past, I promise to be the man you deserve from here on out. To love you unconditionally. To protect you with everything in me. And to be your partner above all else. Will you do this life with me as my wife?"

Before Conrad is even finished with his question, my arms are around his neck, and I'm tackling him to the ground. "Yes! Yes! Yes!" With him on the ground, I forcefully grip his face and crash my mouth against his. Conrad smiles against my many kisses as I paint his face with my lipstick.

Our friends are all laughing and shouting out congratulations, but nothing matters besides the man under me. The man I love more than anyone in this world. The man I'm going to spend the rest of my life with.

My future *husband*.

Our relationship has had its ups and downs, mainly the first year, but none of that matters anymore. We fought our battles and came out stronger because of them. My love for Conrad Dugray is strong, and I know that whatever life throws at us, we can handle it. Together.

Want to read more of the Braxton U crew? Blaire and Camden's story is now available. Check out The Act of Trusting.

THE ACT OF TRUSTING

There was a sadness in her clear, gray eyes that I could see she tried to hide. A fight with her inner demons she didn't want to show anyone...

CAMDEN COLLINS

Life was going well for me. I was on the right track: captain of the soccer team, grades were passing, and I had the respect of my team. Girls threw themselves at me. It was every twenty-year-old's dream.

Then I saw her...

One look at her, and it all changed. Something about her drew me in. A sense of protectiveness to guard this small, sad girl. In her eyes, I could see the fight she had within herself...and I wanted to be there for her. To protect her and be someone to lean on while she fought whatever it was. Nothing else seemed to matter but the dark-haired, beautiful girl I couldn't stay away from.

BLAIRE WENTWORTH

I wasn't the same girl I was four years ago. My life was stolen from me one night and I'd never have the chance to get old me back. Now I was just existing, not living. I went through the motions of my everyday routine, staying quiet and keeping to myself. Trusting and letting people in was a constant struggle.

Until he showed up...

I'd never seen someone like him before. Not once had I described a guy as beautiful, but that's what he was. He struck something in me, and I didn't know how to handle that. I was chasing nightmares no one knew about. Ones I kept to myself for a reason. Could I let this new person into my life that I had kept closed off from many for far too long? What if I let my guard down and he ended up destroying me?

And that became my greatest fear…

Be sure to add the entire Braxton U series to your Goodreads TBR so you don't miss out on the rest of the boy's stories:

The Hurt of Letting Go (Conrad & Emree)

A Memory That Once Was (Maddox & Trazia)

The Power of Resisting (Mateo & Sage)

The Art of Forgiving (Levi & Easton)

ABOUT THE AUTHOR

Lexi Bissen is a new adult and young adult romance author who aspires to write in all genres, including paranormal—which started her obsession with words and fictional characters she cares about more than real people. She's also a coffee snob, reader, far too sarcastic, and dog rescue advocate.

Born and raised in Tampa, Florida, Lexi enjoys spending time with her family, taking in the sunshine with a good book, and giving the voices in her head a story. Writing has always been an escape for Lexi, where she can check out of her life and discover new, exciting places she makes up—but not in a crazy way.

When Lexi isn't writing, you can find her binging the latest Netflix show, laughing at her own jokes, or sipping iced coffee while spending way too much money at the bookstore.

Check out Lexi's website for updates on upcoming releases, current books, and where to follow on social media: https://www.lexibissen.com/.